MORTAL
DECEPTION

LIZBETH LIPPERMAN

MORTAL DECEPTION
Copyright © 2012 by Lizbeth Lipperman
http://www.lizlipperman.com/

ISBN-13: 978-0615542980
ISBN-10: 0615542980

The Story Vault
c/o Marketing Department
P.O. Box 11826
Charleston, WV 25339-1826
http://www.thestoryvault.com

Cover Designs by Kelly Crimi

Publishing History: First Edition
Published by The Story Vault

To Dan, my real life hero since high school.
Without you beside me all the way,
I could not have achieved my dreams.
Te Amo.

CHAPTER ONE

Before the night ends, I'm going to have sex with a total stranger.

Taking a deep breath Dani Perez walked toward the hotel bar, her red stilettos clattering like a *Riverdance* audition on the black marble floor

What are you looking at? she wanted to scream when the desk clerk glanced up with a knowing smile. But she knew exactly why he was looking. The stupid dress damn-near showed the cheeks of her ass.

Dani smiled, thinking when she got home, she'd have to make a big deposit in Abby's pickle jar decorated with commodes. Her daughter called her creation the "potty-mouth jar." Since Christmas, Dani had to pay up every time she cursed. She and Abby were saving for their dream vacation, and at the rate she was going, Hawaii wasn't an unrealistic destination. Hell, the F word alone was worth a whopping twenty bucks.

Dani wasn't proud of the way she talked, but old habits die hard. Five years on the Cimarron Police Force riding with Jerry Spigoretti had added a variety of colorful words to her vocabulary. She'd thought when she left the job last year, she'd clean up her language, but working with Harry Fielding, another hard-nosed, ex-cop-turned-PI, hadn't helped. On a good day, she was able to keep it under control.

Today wasn't a good day.

She stopped in front of the door, a sudden rush of apprehension overwhelming her as she struggled to keep a falling ringlet of hair out of her eyes. Silently, she cursed her twin. Her usual ponytail would have been so much easier, but Nikki had insisted on pulling her unmanageable hair up and curling it around her face—said it was sexy.

How freakin' sexy would it be if she landed on her barely-covered tush because she couldn't see?

The huge purse they'd picked out felt like it was full of rocks, but she needed one this size to hold the equipment she would use. She jerked it higher on her shoulder, glancing back to see if the clerk was still watching.

He was. She fought the urge to flip him off.

Breathe, chica. A lot is riding on tonight.

The minute she opened the door, her eyes widened, a reaction to the darkened room, lit only by the neon signs behind the bar and the candles on the ten or so tables strategically placed around the room. Even in this light, she could see the entire bar area, praying he'd be there, petrified he was. She'd counted on him being a creature of habit and doing the exact same thing he'd done every Thursday for the five weeks she'd tailed him.

Dr. Nathan Randall didn't disappoint her. He was alone as usual, at the far end of the bar, mindlessly twirling a glass on the counter. The lump in her throat threatened to cut off her breathing while she watched him put down the drink and rub his forehead, probably unaware he did that often. She didn't have to see his searing blue eyes to know they were squinted in deep thought, an image she'd captured on film many times.

She hated what she had to do to him.

Eyes finally adjusted to the dark, Dani chose a table far enough to be out of sight from where he sat but close enough for observation. She attempted to sit down gracefully without compromising her dignity in the skin tight dress, but it was a losing battle. She reached behind and tugged at the hem of the red jersey number as it rode up her thighs.

Oh, dammit!

She was sure she had given everyone a peek all the way up her legs to the thong panties she was dying to pull out of her butt. She didn't get the whole thong panties thing. Number one, they'd cost eight dollars on sale. Who pays eight dollars for panties that barely had enough material to qualify as a G-string?

And who wants to walk around with a constant wedgie?

She plopped the heavy purse on the floor and glanced up to see if anyone had seen her flash. Her eyes connected with a middle-aged man sitting at the corner of the bar, facing her. He lifted his glass and smiled.

Christ!

She lowered her eyes. The last thing she wanted to do was call any more attention to herself before she was ready. And she needed a whole lot of courage to be ready.

Liquid courage.

Dani waited until the waitress approached before she looked up again, afraid the guy in the suit might consider any further eye contact an invitation. She'd prided herself on reading people, had actually avoided danger on the job because of that particular skill. Her radar said this guy definitely had the married-but-trolling-for-stray-action look all over his Midwestern face.

"What can I get you?" The flat tone in the waitress's voice conveyed her disapproval.

Dani didn't blame her. Hell, she'd disapprove of herself, too, in this outfit that screamed *I come with a price.*

"What's the latest drinking rage these days?" she asked, knowing the Corona she craved wouldn't go with her on-the-prowl persona.

Marcia, according to the nametag on her blouse, looked surprised by the question. "Depends on what you like."

What does someone whose butt is hanging out of a dress usually drink?

"I'd like to try something different. Can you suggest anything?"

Marcia shrugged. "Cosmopolitans are popular, and apple martini's a favorite with a lot of the single women who come in here."

"Then an apple martini it is." Dani smiled as the waitress pursed her lips in a condescending manner before she hurried back to the bar.

She relaxed her shoulders slightly and leaned back into the chair. For a Thursday night, it wasn't too busy, thank heavens. She didn't know what she'd do if the place was rocking, or if, God forbid, someone recognized her.

Who would? Most people avoided downtown Dallas like the plague. Even though Cimarron was only twenty miles away, she couldn't remember the last time she'd come to town before this. But she wasn't reassured. Even in a city this big, stranger things were known to happen.

Marcia arrived with the drink and set it on the table. "That'll be five fifty."

Dani handed her a ten. "Keep the change."

For the first time, the waitress smiled. Guess she thought a tip that big warranted an attitude adjustment.

The minute the cool liquid hit her throat, Dani raised her hand to her mouth to suppress the cough. *Holy Crap.* She forced down another sip and waited as it scorched a trail of fire from her esophagus to her stomach, the warmth rushing through her gut.

As the tingling sensation raced through her veins, she lifted the glass to her lips and downed the remainder of the drink. Within seconds, she felt her fears slipping away as she savored the hurts-so-good burn all the way down.

She could do this. Hey, she could do anything for one night. She had to. Casey's life depended on it. Just the thought of Nikki's son had Dani fighting to keep her emotions in check.

When she'd dropped Abby off at her sister's earlier, she'd noticed how pale Casey had become. Watching her nephew and her daughter kick a soccer ball around in the back yard, she'd been reminded of the rapid progression of the anemia.

Fanconi Anemia, a killer whose genes she carried in her own DNA, was sucking the life out of Nikki's only child. It had become more and more difficult to see him struggle with everyday activities, stopping to catch his breath every few minutes.

Time was running out for Casey, and she'd vowed to do whatever necessary to save him. If that meant sitting in this bar dressed like a slut, so be it. It wouldn't be her first time undercover, but this was more than a routine stakeout.

This time it was personal. She didn't have the luxury of watching from a parked car, sipping a Mocha Cappuccino, or knowing ten guys were waiting to haul the pervert's ass in as soon as money changed hands.

She glanced up as the waitress reappeared. "Marcia, I'll have another one of these." She pointed to her empty glass. "But this time, make it a double."

Dani knew Dr. Nathan Randall usually only spent an hour at the bar before he retired to his room, always alone. She needed more courage, and she needed it fast.

After the waitress brought her drink, Dani studied him discreetly. She'd been tailing him since she and Nikki had concocted this ridiculous scheme a little over five weeks ago. Every Thursday night, he went from his office in the Schaffer building in downtown Dallas to the free clinic near Fair Park.

She'd seen dozens of people, most of them with kids, some with an elderly person, enter the rundown building every time he was there. No matter how many went in, Randall never left until the last one was gone. She'd watched, week after week, as he'd exit the clinic, his shoulders slumped after the long night. Each time she'd followed him back to this very bar where he'd consume three or four drinks before heading to his room.

By her count, he was on his third.

She felt a momentary twinge of guilt, knowing she was about to deceive him. All her life she'd despised men who cheated. Everything she'd learned indicated Randall was a decent enough guy, but if she was successful tonight, that would all change.

She downed the double martini and stood, clutching the table until her lightheadedness subsided. She never could hold her liquor. That's why she stuck with icy cold Coronas.

But it was now or never. She exhaled slowly before starting across the room. The damn shoes announced her even before she got close to the other end of the bar.

He looked up when she was almost beside him, and Dani smiled seductively. Nikki had made her practice that look in front of the mirror a dozen times. Made her say "hi" in a breathy way that reminded her of Aunt Sophie who had emphysema and never went anywhere without an oxygen tank.

Then she stumbled and smashed into his shoulder, nearly knocking him off the bar stool. She squeezed her eyes shut, thinking she should pretend like she did have emphysema. A doctor would assume her wooziness was the result of a depleted oxygen supply and not because she couldn't handle her first taste of an apple martini. Actually, it was probably that second taste that did it, but who was counting?

She forced her eyes open, only to find his face way too close as he steadied her. Other than the hint of amusement that flashed in those sultry blue eyes, his face was unreadable.

She wiggled out of his clutch and tried that seductive smile thing again. Swallowing the lump in her throat she said a quick prayer to St. Jude. This situation definitely qualified for help from the patron saint of hopeless cases.

Inhaling sharply, she forced herself to maintain eye contact with him as she let the breath out slowly. She was terrified, but it was too late to turn back. She'd just made the first contact with her mark. Now all she had to do was get him into bed.

"Whoa there. You okay?" Randall asked, still holding her up.

It had been a long time since she'd been in a man's arms, she thought, right before someone bumped her and knocked her further into his body.

"Crap!" She raised her hand to her mouth to stifle a giggle. "Buy a girl a drink?" Dani stared into his eyes, wanting desperately to turn and run.

Confusion flashed across his face before a slow grin replaced it. "Sorry. I was just about to head up to my room. I'm sure you won't have a problem finding someone to drink with." He stood up and reached back for his wallet.

Dani frowned. This wouldn't be easy. She placed her fingers on his shoulder, gently pushing him back down. "Now why would you want to go up to your stuffy old room when you could sit here and have a drink with me?" She batted her eyelashes and winked, praying the glob of mascara wouldn't permanently shut her right eye.

He laughed out loud. "Now that's a good question. Unfortunately, I still have to decline. I've had a hard day, and I wouldn't be much company." He rose again.

Dani moved closer, brushing her hand across the front of his jeans. This was not going according to her plan. She licked her lips and leaned in. "Oh, come on. I've had a hard day, too. What's one more drink gonna hurt?"

She held her breath while he glanced at his watch. When he lifted his eyes to hers, she was sure she had failed.

"What's the lady drinking?"

She frowned, then giggled. "Something with apples. The waitress will know."

He raised his hand, and immediately the bartender appeared. "Lily, would you bring a scotch on the rocks and another of whatever the lady is drinking, please?"

"Sure, Nate."

Her voice sounded sweet, but Dani noticed it contrasted with the scowl on her face when she stared at her. Was there a history between the two of them?

After Lily served the round, they sat in silence.

"Do you have a name?"

"Sophie," Dani blurted.

"You don't look like a Sophie."

"Oh yeah? What do I look like?"

"I don't know. Maybe Candy, Desiree, definitely something exotic."

She gulped, before reaching for the martini and taking a huge swallow. "I can be anyone you want me to be, Nate." She placed her hand over his. "Know what I mean?"

She watched as her meaning sank in. After a moment, he reached for the scotch and chugged it. She held her breath, sure he was about to send her on her merry way.

"What'd you have in mind?"

What she had in mind would send her to the confessional before Sunday mass. She lowered her eyes, hoping he hadn't seen the panic. Her heart felt like it would thump out of her chest. She had to calm down.

"Let's play it by ear," she whispered.

She saw hesitancy flash in his eyes, and she leaned in closer, making sure her breasts touched his chest. His sharp intake of breath told her they had. Father Jerome's voice in her head doled out one hundred Hail Marys for her penance.

Nate stood up, pulled three twenties from his wallet and threw them on the counter before turning back to her. "How much, Sophie?"

She looked confused. "How much what?"

"How much for two hours with you?"

Two hours? What in God's name did he have in mind?

Chill, Dani. Walking out of this hotel empty-handed is not an option.

She met his stare. "The same as everyone else."

"I don't have a clue what the going rate is."

She had to think fast or she'd lose him. She ran her tongue over her lips. "Trust me. I'm worth every penny."

He sprang from the barstool. "Christ! I don't care what you charge. Let's get out of here." He guided her toward the door.

Suddenly she gasped and turned back. "My purse."

"Don't move. I'll get it." He raced back to where they'd been sitting and hoisted the large purse from the floor.

"What's in here?"

Panic consumed her a second time "A girl's got to be prepared."

Randall placed his hand on the small of her back and gently pushed her out the door. "I need to stop by the ATM in the lobby," he said, heading for the desk. "Wait here."

While he talked to the clerk, Dani clamped her lips tight and forced herself to take slow deep breaths. Hyperventilating wasn't very sexy, especially if she passed out before stepping into the elevator.

The irony of acting like a virgin on Prom night was that she wasn't even one back then. Having dated Johnny since junior high, they'd ventured past necking long before the dance. So, what was the big deal?

Her solitary mission tonight was simply to have sex with this man. Women everywhere hooked up for an evening of mindless sex. It wasn't like he was a felon packing heat or a freak with bad breath. On the contrary. Ordinarily, Nate was a man she'd notice in a crowd, and he'd passed the bad breath test an hour ago when she'd nearly knocked him off the bar stool.

How hard could this be? Ten minutes, twenty tops, and she'd be headed to the lab with his specimen in her purse.

Then she remembered he'd bought her for two hours.

She froze. Could she have missed his affection for kinky stuff when she did the research on him? A mental flash of her tied to a bedpost drained the color from her face.

Oh, dear God! She opened her purse, then remembered she'd packed everything except a paper bag for oxygen emergencies.

She exhaled slowly, deliberately, like she'd been instructed during relaxation training at the police academy. It was supposed to teach rookies how to remain calm in stressful situations. The older cops called it "The Newbie's Guide to Working Without an Underwear Change." It wasn't so funny now.

She willed herself to relax. Sex with a stranger should be easier than shooting someone. Even though she'd never actually had to do that, she'd faced some of the worst felons in Cimarron without needing a new pair of panties. This should be a piece of cake. Or more appropriately, a piece of tail. Surely, a ten minute roll in the hay with a man who wasn't ugly couldn't be that difficult. She might even enjoy it. Hell, she hadn't been laid in over two years.

Randall turned suddenly, as if to see if she was still there. When their eyes met, he smiled.

Dani gulped. What ever made her think she could waltz into the hotel bar, wearing an outfit that fit her body like shrink wrap, and hop in the sack with a perfect stranger? She'd never been naked in front of anyone but Johnny.

The reality of stripping in front of this man produced tiny drops of sweat on Dani's upper lip. Maybe it wasn't too late to back out. She turned toward the revolving door, ready to kick off her heels and run. Then his hand was on her shoulder, the touch more a soft caress.

"Sophie?"

She whirled around, nearly falling into Nate Randall's arms a second time. She struggled to maintain her balance. Why did she tell him her name was Sophie? That sounded like someone's mother or an aunt with an oxygen tank. Why didn't she at least call herself Sophia? That definitely had a more sophisticated ring to it.

13

"Is everything okay?"

Dani raised her eyes to meet his. Standing close to Randall, she detected a faint whiff of his aftershave. For some ungodly reason, it had a calming effect on her.

She forced a smile. "Why wouldn't it be?"

Nate's eyes darted around the lobby, then fixed on hers as he attempted to smile. If she didn't know better, she'd swear he was as nervous as she was.

"You look a little uncertain. It's not too late to back out," he whispered.

Thank you, Jesus, she wanted to shout. Then an image of Casey lying helpless in a hospital bed flashed through her mind.

She took a calming breath. "Now why would I want to do that?" She slipped her arm through his and gently pushed him toward the elevator. "Let's not keep me waiting too much longer, Nate."

His face lit up. "Yes, ma'am."

For the split second it took for the elevator door to close, Dani contemplated bolting one last time. The final clang before it started rising sounded much like the cell doors in the movies she'd seen where the jailer threw away the key. All hope for a clean break vanished.

Nate pushed the button for the fourteenth floor, and Dani's knees nearly buckled. Could she really do this?

When the elevator stopped, Nate gently nudged her. "My room's this way, Sophie."

They walked in silence to room 1469.

Okay, God, this really isn't funny.

When the door closed behind her, Dani allowed her eyes to scan the room. She knew the Marquee was a high-dollar hotel, but this surpassed everything she'd heard. His suite was as luxurious as she'd ever seen with the massive king-size bed in the middle of the room as the focal point.

Her heart raced. Quickly, she searched for the minibar. This would take way more courage. A soft knock on the door interrupted her panic attack, and she spun around. Nate opened the door and stepped aside to allow the bellman to wheel in a cart.

After signing for room service and ushering the young man out, Nate turned back to her. "I hope you like champagne."

Dani nodded as he pulled a bottle of Dom Perignon from the ice and uncorked it. After he poured two glasses of the chilled drink, he handed her one.

"Cheers."

She didn't know what to make of it. The only other time she'd had champagne this expensive was on her wedding night twelve years ago.

She forced a smile. "What shall we toast?"

He hesitated. "How about to business deals that hopefully, will result in unbelievable pleasure for both of us?"

Dani felt a warm blush creep up her face. "I'll drink to that." She touched her glass to his before lifting it to her lips. The smooth liquid went down without the burn of the apple martinis. She'd never liked the taste of champagne, but this one was delicious. She tossed back her head and chugged it. He was there to refill her glass before she finished.

Is he trying to get me drunk?

She studied his face while he poured himself another. To him, she was a whore, not a first date. He didn't have to get her tipsy to get laid. She'd already agreed to that.

When Nate turned back to her, he smiled nervously while he fidgeted with the glass. For the first time, Dani noticed how blue his eyes were close up. The camera never captured the depth the way the real thing did. Something about them seemed haunted, almost sad. For a moment, she contemplated blurting the truth about why she was in his hotel room in the ridiculously slutty dress.

Damn it, girl, you know what you have to do.

She tilted back her head and downed the second drink.

"Slow down, Sophie. We have two hours. This stuff may seem tame, but it will hit you like a ton of bricks." He poured another round. This time he didn't move away.

His eyes bore into hers. Seeing his desire caused a flutter in her stomach. It had been a long time since someone wanted her, and in a crazy sort of way, she was turned on by his lust.

15

With his eyes fixed on her, he took her glass and placed it back on the cart. "You're beautiful." He lifted her chin with his finger and bent down to touch his lips to hers, slightly at first, then more demanding.

Expecting her mission to be nothing more than a ten-minute deal to get the precious specimen, Dani was confused by the rush of feelings she experienced. She'd only had two dates since Johnny's death, and the perfunctory goodnight kiss at her doorstep had never been anything like this.

She leaned in, her lips parted to welcome his probing tongue. Without thinking, she slipped her hands around his neck, pulling him even closer.

"Oh, God," he groaned. He lifted her into his arms and carried her to the bed. With one hand supporting her body, he pulled the covers back with the other, all the while nibbling on her ear. Gently, he laid her back against the massive pillows while his eyes traveled her entire body.

Suddenly, he lifted his body from the bed and sauntered to the dresser. Reaching into his jeans pocket, he pulled out his wallet and threw several bills down. "Two hours at three hundred an hour. Is that about right?"

Dani was confused. For a minute, she'd let herself enjoy his attention way too much. The money jolted her back to reality. This was a job. She had to remember that. "Perfect. Now come back here and let me show you how I earn it."

Nate hesitated. "How do we do this? Do you want me to undress you?"

Oh, crap. The naked thing.

Dani looked away, hoping he wouldn't see the color creep up her face. When she was more composed, she turned back to him. "Unless you'd rather watch me do it."

That was all Randall needed. In a flash he had the skimpy dress over her head and sprawled across the floor. She heard the catch in his breath when he stared at the black lacy push-up bra and the barely-there lace panties before he lowered his head and captured her lips again. This time, there was no light touch.

Kissing had always been an important part of lovemaking to Dani, and this guy definitely knew how to do it. She felt dizzy, probably lightheaded from the liquor. Or was it from the friction of his five o'clock shadow against her cheeks? Or maybe the masculine scent of his aftershave, faint but definitely there? Whatever it was, it was intoxicating. Maybe this wouldn't be so difficult after all.

His eyes held hers for a moment, giving her one last chance to stop him. Lips parted in a hint of a smile, she pulled his face down. "You're on the clock, Nate."

CHAPTER TWO

A sigh escaped Dani's lips as Nate silenced her with his mouth, tasting, nibbling. Desire surged through her body as every nerve ending came alive with his kiss. She locked her arms around his head and pulled him closer. She'd come this far, she might as well make the most of it.

His hand made a feather-like trail down her neck until it settled on the swell of her breast, bulging out of the one-size-too-small bra, fueling her fantasy about what would follow. Sensing her response, he crushed his body to hers and the kiss deepened. His mouth devoured her, probing, sucking, tasting.

He pulled away long enough to unhook her bra, exposing taut nipples that begged for attention. He obliged, taking first one in his mouth and then the other.

A soft moan escaped Dani's lips as his mouth left the swollen nipples and made a slippery trail lower. His tongue moved over her navel in a slow, hot circle that was driving her wild.

She wanted more. Had to have more. She pulled his face back up to hers, and she explored his lips with her own tongue. Emotions she had buried with Johnny flooded her mind. She thought she'd never feel this way again, but here she was in a stranger's bed, hot and ready.

She felt his hands pulling at her panties.

Rip the stupid things off, she wanted to shout. Instead, she raised her body slightly to make it easier for the material to slide over her hips. With the speed of an ace pitcher's fastball, Nate tore at his own clothes until they were lying in a heap alongside her discarded undies.

Naked and obviously ready to make love, Nate was a work of art. Drawn to his incredible muscles, tan and bulging, she took an inventory of his body exactly the way he'd done to hers only minutes before.

He was the only man she'd ever seen completely naked other than Johnny. If she never saw another one, she would die happy. As gorgeous as her husband had been, his body didn't come close to looking like the one in front of her. It was a given Nate worked out, and as her eyes moved lower, a certainty he wanted her.

A flash of guilt forced her to look away. How could she compare another man's body to her beloved Johnny's?

She didn't have time to wallow in her guilt as Nate threw back the covers and climbed in beside her. When his lips reclaimed hers, he reached down until his fingers touched the fine hairs below her navel. Involuntarily, she shivered as they found what they were searching for. Slowly, he massaged the swollen tissue, gradually increasing the tempo until she begged for more.

Encouraged by her reaction, Nate rose up on his elbows and entered her. Dani gasped as the gentle rocking intensified, nearly taking her over the edge. Her breathing quickened, and she began a slow grind with her hips, pushing her lower body closer to his. When she was positive she couldn't stand much more, she pulled his body to hers, clinging, moaning. Long forgotten were her fears about this night. Long forgotten was her reason for being here in the first place.

Her reason for being here. *Oh my God!*

Dani jerked away and tried to get out from under the weight of his body.

"Sophie?"

"I almost forgot the condom, Nate. Let me up."

Confusion registered on his face, flushed from the lovemaking, but he lifted his body off hers. She slipped out of bed before he could react, and she raced to her purse to dig for the special collection condom the lab had provided.

Keeping her back to him she tried to get control of her emotions. This was not working out the way she'd expected. She'd imagined they would jump into bed, bump and grind for a few minutes, and she'd leave. She was even willing to throw in a few moans for special effect.

But her whimpers just two minutes earlier weren't faked. The man had been seconds away from bringing her to a climax.

What was she thinking? If this was going to work, she had to stay detached, no matter how good he made her feel. She had to keep the upper hand.

Dani walked back to the bed and unwrapped the prophylactic. "State law," she said simply. She watched as he rolled it on.

"It feels weird, like it doesn't fit right."

Dani panicked. Nate was right. The condom was designed to be used by men who had an aversion to the usual methods of obtaining a semen sample. The floppy area at the end was for collection purposes and did look a bit strange. She had to think fast. "It's the only kind we're allowed to use. Something about it being safer."

When he still looked doubtful, she added. "Besides, it's designed to give both of us maximum enjoyment. You do want that, don't you, Nate?" This man wasn't stupid, but she prayed he'd buy the lie.

Nate pulled her down and straddled her. "Let's see if it works."

His kiss deepened, and involuntarily, her legs moved apart, inviting him. A soft gasp escaped her lips as he slid into her for the second time, and she arched her hips to allow him to go deeper.

He lifted up, balancing his body on his forearms as he made love to her, slowly at first, then increasingly demanding. She opened her eyes long enough to see his face contorted with passion. She didn't want this to end, but her body screamed for release.

Pulling his face down, she turned on her side and wrapped her legs around his frame. Thrust after thrust, she matched his passion, her breath now coming in short frantic spurts, until both of them cried out. She clung tighter as the orgasmic spasms rocked the bed.

When her muscles began to relax, she opened her eyes and met his stare, still close enough that their lips nearly touched.

"I've never done anything like this before."

She closed her mouth before she confessed this was her first time, too. He pulled away slightly and reached down to remove the condom.

For a moment, Dani was caught up in the spent passion as she tried to normalize her breathing. Then she sat up in the bed. "Let me do that, Nate." She rolled the used condom off, protecting the semen that had collected in the end. "You get comfortable while I flush this. You've got time left to entertain me, so you'd better rest while you can." She winked.

She lifted her body from the bed, suddenly embarrassed by her nakedness but unable to cover herself and protect the specimen at the same time.

She walked into the bathroom and placed the condom on the counter before she flushed the commode. Then she wrapped a towel around her body and walked out.

"I'm going to hop into the shower, Nate. I just need a few girly things from my purse." She smiled as she watched him watching her. He looked like a teenage boy who had just lost his cherry.

He smiled when he caught her looking. "Hurry back, Sophie. I already miss you."

Dani closed the bathroom door and hoisted the purse to the counter. She pulled out the metal container and the glass tube, turning on the water in the shower to cover any noise she might make. Within minutes, she had the precious semen out of the condom and into the test tube exactly the way the lab technician had instructed. She opened the container, and watched as the frigid steam from the dry ice clouded the mirror. Quickly, she inserted the tube into the canister and slammed it shut.

She glanced into the mirror, feeling a sudden twinge of guilt. Nate didn't deserve this kind of deceit.

His voice outside the door startled her. "You want company in there?"

Dani jammed the canister back into the purse and carefully placed it on the floor under the counter. Forsaking her guilt, she pushed it further back with her foot. Letting him discover her equipment was not such a great idea.

"I'm almost finished, Nate."

She threw the condom into the toilet and flushed again. Yanking off the towel she stepped into the shower. The hot water slid over her skin, reminding her of the way his fingers had done just minutes before. She scolded herself for even thinking about that. This was a job, nothing more.

She reached for the shampoo and lathered her head. It felt good to get all that hair spray out of her hair. When she heard the shower door open, she froze. Instinctively, she opened her eyes then quickly squeezed them shut as the shampoo set them on fire.

Then she felt his body behind her, his skin warm against her slick body, his erection moving against her back side. She leaned into him, enjoying the friction created by the hot water.

Silently, he nibbled on her neck, sending shivers down her entire body. When she could take no more of his teasing, she turned and pulled him close. With her left hand, she braced her body against the wall. The sensation when he entered her nearly sent her over the edge, and she gasped. Under the steady pounding of the hot water on their bodies, they made love again, quickly this time, but no less intense.

Exhausted, they dried off and slipped back under the covers, still without conversation.

"Sophie, I haven't made love like that in a very long time. I didn't realize how much I missed it."

She wanted to admit feeling the same but couldn't. "That's what I get the big bucks for."

They lay in silence, each in their own thoughts until she heard his breathing deepen. She eased out of bed, grabbed the discarded hooker clothes and quickly dressed.

For a minute she stood over him, watching him sleep, wondering if she filled his dreams.

She sighed and reminded herself again that was not her mission. Walking out the door with his specimen was.

She tiptoed across the room, the heavy purse slung over her shoulder. After one final glance at Nate Randall, she slipped out, leaving the money behind. She didn't need to feel any dirtier than she already did.

Dani tossed back the sheets and grabbed her robe. "I'm coming," she hollered, rubbing her eyes. Then she glanced at the clock on the nightstand. "Oh, crap." Seven thirty. If she hurried, she still might get to see Abby before Nikki dropped her off at school.

Tying the robe tightly around her naked body, she hurried down the steps, stumbling over one of the heels she'd flipped off on her way to bed. As she thought of the shoes and what had happened last night, her face heated up.

The glow evaporated when she opened the door. Johnny's ex-partner usually didn't come around this early.

"Tino, what's the matter?" An overwhelming sense of fear drained the look of surprise on her face. "Abby's okay, isn't she?"

"Abby's fine, or at least she was when I saw her last night at your sister's." He turned to Dani, his eyes accusing. "Where in the hell have you been all night?"

Ramon Florentino walked through the door, brushing against her body as he passed. The gesture wasn't accidental, making Dani even more self conscious of her nakedness under the robe. She never slept in the buff, but last night she'd been so grateful to lose the stupid thong, she'd tossed it in the trash and hopped into bed.

Dani ignored him and strolled into the kitchen, positive she didn't like the tone of his voice. Tino had been really helpful to her and Abby since Johnny died, but that didn't give him the right to demand details.

"What do you mean?"

"I drove by last night to check on you. When you weren't here, I went over to Nikki's. She was pretty evasive about where you were."

Dani hesitated. "I was on a stakeout."

"Until three in the morning?"

Dani whirled around to face him, anger blazing in her eyes. "How do you know what time I got home?"

Tino's glare softened, then he smiled. "I was worried, that's all. When Nikki wouldn't tell me where you were, I parked down the road and waited. After I was sure you were safely in the house, I left."

"I already have a father, Tino. I don't need you keeping track of where I go or when I get home like I'm some damn teenager."

As soon as the harsh words left her mouth, Dani regretted them. She touched his arm. "Sorry. I didn't get my eight hours last night as you know, and I'm crabby. I'm grateful you look out for Abby and me. I honestly am."

Tino covered her hand with his. "You're always crabby. What else is new?"

Dani released her hand and jabbed him playfully. "Is that why you come around so much? You some kind of glutton for punishment?"

His expression turned serious as he grabbed her hand again. "Truth is I worry about you. I wish you'd let me show you how to have fun again."

Dani reacted as if his touch were a lit torch. "Tino, don't go there." Despite him being a great looking guy, she wasn't the least bit attracted to him. Not sexually, anyway. He was simply her husband's old partner and a good friend. She didn't know how she would have made it without him those first few months after Johnny was killed by a drug dealer.

She moved closer and put her head on his shoulder. "You have to know how I feel about you, Tino. I love you like the brother I never had. You sit beside me at family dinners as if you are that brother. Abby loves you, too. But we're just friends. I'm not ready for anything more. Besides, I still talk to Alana and the girls two or three times a month."

"She and I have been divorced almost a year now, Dani. I've moved on, and you need to do the same."

Dani sighed. "I know. When I'm ready, I will. I just don't think it's a good idea for you and me to get anything started." She kissed him on the cheek. "Come on, Tino, a guy like you must have the ladies crawling all over him."

He held her stare for a moment before heading toward the door. "I'll drop it for now, but I'm not giving up. I'm betting Johnny would be happy knowing you were with someone he trusted."

Dani lowered her head. Her heart still ached every time she heard Johnny's name. "You are kidding, right? The absolute last thing he would want is for me to be with someone else. He always said if anything happened to him on the job, I should join a convent and take Abby with me." She laughed, then remembered last night at the

Marquee, and the warmth crept up her cheeks. How could she have felt that way with someone other than Johnny?

"I think you're wrong about that."

Dani grew uncomfortable with the direction of the conversation. "Hey, anything new with the investigation?"

He pursed his lips. "Nothing good. IAB is convinced Johnny had something going on with the dealer. They still think he was stealing heroin from the pushers he arrested and selling it to Apollo. The working theory is that Johnny wanted more and threatened to bust him if he didn't get a bigger cut. Apollo killed him, instead."

Dani shook her head. "Anyone who knew Johnny knows how ridiculous that is. If I have to investigate for another twenty years, I will. I'll clear Johnny's name or die trying. He was not a bad cop."

Tino sighed. "I know. I've talked to IAB until I'm blue in the face, but it's hard to argue with the evidence, Dani. They found a secret bank account under his name with five thousand dollars in it."

"Doesn't it seem strange that a guy taking kickbacks from a big dealer like that would have so little tucked away? Look around." She made a wide sweep with her arm. "Does this look like the digs someone would live in if they were rolling in cash? I think not."

"You don't have to convince me."

Dani shook her head. "It makes no sense, Tino. Besides, they can't even prove the bank account was really his. The manager wasn't able to positively identify Johnny as the one who opened the account."

Tino blew out a breath. "The security tape shows a man that looks a lot like Johnny."

"Yes, but by the bank's own admission, the recorder had been malfunctioning, and the picture is fuzzy. They can't say for sure it was Johnny."

"As encouraging as that sounds, hanging on to every new lead, hoping each one will be the one that clears him only to have it fizzle out can't be good for you or Abby. Where'd you hear that, anyway?"

"You're not the only one with inside information. My sources tell me something isn't right about the whole thing. It seems a little too convenient. Besides, Johnny was a smart cop. Do you really think he'd open a bank account this close to home if he was trying to hide money?"

"You and I both know the answer to that, but IAB can't get past why someone else would put money in the bank in his name. And why didn't you know about the account?"

Dani shook her head. "I can't figure that out, either, but I promise, I'm going to."

"How? All the leads have dried up. They've got nothing. I almost wish I hadn't put that bullet between Apollo's eyes when shots started flying. Maybe if he'd lived, we could have found out the truth."

Dani met Tino's stare. "I'm glad you killed him. I might have tried to do it myself if you hadn't. But that's not going to stop me. Last week I got a call from an old snitch of mine who sold for Apollo. He said the word on the street is that Apollo's death was a setup. Said Johnny was in the wrong place at the wrong time."

Tino frowned. "Tell me something I don't already know. Give me a name, and I'll look him up in the system. Maybe I can find something new."

"He's just a low guy on the totem pole in Apollo's camp. Said he's got a friend who knows the whole story. I'm waiting to hear back from him."

Tino's face tightened. "Dani, you're not thinking of doing this by yourself, are you? You're not a cop anymore. You have no business being in that part of town alone, much less talking to a pusher without backup."

The loud ringing of the phone startled Dani, and she glanced at Caller ID. Nikki. No way could she talk to her sister with Tino right there.

After her machine picked up, she turned back to him. "I know your opinion of a PI isn't all that great, Tino, but jeez. I was a cop for a lot of years. I know how to handle myself."

Tino snorted. "Don't I know that. But even the best cop alive is smart enough to have someone watching his back. At least let me go with you. There's something about a uniform that's as intimidating as hell."

There was no use arguing when Tino was determined. "Okay, I'll call when I hear from him. Now, I need to go before my daughter leaves for school."

"Too late. Abby had to be there fifteen minutes ago for a field trip." After seeing the confused look on Dani's face, Tino added, "Sara goes to the same school, remember?"

Dani chastised herself for being a bad mother. Her daughter's field trip had been the very last thing on her mind last night. "Right. I forgot about the trip." She opened the door and nudged him out. "Now, leave. Harry will have my head if I don't get to the office. Catch you later."

Reluctantly, Tino walked out and sauntered to his car as Dani studied him. He really was a hunk, especially in uniform. His dark hair peeking out from beneath the cap and his chiseled buns that always caught the attention of females were outlined even in his baggy police-issued pants. He'd make a good catch for some lucky girl one day. Just not her. Lately, he'd been showing up more often, mostly uninvited, and it worried her. She'd have to address that in the near future. But for now, she was dying to call Nikki.

She slammed the door and reached for her phone. Nikki answered after one ring.

"Dani, where are you?"

"Home. Where do you think?"

"Why didn't you answer the phone? I've been trying your cell and your home phone. Harry said he hasn't heard from you, either. Said if I find you to tell you to get your skinny little ass down to the office. He's swamped. But you're not going anywhere until I find out what happened last night. I've been going crazy. Where were you?"

Dani smiled. She enjoyed keeping her twin sister in suspense a little longer. "Overslept."

"Dani, I'm gonna kick your butt if you don't start talking. Do you realize how worried I was about you? I almost called to tell you to abort the whole stupid plan."

"I'm glad you didn't."

An awkward silence fell between them. "That's it? No details?"

"If you show up with a Grande White Chocolate Mocha, I'll tell you anything you want to know."

"Done. But give me something to hang on to. Did you do it?"

"Do what?"

"I really am going to kick your..."

"Twice."

Nikki gasped. "Don't you dare move. I'm on my way."

CHAPTER THREE

"Dr. Randall, the patient's ready."

Nate couldn't stop thinking about last night. Visions of soapy, hot sex with Sophie's hair, wet and free in his hands, brought a crinkle to his lips and a familiar tightness inside his scrubs.

"Dr. Randall?"

He glanced up at the nurse. "What? Oh, yeah."

Jesus. He was about to put a seventy-year-old woman under. He'd better get his head into what he was doing. It had been bad enough his stomach churned like it was running the Indy 500. "In a minute, Kelly."

He pulled the surgical mask over his nose and tied it in back. It had been a long day, and this was his last case. He didn't need to be fantasizing about some hooker he'd never see again.

He pushed through the door into the operating room and walked directly to the patient. Mrs. Smith was already asleep from the sedative he'd given her in the pre-op area. This was her first surgery, and the sweet thing had been so afraid she wouldn't wake up afterwards, she'd nearly cut off the circulation in his hand squeezing it.

He sat on the stool behind her head and reached for the medicine. After drawing it up, he checked the monitors before he injected it into the IV line. Then he reached behind and turned on his CD player. Today, he decided to listen to something soft. He put in a Boyz 2 Men CD and hit play before checking Mrs. Smith's monitors again.

Certain she was under, he injected Vecuronium, another anesthesia drug and inserted the breathing tube. Then he signaled to Jake DeLeon, the orthopedic surgeon scrubbing up outside the OR door.

His arm caught the edge of the metal table holding the anesthesia drugs.

He hopped off the stool as the vials and syringes hit the hard floor with a bang, scattering broken glass everywhere.

Kelly rushed over with a towel, barking orders to the circulating nurse to call for Housekeeping. "Do you need new scrubs, Dr. Randall?"

Nate, embarrassed by his clumsiness, dabbed at a wet spot above his knee. "I'm fine, Kelly. Sorry about the mess." He glanced at the monitors before moving aside as a man wheeled in the clean-up cart.

"What's with you, Randall?" Jake asked when he came through the double doors. He held his hands in the air as a nurse shoved the sterile gown over his scrubs. "I've never known you to be so klutzy." His forehead creased. "And since when do you listen to R & B? Usually, you torture us with jazz."

Nate lowered his eyes. He had to chill. The last thing he needed was for anyone, especially his friend Jake, to think his behavior was unusual. God forbid if anyone discovered he'd paid to spend the night with a woman. He'd be razzed to death.

He grinned. Why would they think that? He wasn't wearing a sign or anything. "Apparently, I get nervous waiting for you orthopedic guys who are never on time."

"Yeah, right." Jake positioned himself over the patient. "We go on your say, Nate."

Nate reached for the new vials Kelly handed him and quickly drew up the medicine. Mrs. Smith was already under, but he liked to be ready just in case. He nodded to his friend.

Jake made an incision at her hip, humming to the CD. "My wife loves these guys. Makes her really friendly." He snorted. "Trust me. That's been one uphill battle lately."

"I hear you," Nate deadpanned. "Hey, how is Nancy?"

Jake frowned. "Let's just say I've been working way too many hours. Guess I'd better bring out the old cheesy CDs and try to warm her up again."

Nate grinned. "Take mine. You need all the help you can get."

"Don't I know it? Okay, let's get this show on the road so this pretty young lady can walk without pain."

For the next hour or so, the talk centered on mostly hospital politics. Jake was an old friend from medical school, had even been the one who'd introduced Nate to Janelle. Although Jake knew Nate and his wife were having problems, he didn't know the grizzly details. Some things were better left private.

Like spending the night with a call girl.

Both Nate and Jake turned when the door to the operating suite opened and one of Nate's partners poked his head in.

"Hey, what was all the noise earlier? Is everything all right in here?"

Nate laughed. "It's fine, Paul. Apparently, I've had a little too much caffeine today. Made a total mess for Kelly." He mouthed, *Sorry*, to the nurse before turning back to his partner. "You through for the day?"

Paul Gerard walked further into the room and closed the door. "Yep. I'm headed to the office now."

"We're finishing up here, so I'll see you shortly." Nate hung another IV bag and adjusted the drip.

"Doubtful. I'll be in and out and long gone before you get there."

"Big night with the missus?" Jake asked.

Nate glanced up in time to see the look that passed between Paul and the operating room nurse.

"Business meeting," Paul replied, heading toward the door. "See you in the morning, Nate," he said over his shoulder as the door closed behind him.

Nate blew out a slow breath. Like hell, he had a business meeting, although that's probably what he'd told his wife. The sudden flush on Kelly's face spoke volumes. His partner was up to his old tricks again, even after all the grief he'd taken when his wife had caught him playing house with the new, hot-looking pharmacist a few months ago. That had bought him several trips to a marriage counselor and a lot of high-dollar, mea culpa purchases.

Nate thought Paul had changed. Obviously, he was wrong.

"Kelly, where's the pulsator?" Jake said, interrupting Nate's thoughts. After the surgeon reached for it and irrigated the wound, he glanced back at Nate. "Hey, how was last night?"

After recovering from his initial shock, Nate scrutinized Jake's face. Had his friend just read his mind? How could he possibly know about Sophie? Had someone seen him? He was already feeling remorseful about having sex with a prostitute. Hell, with anyone.

"What do you mean?"

"The clinic. Isn't Thursday the night you work at Fair Park?"

Nate hoped the relief didn't show on his face. "Yeah. It was a zoo, as usual."

"I wish I could find the time to give them a few hours. Last time I tried, I got called out for an emergency amputation and left about fifty patients who didn't get seen. They deserve better than that. So, I replenish their medical supplies once or twice a month, and thank God for guys like you."

"That's more than most people do, Jake."

Just then, the monitor alarm sounded indicating an increase in Mrs. Smith's heartbeat. Nate grabbed the pre-filled syringe and injected the medicine into her IV. After a few seconds, the rate decreased, and Nate relaxed.

Once he was sure Mrs. Smith was okay, he allowed his mind to wander back to the events that had taken place after he'd left the clinic last night. What was he thinking, having sex with a prostitute without some kind of protection?

My, God! He was a doctor, not some horny teenager. He'd have to get tested in the morning and again in a few weeks. He took little comfort in the fact that a high-priced hooker like Sophie probably had herself tested religiously. Still, he should start the HIV cocktail just to be on the safe side. He could blame it on a careless needle stick if anyone found out.

He settled back and concentrated on Mrs. Smith and her vital signs, all of which were fine. Without warning, he reached back and turned off the CD. Hearing the Boyz sing about taking off clothes and making love was more than he could handle today.

32

"Hey, I was just getting into them," Jake said, a little annoyed. He turned to the orthopedic resident assisting him. "Close her up, then send her up to ICU overnight, so they can monitor her heart rate just to be sure the tachycardia was an isolated incident. Hopefully, our Mrs. Smith will soon be walking like a teenager again."

He stepped away from the operating room table and pulled off his gloves. "Were you serious about lending me that C.D., Nate?"

Nate reached back again and ejected it. "Tell her I'm available if this doesn't work."

"Not in this lifetime, pal." Jake started for the door, then turned back. "Must have been one helluva night. You look like you haven't slept in a week."

"Wouldn't you like to know? Now, get out of here before I change my mind about the C.D.," Nate bantered, knowing his friend was right about the way he looked. He should never have mixed champagne with scotch, but Jake was wrong about the lack of sleep. Spent passion was better than any sleeping pill on the market, and he'd slept like a baby, nearly missing his wake-up call.

After the resident finished with Mrs. Smith, Nate reversed the anesthesia drugs as much as he could and prepared her for transfer. An hour later, confident she would have no further problems with her heart rate, he settled into his car and started for his office to wrap things up before heading home for the day.

Home? Could he really call living in the guest house on his wife's property home? When he'd told her he was moving out a year ago, Janelle had talked him into staying until he found a place of his own.

Somehow, a year had passed, and he still hadn't done a thing about getting out. He'd known it was a bad idea to start with, but he'd thrown himself into his work and had allowed things to remain as they were. Janelle interpreted this as a possibility they might be able to patch things up and start fresh.

How could you start fresh when your whole relationship was based on one lie after another? When he'd found out she'd been lying to him all along about the fertility treatment, he'd gone ballistic. All those years they'd been trying to conceive, all the disappointments and tears, all the outright lies.

33

None of that mattered anymore. It was time to move on. Despite the twinge of guilt he felt about last night, despite the fact he'd have to pay a visit to Father Anthony, his night with Sophie had convinced him that he had stopped living a long time ago. He merely existed.

Last night he'd had his first taste of champagne in over five years. The old Nate would never consider spending the night with a prostitute. The new Nate wished Sophie had left a number so he could give her the money she'd left on the dresser. Probably had been in too big a hurry to get to her next john.

He smiled. Okay, maybe that wasn't the only reason he wished she'd left her number.

Thoughts of Sophie and her shiny black hair highlighting the chocolate eyes in the dim light of the bar returned with a vengeance. He had come damn close to saying no when she had literally fallen into him. His conscience still nagged him that he hadn't.

Although he'd made the decision over a year ago to end his unhappy marriage, the fact remained that he still wasn't single. Maybe if Janelle hadn't freaked out when he'd suggested she find a lawyer, or if he hadn't procrastinated like an idiot, things might be different now.

But they weren't. Nate knew casual sex didn't bother some people, but unfortunately, he wasn't one of them. At least, he hadn't been until Sophie had rubbed against his chest, and his testosterone level won the battle with his conscience.

He'd never paid for sex before in his life. He'd never had to. College girls at Southern Methodist University had been more than willing to spend the night with him. Then he'd met Janelle, six feet of the most gorgeous female he'd ever seen, and that had been the end of his one-nighters.

Don't go there, Randall.

He turned down Gaston Avenue, and his thoughts returned to the previous night. Sophie hadn't come cheap, but it hadn't mattered. For one thing, he still had the money, but more importantly, sex with a woman who looked like that and only knew his first name had been worth it. His head had warned him it was a bad idea from the get-go, but the bulge in his pants had trumped his better judgment.

His initial impression had been that Sophie was too skinny for his taste. Too skinny for his taste? Since when did he have a taste? For the past ten years, he'd been faithful to Janelle. Not that he was a saint. God knew he wasn't. He appreciated a great-looking woman as much as any red-blooded male, but his Catholic upbringing had always stopped him cold. Even now that he and Janelle hadn't shared a bed in over a year, he hadn't looked elsewhere.

So, no. He hadn't cultivated a taste in women. Instead, he'd thrown himself into his work, spending twelve hours or more at the hospital or his office six days a week. But even that hadn't filled the void in his life. That job belonged to his old friend, Johnnie Walker Red.

Nate pulled the Mercedes into the underground parking garage and slid into his slot, noticing his partners were already gone for the day. He breathed a sigh of relief. He had several hours of paperwork ahead of him, and lately Paul seemed hell-bent on making small talk. Nate found getting him out of his office without being downright blunt a chore. And even Roger, his other partner who usually kept to himself, had been hanging around lately.

The ride in the elevator took only seconds, but in that short time, Nate made the decision to call a real estate agent in the morning. He'd check out one of the suburbs north of downtown Dallas, as far away from Swiss Avenue and his old life as he could get.

When the elevator doors opened, the first thing he noticed was the silence. No phones ringing off the hook, no usual hustle and bustle, just quiet. He glanced at his watch. Seven thirty. With a little luck, he could be home and in bed before midnight. His light schedule had been shot to hell, thanks to three emergency surgeries.

Stifling a yawn, he walked into his office and turned on the light.

"Hello, Nate. Did you have a good time last night?"

He whirled around and came face to face with his wife, dressed to the nines and sporting the most venom-filled eyes he'd ever seen.

"What brings you here, Janelle?" Nate asked, after the shock of seeing her in his office wore off.

"I own the building. Remember?" A smile covered her face but didn't mask the anger in her eyes.

Nate walked to the small refrigerator, feeling the heat of her gaze on his back, sensing her rage. He reached in for a beer and offered it to her. When she declined, he popped the top and took a long swig. This could get ugly. "How could I forget? You bring it up every chance you get."

Her smile faded. "Who were you with last night?"

Her comment caught him by surprise. "You know I'm always at the clinic on Thursdays," he said, buying some time until he figured out if she was fishing or if she really knew something about last night. Had she paid someone to tail him?

Janelle pulled a cigarette from her purse and lit it, obviously in no hurry to end his speculation. She blew the smoke out in one long breath before she smiled again. "I'm talking about after the clinic, Nate. I'm talking about the whore you took up to your room."

Question answered. She did have someone watching him. He vaguely remembered a guy in a suit at the other end of the bar, but he was gone before Sophie showed up. The only reason he remembered the man at all was because Lily had said he'd hit on her.

Nate racked his brain. Was Lily the spy? She'd been serving drinks at the Marquee since he'd started spending his Thursday nights there. Occasionally, they were the only two in the bar. He knew all about her kids, the problems with her ex, even about her love life. It couldn't be her, could it? Knowing how persuasive Janelle could be when she flashed a wad of cash at someone like Lily, he realized there was a real possibility it was. He'd have to be more careful around her.

"I don't think that's any of your business, Janelle. Our marriage is over. Has been for a long time."

"I've got a piece of paper that says you're still my husband. That makes it my business."

Nate sighed. His procrastination had given her the right to probe. "My mistake. I figured that sooner or later, you'd get pissed off enough to call your lawyer. Guess I was wrong. I'll take care of it first thing Monday morning."

She laughed. "Do you really think that's what I want? That I'd give you up so easily?"

"There's no giving me up, Janelle. The simple truth is, I don't love you. Haven't for a long time." He knew his words were hurtful, but they had to be said. "We were just kids when we married. We gave it our best shot, but we've grown apart. If you were being truthful to yourself, you'd admit you have no love left for me either. We've been living a lie for a long—"

"That's not true. I've loved you from the minute I laid eyes on you, back when you were a struggling med student, worried you'd have to leave school because you were so far in debt. You loved me then. I know you did. You loved Daddy's money, too. How can you forget that without him or me, you'd probably be in some hick town in southwest Texas pumping gas?"

How indeed, when she reminded him every chance she could that she was now sole owner of the building housing his office and that she sat on the boards of the two hospitals where he was on staff? Early in his career, he had sold his soul, and now the devil herself was demanding her due.

Janelle got up and walked around the desk. "We can fix anything, Nate, if we try." Her voice softened. "Just tell me what you want me to do." She stepped behind his chair and began to massage his neck.

He jerked away as if her fingers were blades. "Stop it, Janelle. We've been down this road too many times before. What's been wrong with our marriage—what's been wrong between us for a long time—can't be fixed."

"I'll get pregnant, Nate. I promise. I know how much you want a baby. This time, I'll really try. You can go with me to Dr. Sheffield's office."

Nate studied her with genuine sadness. She really believed having a child would make everything right between them. He couldn't blame her. For a long time, he'd believed it, too. But no more. Bringing a child into a house without love wasn't fair to anyone, and it certainly wouldn't fix a dying relationship.

One thing was for sure. He'd fallen out of love with her long before he'd discovered her deceit.

"I realized years ago, Janelle, that motherhood wasn't your thing. Maybe that's the way it's supposed to be. I don't know. I only wish you'd confided in me before I discovered your little secret. We might have been able to work it out had you been truthful. Now it's too late. It's time we move on."

She grabbed his hand and pressed it to her breast. "Don't say that, Nate. We love each other. We used to have a pretty good time in bed." She moved his palm to her other breast.

He pulled his hand from her grasp. "That's ancient history, Janelle."

"No." She parted her lips in a determined smile. "I'll never let you go."

"You have no choice. I'll pick up my things tonight and move into the Marquee until I can find a place of my own." He raised his eyes to meet her gaze. "Don't worry. I don't want you *or* your money."

He reached for the stack of files on his desk. "Now, if you'll excuse me, I've got several hours of work here. I'll stop by tomorrow for my stuff."

Hope faded from her eyes, only to be replaced by rage. She stood and stretched her long body across the desk until her face was close enough to touch.

"No one leaves Janelle St. Clair, especially a spineless, self-righteous man like you. You'll come begging, I promise. I'll make your life so miserable you won't know what hit you." She stormed out the door, stopping only to blow a kiss before she slammed it, rattling the entire office.

Okay. That went well.

Janelle would never change. If he had any doubts before, he was convinced now. Their relationship could never work no matter how hard they tried.

He sighed. Despite her threat, he felt alive for the first time in months, as if a two-ton weight had been lifted from his shoulders.

He studied the chart in front of him but was unable to concentrate. He was in for the fight of his life. But it was a battle he could not lose. He wanted out, no matter what he had to do.

Chapter Four

He lay back on the pillow, smoking the joint he'd scored an hour ago, before turning to the young girl sprawled across the bed.

"Time to pack up and go, sugar." He nudged her off the side. The bitch was so stoned, she probably didn't even feel her head thump against the hardwood floor.

When she didn't move, he slid out of bed, jerked her upright, and threw her wrinkled clothes in her face. "Get dressed. I'll drive you home."

The hurt look she gave him when she stumbled past on her way to the bathroom didn't faze him. He'd picked her up at some teeny bopper joint with the promise of good weed.

Women were sluts. All of them.

He pounded on the bathroom door. "Hurry up, bitch. I don't have all night."

As he waited, his mind was on someone else. Someone whose name he'd called out as he'd exploded into the young girl's mouth moments before.

Someone who was getting too damn close.

The front door opened and Dani hurried to pull on her jeans.

"Dani?" Nikki yelled from downstairs.

"In a minute."

"Hurry. I'm dying to find out about—" She stopped abruptly when Dani appeared at the top of the stairs. "You don't look any different."

Dani laughed. "God, I hope not. Although I gotta tell you, I'm probably walking a little funny."

"Ohmygod! You actually did it. Did you take the canister to the lab?"

"The guy said I had up to twenty-four hours to bring it in as long as I kept it in dry ice. I'll drop it off on my way to the office."

Tears welled in Nikki's eyes. "I thought last night would never end. I worried so, thinking maybe something had gone wrong and the plan got scrapped or worse, that it really was happening and you were in trouble. Was it a total nightmare?"

A slow smile spread across Dani's face. "If you call having mind-blowing sex with a gorgeous guy a nightmare, then yeah, it was."

Nikki's eyes widened. "Oh, Lord, Dani. What were we thinking sending you off to a bar to seduce him? In downtown Dallas, for god-sakes! He could have been a pervert."

"True." Dani scrunched her lips to hide the grin. "I probably wouldn't have noticed."

Nikki's eyes glistened. "That hot, huh?"

"Oh, yeah. Even with the powerful lens I used, the photos didn't do him justice." Dani frowned. "Oh, Nik. I can't believe I really did it. And the worst part is that I actually enjoyed it. That wasn't supposed to be part of the deal." She sighed. "He was so cute and nervous, I couldn't help myself."

"I said a prayer he wouldn't be butt ugly."

Dani snorted. "It worked. If the fertility clinic had to screw up, thank God they did it with someone whose genes are top quality."

At the mention of the fertility clinic, Nikki lowered her eyes.

Dani touched her arm. "Sorry. I didn't mean to make light of something that has devastated you and your family. I only meant—"

"I know what you meant, Dani. I don't know what I would do without your humor sometimes."

Dani put her arm around Nikki's shoulder. Her sister and her family had been through so much since they'd diagnosed Casey with the rare genetic disease. A disease that would eventually kill him if he didn't get a bone marrow transplant. Even more devastating had been the discovery that Casey did not carry Bobby Romano's genes.

Dani remembered that night as if it were yesterday. She'd nearly wrecked her car on the drive to Nikki's house. But after hearing the anguish in her sister's voice, she'd known something was terribly wrong.

"Bobby's not Casey's father, and I'm not a match," Nikki had said between sobs.

"How could that be?" Dani asked. Since her senior year, Nikki and Bobby had been inseparable, even in Austin where college parties could get rowdy.

Nikki lowered her eyes. "I don't know." She'd turned to Bobby. "I know you think I betrayed you, but I swear you are the only man I've ever been with. Now our son is going to die, and you have no reason to believe me. I don't think I can live with that."

"Nikki, don't," Bobby had whispered, caressing her hair. "We'll find out how this happened, I promise. Casey needs us both to be strong."

Watching her sister and the brother-in-law she loved in so much pain had nearly killed Dani. They had kept her sane when she'd gone through her own grief, and she'd felt helpless when they'd needed her.

That had been three months ago. Three months of traveling all over the country with Casey to the few Fanconi experts out there. None had offered much hope without a transplant until Casey had seen Dr. Juliana, a research doctor from the Mayo Clinic. He told them there had been limited success with a new procedure using cord blood after the birth of a perfectly matched infant. He'd said that since both Nikki and Casey's father were carriers of the fatal disease, the procedure to genetically engineer a Fanconi-free embryo that was also a match would be tedious but not impossible. So far, it had worked in nearly seventy percent of his patients. They called it *pre-implantation genetic diagnosis*. Dani remembered how Nikki's eyes had brightened with renewed hope.

"It was a miracle you were able to find Randall with so little to go on," Nikki said.

Miracle, my butt!

Dani had spent long hours pouring over the list of donors at the fertility clinic much to the dismay of the owners who initially were uncooperative. But after Dani had picked up the phone to call the local

TV station with her suspicions and threatened a multi-million dollar lawsuit, they had changed their tune.

A mix-up at the clinic was the only explanation that made sense. She'd believed her sister immediately, knew she wouldn't lie about something as important as this. They might never have discovered the error if it weren't for the diligence of a young man who took pity on them and delved deeper into the files. When he came up with two possible specimens, Dani took over.

The first name on their short list was a middle-aged man who was undergoing chemotherapy for early-onset prostate cancer. He had preserved several sperm samples at the clinic in case the powerful chemo drugs rendered him infertile. The other was a doctor whose wife had been undergoing fertility treatments.

Dani had tracked down the doctor first and followed him for two weeks before striking gold with DNA from a retrieved Starbuck's cup. The test results left no doubt that Dr. Nate Randall was Casey's biological father, his sperm mistakenly used to fertilize the embryo that was then implanted into Nikki's uterus.

"I am so grateful to you, Dani, even if this doesn't work. At least we tried." Nikki paused and took two cups out of the sack. She handed one to Dani. "Here's your coffee. Now give it up."

Dani reached for the steaming brew and sipped. She sat at the table and waited for her sister to do the same before she gave her a rundown. "Nik, he was one of the nicest men I've ever met. I can tell you with certainty, Casey's sky-blue eyes didn't come from Mom's side of the family like everyone thinks."

"Were you terrified?"

"Yeah, the bar thing was scary, but I made sure I drank enough to drown my inhibitions. Ever taste an apple martini?"

"Dani, I don't give a rat's behind about apple martinis. Get on with the story," Nik said, unable to hide her impatience. "Were you drunk?"

"A little. He bought the whole hooker routine. Guess you were right about the dress. Told him my name was Sophie."

Nikki spit out a mouthful of coffee. "Sophie?"

"Don't ask. Anyway, we got up to his room, and I nearly freaked out. The king-size bed was massive, and I wanted to bolt right then and there, but I'd come too far to turn back. Then room service arrived with a bottle of Dom Perignon."

"No way!"

"Way! By the time I had downed two glasses, in addition to the martinis, I was feeling really mellow, and the good doctor was looking pretty damn inviting." Dani touched her sister's arm. "I can't even begin to tell you how good the sex was."

"And you used the condom they gave you, right?"

Sort of. "Yep. I had to think fast when he saw it, but fortunately, the guy was so horny, I could have said it was made of licorice, and he wouldn't have cared. I think I told you the reports I got on him implied he and his wife were having some kind of marital problems." Dani paused before adding, "Plus, he was a little snockered, too."

"That always helps." Nikki grabbed Dani and planted a big kiss on her forehead. "I love you so much for doing this."

"It had to be done," Dani said, her voice almost a whisper. "I'd do it again in a heartbeat. I just didn't expect to feel anything. What does that say about me?"

"That you're the best sister in the world. I'm so sorry for putting you through this. Even though it was your idea, I know how it goes against everything you believe in. You know, the sanctity of marriage and all that. Johnny would be so proud."

Dani nearly choked as she coughed and laughed at the same time. "What's with everyone thinking Johnny would be happy to see me screwing around? My Johnny, who beat the crap out of the poor skinny guy who moved down the street senior year and was stupid enough to flirt with me?" She laughed.

"Forgot about how jealous he was. You couldn't pay a boy to look at you after that."

"No, Johnny would *not* be proud of me," Dani continued. "I fact, he'll probably come back and get revenge." She stopped, her eyes squinted in thought. "I'll probably get some kind of STD."

"You said you used the condom."

"The first time."

Nikki gasped. "Oh, Dani, don't tell me you were dumb enough to have sex with a stranger without protection."

"It happened so quickly. We were in the shower." She turned to her sister, her eyes challenging. "Did you use a condom with Bobby before you were married?"

"Point made, but that was almost ten years ago. We weren't so smart back then." Nikki clucked her tongue. "Had I known it would be so hard to get pregnant, I could have saved myself a lot of sleepless nights worrying I was knocked-up back in college."

"Can you picture Dad holding a shotgun on Bobby at the altar?"

Both girls cracked up. Then, the light moment over, Nikki put her head in her hands. "You do know you'll have to get tested and take some pills, right?"

"What? Oh, yeah. He's a doctor, Nik. I'll go somewhere in Fort Worth and have the test done, but honestly, I'm not that worried about it."

Dani hoped her sister would believe the lie. They'd never been able to keep things from each other for very long. The fact was it was the twenty-first century and anybody who wasn't an idiot knew better than to have unprotected sex. Even more idiotic, she had a spare condom left in her purse.

"We still should have gone to him straight out and begged if we had to. He would have been tested, I know."

"It isn't that simple. We all agreed right here at this table—you, me, and Bobby—that Casey was already going through enough without telling him the father he loved wasn't related to him at all. Can you really imagine a perfect stranger becoming a part of your son's life right now, telling you how to raise him, demanding holidays with him?"

Dani softened. Now was not the time to bring this up. Nikki's emotions were too fragile. Even though Casey was doing better, they all knew they were in a race with time.

Nikki shook her head. "It all sounded so easy that night. You have sex with a great looking stranger, and my son gets a chance to become a teenager. We never considered the down side. I still can't believe you had unprotected sex, Dani. What were you thinking?"

"How his fingers set every nerve ending in my body on fire. How his five o'clock shadow burned against my cheeks, my breasts."

"Stop! I get it. Promise me you'll get tested today."

"Can't today. Harry's already having a hissy, plus I have to go by the lab."

"Do you want me to drop it off?"

"The place is in downtown Dallas, Nik. You don't even drive in downtown Cimarron. No, Harry will just have to wait a little longer." Dani chugged the last of her coffee and stood. "Gotta go. I'll see you Sunday at Dad's."

"I'll never forget what you've done for me," Nikki said, wistfully. "I'll pay you back."

"That's what sisters are for. Besides, seeing my only nephew and favorite godchild live long enough to put you through hell when he's in high school, the way you did to Dad, will be enough payback." She grabbed her car keys and headed out the door. "Lock up when you leave. Love you."

Nikki finally smiled. "You are walking a little funny."

Dani blew her a kiss. "Now there's that wild child I knew way back when. See ya."

She hopped in her car, glancing at her watch as she backed out of the driveway. The trip to the lab would take an extra forty-five minutes, and Harry would fume. She pushed on the gas pedal, and the pick-up burned rubber as it sped off. It wasn't until she hit the interstate that she relaxed and let her mind replay the night before with Nate Randall.

She hadn't lied to Nikki about him being a nice man. A nice man with great hands! He could put her to sleep anytime for free with those fingers.

Girl, what's the matter with you? You're never going to see that man again.

She couldn't, not if their plan was going to work. Randall could never know he had fathered not one but two children he would never see. She hated that part.

By all accounts, he really was decent—at least, according to the people with whom she had spoken. Without exception, they'd all agreed he was married to the wicked witch of Dallas. Janelle Randall, heiress to the St. Clair real estate fortune, was not the favorite person of anyone she'd questioned. In every conversation, the word *bitch* had been used extensively to describe her. One of Dani's informants had mentioned that Nate wasn't even living in the same house as his wife. Hadn't been for nearly a year. That would explain why he had been so easy to deceive. He had obviously not been thinking with his brain.

All the same, she'd say a special prayer for him at mass on Sunday. She owed him that much.

Just then, a Toyota cut in front of her car, and she slammed on the brakes. Nothing.

"Shit." She shoved her foot all the way to the floor in an attempt to activate the brakes. Still nothing.

She watched, almost in slow motion, as her car plowed into the Camry and bounced off the concrete barrier, sending her careening across the two right lanes, through the guard rail, and over an embankment. The last thing she remembered before she blacked out was reaching for the canister on the front seat.

"Dani?"

Dani tried to open her eyes but squeezed them shut as the pounding in her head intensified with the light. Slowly, she turned in the direction of her sister's frantic voice. "Nik?"

"Oh, God. I was so worried about you."

"Where am I?"

"ICU at Grace Memorial. You were in an accident about ten hours ago."

Dani tried to raise up, but the pain in her head forced her back onto the pillow. A soft moan escaped her lips.

"Easy, Dani. You have a nasty concussion."

A rough hand slid over hers.

"Dad?"

"I'm here, sweetheart. Don't try to talk. The doctor doesn't want you to move very much for the next twenty-four hours. We're only allowed in here five minutes every few hours. Oh, God, I thought we'd lost you. I couldn't bear—" His voice cracked.

Dani tried again to open her eyes, but she couldn't. The only other time she'd heard anguish like that in her dad's voice was when he'd told her and Nikki their mother had been killed in a four-car, pile-up on Central Expressway. She knew her injuries must be bad. "Am I okay?"

He squeezed her hand. "You were unconscious when they found you, but other than the concussion and about eight stitches in your forehead, you're going to live. Your mother must have been watching over you. It's a miracle you're here. It took the firemen more than two hours to cut you out of the—" His cry choked off the rest.

She patted his hand with her free one. "Daddy, don't." A sharp pain sliced across her chest, nearly cutting off her breath. She bit her lip to keep from screaming.

"Be still, child. You took a pretty good hit in the chest with the air-bag. The nurse said you have a huge bruise from that and the seatbelt."

"She's awake?" a woman asked.

Someone lifted her arm. "Are you in pain, Mrs. Perez?"

"A little," Dani lied.

"I'm Katie, your nurse until midnight. I've got something that will take the edge off. I'm putting it right into your IV line. You should get some relief in just a few minutes."

"Okay," Dani said, her eyes already growing heavy. She racked her brain for answers about how she had ended up at the hospital, but the medicine was already making her groggy. Then she remembered why she'd been going to downtown Dallas in the first place.

"Nik?"

"Relax, honey," Katie said. "I sent them out so you can rest."

Dani needed to talk to her sister. Needed to tell her the specimen was still in the car. She tried but couldn't open her eyes, couldn't form the words. Her tongue was so heavy. With every slow breath, her body relaxed a little more, the morphine taking her to a place where she would have no worries, no pain.

CHAPTER FIVE

"Come on, baby. Come to Mama." Janelle's throaty voice promised everything he could imagine.

She snorted the line and lay back on the pillow. His self control lasted all of two minutes before he caved. God, he wanted her.

Get it over with. Don't let her take the last bit of dignity from you.

He was here to do what he had tried unsuccessfully to do many times before. He was here to end it, once and for all.

He forced his eyes from the bed. "I didn't come here for that, Janelle."

"Then why did you come, baby?" She pulled the sheet away from her body, exposing her see-through thong panties that matched her black lacy top.

His mouth watered. She was six feet of raw sex. That come-on look is what had gotten him in this situation in the first place. He had to stay strong. Even though sex with Janelle was dynamite, she'd become more demanding every day. It was one thing to let her control what went on under the sheets, but lately, she'd pressed for more control over the rest of his life. She'd even made threats.

"It's over, Janelle. I wanted to tell you in person."

The sound of her bitter laughter cut through his words. "Honey, it's not over until I say it is." She paused. "I thought you understood that, especially since you came here with your dick out looking for action and your hand out looking for more money." She ran her index finger over her tongue slowly, seductively, and then spread her legs.

As hard as he tried, he couldn't pull his eyes away, anticipating her next move as she pushed the triangular lace to the side, exposing her greatest asset. Mesmerized, he kept his gaze on her as she performed for him, his breathing coming faster with each stroke of her moistened finger.

"Come here, baby, and convince me to keep you around," she whispered, her voice dripping with lust.

God help him. He tried and almost succeeded until she moaned softly and moved her hips slowly over the satin bed sheets. He tore at his clothes, heaving them across the room as he climbed on the bed and positioned himself between her long legs.

"That's it, baby. Make Mama sing."

As he ravished her with his tongue, every ounce of will power dissolved. She was a work of art.

He tightened his grip on her thighs and upped the tempo. She responded by grabbing his hair and pushing him further into her, moving her hips, shaking the entire bed until she screamed in orgasm.

"You're good, baby. Now come up here and let me show you how good I am," she whispered, still trying to catch her breath.

He wished he had the balls to get up and walk away. Leave her begging for more like she always left him. He wanted to tell her she would never see him again. That she'd have to find someone else to be the outlet for her insatiable appetite for sex, which almost always turned kinky.

But he couldn't.

He rose up and plunged into her the way she liked it—hard and fast. He was so weak, so easy to manipulate. Say what you wanted about her—she was one great piece of ass. Plus there was the money thing.

Shit.

He could always end it tomorrow.

Thrust after thrust, he pushed deeper into her, his eyes on her face as it contorted in the throes of passion. She liked it rough. He'd give her what she wanted.

"Ride me hard, baby. Don't make Mama wait any longer. Bring me home."

With one last thrust, he exploded into her, pushing, pumping. When the orgasm finally rode its course, he rolled off and stared at the ceiling. Now is when the self-loathing usually hit. When he remembered what a bitch she really was. When he paid the price for being with her.

"You don't really think I'm going to let you leave me, do you, baby?"

Dani stared out the window, her mind unable to focus on the scenery flashing by as Bobby drove.

"Honey, you okay?" Nikki asked from the back seat. "Are the bumps killing you?"

Dani sighed, wishing that was the reason she was down. "I'm fine, Nik. Really." She glanced back as Abby suddenly giggled at something Casey had said, and Nikki's eyes met hers.

I'm sorry. Dani mouthed the words.

Nikki reared up, edging close to the front seat so the two kids in the back couldn't hear. "For what? You went above and beyond, and I love you for it."

"I'm sorry about the accident."

"Like it was your fault your brake line had a problem. Dad said there was a crack in it, probably from a big rock or something. Come on, Dani, quit blaming yourself."

Dani tried to turn and face her sister, but searing pain raced through her at the slightest movement.

"Don't move your head so fast. The doctor said to go easy for at least another week. You had a nasty concussion."

Once the pain subsided, Dani forced a smile. "So now what's our big plan?"

"What we should have done in the first place—go see Randall and tell him the truth."

Dani frowned. That's exactly what all the elaborate scheming had been about, to keep from doing that. They had to find a better way. "And the lab is positive the specimen can't be used?"

"The container got pretty mangled in the accident, and the dry ice leaked out. The car sat in the tow yard about twenty-four hours before

I could get to it. The guy at the lab said there was no way the sample could still be viable, but he checked anyway. Twice."

Dani eased her head back around and gazed out the front window again, careful not to let Nikki see the tears pooling in the corners of her eyes. All that planning and work, not to mention the deceit, and they had failed. *She* had failed. Her promise not to let her nephew down had been destroyed along with the canister from the lab. All she'd accomplished was to get a giant headache while Casey still struggled for each breath.

She couldn't give up, though. Not yet. Their plan would have to go on the back burner for now, at least until she could move her head without it throbbing. For some reason, a mental image of the wild sex that night flashed in her mind, and she grimaced. Even thinking about it hurt.

For the next ten minutes, they rode in silence with only chatter between Casey and Abby audible in the car. The sound of Casey's occasional laughter was music to Dani's ears, but she knew it wasn't permanent. The doctor had warned them not to get too hopeful. Casey was in remission that could end at anytime. He needed a bone marrow transplant, and no amount of wishful thinking would help.

That was the cold hard fact about Fanconi's. It killed.

Dani vowed to do all in her power to see that her nephew got that transplant. Just not today. Today, it was all she could do to keep a smile on her face in front of her family, none of whom except Nikki and Bobby knew the real reason why she was depressed.

She loved their weekly family dinners, but today, she should have stayed home. They would have understood.

No, they would have all rushed over to her house and smothered her with food and tender loving care. She wasn't in the mood for either.

Too late. She was met at the door by her Dad and his two sisters, Carmella and Sophie.

"Child, you are as pale as a ghost," Aunt Carmella said, pulling her into the house. "Come sit on the couch and tell us all about the accident."

Aunt Sophie pushed her portable oxygen tank out of the way and grabbed Dani by the arm. "Let her at least get in the door, Carm." She frowned at her younger sister.

Dani looked to her dad for help.

He shrugged. He had no control over his two spinster sisters who had helped him raise the twins after their mother died when they were in junior high.

Aunt Sophie positioned herself on the couch between Aunt Carmella and Dani. "What in tarnations were you doing way down there anyway?" she asked, in between noisy gasps of oxygen.

The truth would have sent her aunt into respiratory arrest.

When Dani finally climbed into bed, her thoughts returned to what little she could remember of the accident. Thank God, no one else had been badly hurt, although the driver of the Toyota had plowed into the guardrail after she'd hit him. With only a pretty good lick to his chest from the seatbelt, he had been treated and released that night.

No charges were filed against either of them, and his plans to sue Dani had been temporarily squashed when two witnesses came forward and fingered him as the one who had cut her off and caused the accident in the first place.

Not that he would have gotten much from her.

When Johnny was killed, she had received only a small insurance settlement. Young people always think they have time for everything. Increasing his life insurance was one of those things Johnny had put off until it was too, late. What little money Dani had received was tucked safely away in a college fund for Abby.

She'd counted on Johnny's police pension, but that had been withheld because of the investigation into his possible dealings with Apollo, his killer. It could take years to clear his name and receive the pension. She and Abby had to make do on her salary, which meant living on the cheap.

She'd lasted a year with the police department before finally quitting her job. Although her coworkers had said they didn't believe

Johnny was on the take, the air of suspicion hung over her like a black cloud.

From the minute IAB had first walked into the squad room and interviewed the entire force, Dani made proving Johnny's innocence her mission. Despite his flawless record, they had assumed the worst. After they'd found the bank account in his name, they'd gone after Dani as if she were a bad cop, too.

Five thousand freakin' dollars. Like that was the smoking gun.

Dani closed her eyes and mulled it over. Where had that money come from? Although she and Johnny's combined income had allowed them to live decently, they'd never had any leftover cash. With their house payment and two car notes, they'd lived from paycheck to paycheck like just about every other cop at the station.

When her boss had started to question the time Dani put in on her own investigation into Johnny's death, she couldn't take the pressure anymore. She'd quit the only job she'd had since Abby was a toddler. Criminal Justice was all she knew.

"Mom?"

At the sound of her daughter's voice, Dani glanced up. Abby stood in the doorway, her face crinkled with worry. "What's up, honey? Couldn't sleep?"

Abby shook her head, trying unsuccessfully to smile. "I was thinking about how scared I was when you were in the hospital."

"I was thinking about that, too." An outpouring of love flooded Dani's heart. "I'm not sure I'll be able to get to sleep tonight, either. Maybe we'd better cuddle." She patted the mattress next to her.

Abby's smile finally broke through, and she scrambled onto the bed and climbed under the covers, sliding as close to Dani as she could get. "What would happen to me if you..." The child couldn't continue.

Dani squeezed her closer. "Nothing's going to happen to me, I promise. Now close your eyes and try to sleep. You've got a big day at school tomorrow." She rubbed her daughter's back the way she had when Abby was a toddler, a trick that worked every time. Before long, the child's breathing had slowed, and she fell asleep.

Dani hated the fear in her daughter's voice, especially because Abby had done so well since Johnny's death. Apparently, the accident had affected her more than Dani realized. She'd talk to Harry tomorrow about taking a few days off, so she could get Abby through this.

Harry Fielding was her dad's old partner who'd retired about the same time he had. When he'd called to see if she was interested in working for him, she'd jumped at the offer. She'd known Harry since she was a little girl, remembering how he and his wife, Maria, had come to almost every family dinner they had. Since they were childless, they'd treated Dani and Nikki like they were their own.

At first, Dani was unsure if she would enjoy being a private investigator. She'd loved being a cop. Loved the fast pace of it all, the danger. Even loved the high pressure. To her surprise, she'd taken to her new job quickly and was soon Harry's best investigator.

The best part of the job was that Harry believed Johnny had been set up, too. Not only did he allow her to investigate on his time, he'd even pulled strings to get information from his old buddies still on the force.

Dani touched the small bandage on her forehead when the pain returned. After easing her arm from under Abby's head, she slipped out of bed. On the way to the bathroom, she caught a glimpse of herself in the mirror. She was a mess. Although the swelling around the stitches had gone down, blood had pooled under her eyes, giving her two huge shiners. She looked like she'd gone a couple of rounds with a prize fighter.

No way could she go to Randall now to try to get another specimen. She'd have to be content with tailing him for a few more days, until the stitches came out and her eyes returned to normal.

She swallowed a pain pill and headed back to bed. The realization that she was already thinking about taking another shot at getting the precious semen brought a smile to her face, despite the throbbing. That was one sacrifice she'd gladly make for her family any day of the week.

And that sacrifice was the only reason she was smiling. Her gleeful anticipation had nothing to do with wanting to feel a certain someone's arms wrapped around her again.

She closed her eyes and waited for the pain pill to work.

He slammed the druggie against the chain link fence, making sure his face took the brunt of the hit.

"How many times do I have to warn you about selling on this corner, dickhead?" He jammed his hand in the young kid's back pocket and came up with six balloons. Jerking the kid around, he slapped him in the face. "Where's the rest?"

Sweat began to trickle down the drug dealer's face. He couldn't have been older than fifteen or sixteen. "That's all I have," he stammered, sniffing to hold back the tears.

This time he balled his fist and punched the spaced-out kid in the stomach, laughing when he doubled over and threw up. "You must not have heard me. I'm only going to ask one more time." He pulled out his weapon and stuck it against the side of the dealer's head. "Where's your stash?"

The smell of urine assaulted his nostrils, and he backed away slightly, noticing the spreading stain on the front of the druggie's pants.

He cocked the revolver, and the kid screamed, pointing to an abandoned warehouse.

"It's under the floor board near the front."

He lowered his gun and shoved the kid in that direction. "Why don't you show me exactly where it is, loser, and maybe I won't kill you tonight?"

Walking behind, he had to laugh. This was getting too easy. Where was the challenge anymore?

An hour later, he was in his car, the heroin tucked safely under the front seat as he headed down Division Street.

Maybe he'd ride past Dani's house to make sure she was in for the night.

He banged his fist against the steering wheel. Stupid bitch wouldn't give up. Next time, she wouldn't get off so easy. Next time, he would use more than a sharp rock on her brakes.

Chapter Six

Poised and ready, Dani focused the camera as the man and woman exited the ratty hotel near Bachman Lake, her camera focused.

Click. Click.

Turning at the bottom of the stairs, the man pulled the woman close and kissed her. A long, tonsil-touching kiss that should make Mrs. Hamilton very happy. *Click. Click.*

Dani had been tailing Joe Hamilton the entire week, the only job Harry would allow during the doctor-ordered, take-it-easy week. He'd tried to keep her in the office but had relented when she'd pitched a fit.

She hated this part of the job, but it was way better than answering phones and pushing pencils. She despised the creeps who seriously believed they could get away with scamming their wives while balling their secretaries.

Joe Hamilton was one those guys, ranking high on the list of cheating scumbags. He'd charmed his way into Ellen Tresler's life then manipulated her inheritance, so he controlled all her assets, which were huge. But he'd underestimated the petite woman, twenty-eight years his senior and heiress to a multi-million dollar pharmaceutical empire. Soft-spoken Ellen had managed to slip in a one-line disclaimer at the bottom of the pre-nup. Nothing fancy. Just a simple statement, cut and dried.

If Joe screwed around, he would leave the marriage exactly as he'd come into it. Dead broke.

Either the ex-car salesman imagined he was smarter than the average bear, or he'd stuffed his brains into his boxers when he indulged in a nooner with his big-busted secretary, Sara Jane. Probably never dreamed a slick guy like him would ever get caught in a cheap motel doing the horizontal boogie.

Dani snapped picture after picture as the pair stopped beside a red and black Mustang parked on the side. When the woman smoothed her hair, she turned right into the camera. *Click.* She was almost pretty in a carny sort of way, with flaming red lips and a dress showing cleavage that nearly hit her chin.

Note to self. Find out where she buys her push-up bras.

Joe patted her ass before holding the door for her to slide in the driver's side. Seeing Joe in the afternoon sunlight, Dani wondered why any woman would consent to a quickie with a guy who looked like him in a cheap motel that probably rented by the hour.

Yikes!

A vision of DNA samples and God only knew what else on the sheets popped into Dani's brain. Was Hamilton phenomenal in bed, or had Mr. Big Spender convinced Sara Jane he would leave his wife and marry her? Dani voted for the latter, shivering at the notion that pudgy, bald, slime-bag Joe might be a stud muffin.

Dani snapped another dozen pictures as they drove off. She had no reason to follow them back to the club. More than likely, Sara Jane would drop Joe off on the side so he could enter through the back and walk out the front door. Maybe he'd even use a toothpick like he'd just finished a rare steak. No argument he'd had meat, just not the kind with nutritional value.

Dani had more than enough evidence to guarantee Ellen's financial portfolio would stay healthy. Despite her dislike of this type of surveillance, she grew giddy with success. She really was getting good at this.

Harry had assigned one of the younger guys on the Hamilton case two months ago and then pushed it on Dani during her week of recuperation. In all that time, Joe hadn't slipped up once. No unusual phone records, no trail of credit card charges.

Nada.

Still, Dani had gotten a gut feeling about him the minute she walked into Ellen's corporate headquarters near the Galleria, posing as a potential buyer, earlier in the week. Maybe it was the eye contact between Joe and his secretary just before he went back into his office and closed the door. Eye contact that had only lasted a second and probably would have gone unnoticed if Dani hadn't been studying Hamilton from a discreet vantage point in the waiting room.

Whatever it was, her radar for something-not-quite-right had been activated. She'd tailed him the first few days without finding anything. He'd come across as a boy scout compared to the usual cheaters they investigated. Until she decided to follow Sara Jane instead.

Bingo!

She'd tailed the blonde to the prestigious golf club where Joe had lunch two or three times a week. It never ceased to amaze her how far people would go to deceive others. The memory of her own deceit last week was quickly pushed from her mind as she made excuses for her own behavior. That was different. That was life or death.

Instead, she'd focused her attention on the Mustang and slid her car into a space with a great view beside the exclusive club. Within minutes, Joe had exited the back door and headed for his car, parked in the last row a few aisles from hers. When his lover pulled up beside him, he'd quickly hopped in, and they were on their way to the Bates Motel look-alike for an afternoon romp.

The rest had been a piece of cake. Harry would be ecstatic since he'd taken a liking to the petite Mrs. Hamilton.

Dani started the car, a rental she was stuck with until the insurance money came through. Then she headed back to the office to download the pictures and share the good news with Harry.

Out of the blue, she veered the car off the interstate, down the ramp near the West End in downtown Dallas and headed toward the big medical office complex near Baylor. Pulling into the parking place she'd grown quite familiar with, she turned off the motor and stared at the building in front of her.

Thursdays, Nate spent the afternoons in his office before heading to the free clinic. Knowing he was in there poring over charts made her smile. If she had any sense, she'd walk right into the building, take the elevator to the eighth floor, and spill her guts. But was she ready to cry *uncle* and fess up to Randall?

Not hardly. She had no idea what her next move would be, but the consequences of revealing to him that Casey was his son were too monumental to think about. Having Nate become part of her family, seeing him at Casey's soccer games would be too much for all of them. The list was daunting.

For God's sake, she'd exchanged body fluids with the man. How could she seriously turn to him at a family function and say, "Pass the bread, please." And the simple question, "What can I do for you?" would take on a whole different meaning. No, she wasn't ready for that.

She was a hopeless overachiever. Always had been. She hated to admit defeat, and it was still too soon to throw in the towel. There had to be other options.

She glanced at her watch. Twelve-thirty. Her growling stomach told her a piece of muffin was not enough breakfast.

What in God's name am I doing here anyway?

Nate would be holed up in his office until sometime after five. Then he'd drive toward Fair Park and stop off at Taco Castle for a quick bite before putting in his time at the clinic. He was a creature of habit.

She turned the key and backed out of the parking space.

Then she spotted a navy blue Mercedes pulling out of underground parking and heading north on Washington Avenue.

After six weeks of tailing Nate, she'd know that car anywhere. As he passed, she slid down in the front seat, hoping he hadn't seen her. His heavily-tinted windows prevented her from knowing if he had.

She ignored the rumbling in her stomach and gunned the engine. God only knew why! She'd already made the decision not to confront him yet, and although her bruises were receding, she didn't want him to see her this way.

Oh, that's rich. The man saw you naked, and you're worried about him seeing a black eye?

She blended into the flow of traffic, staying safely behind him. The street signs hinted he was probably going to his house on Swiss Avenue.

She guessed right. As the Mercedes turned into the driveway of the massive house, she parked across the street and watched while he pulled into the garage and lowered the door.

This was a first. Every other time she'd followed him, he'd always driven around to the rear and out of sight. According to her sources, he lived in a house on the back perimeter of the property, but she'd never been able to get close enough to verify that. She'd assumed he and his wife were estranged. Could she have been wrong? Could this be a booty call?

A sudden pang of jealousy washed over her as she imagined what he was probably doing in there right now with his wife.

Seriously, Dani, you're as bad as that big-busted secretary you caught on tape at the sleazy hotel earlier.

She leaned her head back and closed her eyes, trying to get comfortable. If she was right about why he was here, this might take a while. A mental image of Nate kissing his wife's body the way he'd kissed hers flashed into her mind. She shook her head to erase it, paying the price immediately with a sharp pain near her stitches.

You are one sick puppy, Perez.

A noisy protest from her GI tract distracted her. She checked the glove compartment for crackers.

Dammit. Her emergency stash was in her pickup waiting to go wherever trucks go when they die.

What did she expect to accomplish here anyway? She should leave, find a Taco Castle herself, and soothe her noisy stomach. She glanced at the house, scanning the front with binoculars, hoping the bedroom faced the street.

Still no activity. She ignored the hunger pains and settled in. What would it hurt to stay a few minutes longer?

She tried to distract herself by thinking about how she was going to find a car as reliable as the Chevy pickup on her budget. About her possible meeting with one of Apollo's drug dealers sometime soon. But her mind kept coming back to Nate kissing a trail up Janelle's thighs.

She reclined the seat, setting off another chorus from her stomach and a pounding in her head. What she wouldn't give for a couple of ibuprofens, a Twinkie and a White Chocolate Mocha.

Janelle stood in the kitchen facing the garage door when he entered, a smug look on her face.

"Hello, darling," she cooed.

"Do you have it?" He slid past her and walked to the refrigerator. Taking out a Bud Light, he unscrewed the cap and took a long swig before glancing back at her.

Her eyes were slits, filled with displeasure. "What? No 'glad to see you, Janelle'? No 'you look like a million dollars, Janelle'? Right to, 'Give me the fucking money.'" She spit out the words, her voice no longer sweet.

He looked into her eyes. Despite the fact she was a class A bitch, she was freakin' beautiful. Everything he'd fantasized a woman should be.

But he was here for one reason. He forced a smile. "You know how I feel about you. Why else would I come crawling back every time you snap your fingers?"

She moved closer, rubbing her chest against his. "Oh come on, baby, you're in this for exactly the same reason I am. Sex." She paused. "And in your case, a handout."

She untied the robe and let it slide to the floor. Her naked breasts moved slowly up his chest. Her hard nipples poked through his shirt.

Christ!

He took a step back. "The auditor called this morning. Said you wanted him to go over the books. Why'd you do that, Janelle?"

Her eyes creased in anger. "It's my damn prerogative. I own everything, remember? Thought it was about time I acted like an owner."

He smiled. "Do you honestly expect me to believe this isn't your way of keeping me on a leash?"

"I don't care what you believe. You're nothing. Never have been. I've compensated you well for anything you've ever given me, which by the way, hasn't been too fucking much lately." She opened the refrigerator and grabbed a Michelob.

Throwing him one last glance, she walked to the bedroom, and he decided her heart was as cold as the bottle she carried.

"Coming, darling?"

He stood silent a few moments. Was he really capable of doing what he'd come here to do?

"You know how I hate to be kept waiting," she shouted from the bedroom. "I don't pay you for drinking my beer."

God, he hated her. How had he let himself get so indebted to her? He was like a puppet, and she held the strings. What had started out as great sex and money when he needed it had become something he dreaded every time she called. Now she was taking over his life. Would ruin him without blinking an eye. He couldn't let that happen. *Wouldn't* let that happen. When she'd hired the auditor, he'd had no choice.

He entered the bedroom and glanced around the room. She was sitting at the dresser, a line of coke ready to inhale.

Perfect.

"Let me. An old buddy of mine gave me some high quality stuff he got exclusively from his dealer. He said an orgasm is unbelievable when you're on this shit. I sniffed a line myself before I left the office." He pulled a small container from his pocket and flipped off the lid. "Cost two hundred a hit."

He emptied the contents onto the dresser and mixed the powder with the cocaine. Then he cut two lines with a razor. "My treat," he said, nodding his head toward the two rows of white powder.

Janelle smiled. "You do know what Mama likes, don't you, baby?" She leaned down and snorted first one line, and then switched nostrils and snorted the other.

Then she walked to the bed and lay spread eagle on top of the comforter. "Take me over the edge, baby." Her words were already slurred.

Impatiently, he glanced at his watch. One-ten. It would take about five minutes for the drug to work. He had to get back to the office before anyone missed him. He looked back at Janelle, noticing the effects already. Silently, he watched as she struggled to breathe. The panic crept into her eyes as she stared. She must be wondering what was happening.

"You really didn't think I would let you fuck up my life, did you, baby?" he mocked.

Realization flashed in her eyes, but she was unable to speak. Unable to move. Unable to breathe. It took only a few more minutes before her eyes went blank.

He pulled a handkerchief from his back pocket and wiped down everything he had touched. He'd take the beer with him back to the office. Might as well finish it to celebrate. Good riddance to the biggest pain in the ass of his life.

When he was sure he had left no evidence, he headed for the kitchen. Then he remembered the money. She had lured him here for twenty-five thousand dollars. He needed it to pay the goons who had come sniffing around on Monday. He'd told them he would pay everything back by the end of the week, expecting to hit big on a Trifecta at the racetrack yesterday. The favorite didn't even show. Pathetic horse should be sent to the glue factory after a run like that. He'd had to put his tail between his legs and come begging to Janelle before the big boys returned on Friday to collect.

He walked back into the bedroom, keeping his gaze straight ahead so he couldn't see her eyes. First, he searched the drawers, careful not to mess things up. Where could she have hidden it? That money would keep him from getting hurt or worse. He had to have it.

Finally, he found it in the nightstand under her Bible. What did a whore like Janelle need with a Bible?

He forced himself to take one last look at her lifeless eyes. "See you in hell, baby."

He walked through the silent house to the garage and got into the Mercedes, an overwhelming feeling of relief flooding him. He caught himself humming the old *Wizard of Oz* song, *Ding Dong! The Witch is Dead*, and he laughed out loud. He was free at last.

The sharp ringing of Dani's cell phone scared the bejesus out of her.

"Dani Perez."

"Dani, it's Harry. Any luck?"

"You owe me big, old man. I nailed him."

"You're sure?"

"Positive. I captured his ugly mug coming out of Sperm Count Motel with his hands all over her ass."

"That's my girl. How soon can you get back here? I can't wait to call Ellen."

Dani laughed. "So it's Ellen now?"

He paused. "I feel sorry for her. That son of a bitch went after her when she was the most vulnerable. She'd just lost her only sister."

"Don't forget you're a married man, Harry. I would hate to see you if Aunt Marie thought you were sniffing around another woman."

"Don't even go there. You know I only have eyes for the gal I married. Actually, I was thinking about hooking Ellen up with your dad."

"Oh, dear God! As much as I love my dad, I wouldn't wish him on anyone. He's like the king of curmudgeons."

"I heard that. Maybe I'll rethink it. So how long will it take you to get back here?"

Dani glanced at her wrist. One forty-five. "I'm leaving now, but I'm starving. I can be at the office by three."

"Good. I'll call Ellen and have her come by around four. That will give you time to print the pictures." He paused. "Yep, I think I might even kiss you."

"That will be the most sex I've had in—" Dani paused. Her usual response to his daily kissing threat was interrupted when Nate pulled out of the garage. "Gotta go, Harry. See you at three."

She grabbed her camera and snapped a picture of him as the car stopped at the end of the driveway before pulling onto Swiss Avenue. Turning her head away from him, she snapped several more. After he passed, she switched her camera over to view the pictures, hoping to get a look at those incredible blue eyes once again.

She hated tinted windows.

Chapter Seven

"A pretty girl like you shouldn't have a problem catching a man, Danielle." Aunt Carmella smiled from across the dinner table. "It's been long enough, don't you think?"

Here we go again.

Ever since she'd passed their mandatory year-long grieving period after Johnny's death, both aunts had rallied around the let's-marry-Dani-off campaign.

"I'm looking, Aunt Carm. Really, I am. Matter of fact, right before the accident, I had a date with a doctor."

When Nikki gasped, all eyes turned to her. It took the heat off Dani for a couple of minutes.

"Nicole, what's wrong? You didn't bite into one of those jalapenos poppers I made, did you?" Aunt Sophie asked.

Nikki recovered quickly and frowned at her sister. "Thought Dani's date with the doctor was a secret."

Dani winked. "Might as well let the cat out of the bag, Nik."

She turned to the spinster aunts now leaning halfway across the table in anticipation of juicy news. For the past six months, Dani had been making up stories about imaginary dates with only-in-your-dreams kind of men to satisfy their desire to marry her off. Last month, it had been a politician. The month before, a lawyer.

That one had almost backfired when Aunt Sophie wanted his phone number. She was pissed at Piggly Wiggly because her riding grocery cart had plowed into a huge cereal display, and a box of Cheerios had bopped her on the head. She'd tried to weasel free groceries out of them, but when they wouldn't budge, she'd threatened to sue.

"What kind of doctor?" Aunt Carmella pressed.

"A brain surgeon."

Sophie's eyes lit up like a birthday cake in a nursing home. "How'd you meet him, child?"

Dani made eye contact with her brother-in-law who looked ready to crack up at any minute. Every week she told the most outrageous stories. Every week those ridiculous stories appeased the amateur matchmakers, at least until the next family dinner.

Dani decided to have a little fun. Maybe they wouldn't be so anxious for details next time.

"At a bar."

Not entirely false.

"Oh my God, girl, what in the hell were you doing in a bar? Only loose women go to bars alone."

Nikki coughed and nearly choked. Bobby slapped her on the back, fighting desperately to contain his laughter.

"What do you usually do in a bar, Aunt Carm? Have a nice quiet drink."

Aunt Sophie halted just before she shoved the third taquito into her mouth and squinted her eyes with displeasure. "Good girls don't have drinks in bars with strange men, Danielle. Your father didn't raise you that way."

Dani decided to toy with her. "He owns a neurosurgical hospital in Fort Worth."

Both women perked up. After taking a minute to digest this new development, Aunt Carmella smiled. "Well, I guess things are different than in our day, huh, Soph?" She turned back to Dani. "So, when do we get to meet him?"

Dani glanced at her dad. He knew exactly what she was doing, and he smiled. His sisters had been a huge help when he faced the overwhelming job of raising two teenage daughters alone, but even he got frustrated by their meddling. He once told Dani it was better they interrogated her about her love life than him. They'd been trying to fix him up with widow ladies ever since his own year-long mourning had ended. Dani didn't expect any help from him.

"How come I haven't met him yet, Mom?" Abby's eyes sparkled with glee.

Dani turned to her daughter. The little shit was biting her lower lip to keep a straight face. "I only had one date, guys. Let's not scare him off."

Dani's hand darted under the table and gave Abby's knee a playful squeeze. "You are so in trouble," she whispered.

"Aunt Dani, I want to meet him, too," Casey said.

Dani snapped her head in her nephew's direction. His dark eyes twinkled. It was good to see him so tickled, even if it was at her expense. She pointed her finger his way. "You are *so* in trouble, too."

He laughed out loud, stopping after a few seconds to catch his breath. Concerned, they watched as he took a few quick breaths to get the oxygen he needed. Dani glanced at Nikki, seeing the same worried look on her face she knew must be on her own. Casey's anemia was supposed to be in remission.

With the light-hearted moment gone, they ate the rest of the meal in silence. As Dani and Nikki loaded the dishwasher, Hector Ramirez walked into the kitchen and enclosed both his daughters in a bear hug.

"Is Casey's lab work still okay, Nik?"

"Yeah, Dad. So far so good. I think he was just having too much fun teasing his favorite aunt. He's okay."

He held her stare, the cop in him probably analyzing her face to see if she was lying. Finally, he focused on Dani. "So, my little bar-hopper, how is your love life really?"

Dani picked up the big stack of dirty dishes.

Hector was at her side almost immediately. "Dani, you just got out of the hospital. Let your sister do that."

"Give it a rest, Dad. I had a concussion, not brain surgery, although I do know a great neurosurgeon." She grinned and slumped as if she were about to drop the dishes.

Her dad lurched forward to catch her arm. Both sisters doubled over with laughter.

"Dammit, Dani, that wasn't funny. I should have left you in the hospital." A grin finally appeared on his face. "Should have sent your Aunt Carmella over to help you recuperate."

"Oh, Lord, I would never speak to you again." She handed the dishes one by one to her sister. Nik had always been better at loading the dishwasher. She could get about thirty-three percent more dishes in than Dani could.

When the last one was worked in, Dani stood up and smiled at her dad. "You're right. That was mean. I'm sorry, but I had to get your mind off my social life or the lack thereof."

"So, you have nothing to tell your old dad."

"Let's put it this way. My love life is the same as yours. Nonexistent."

He laughed. "What makes you so sure I'm not enjoying a lady's company every now and then?"

"Get real, Dad. You're always at my house or Nik's, either waiting for the kids to get home from school or carting Abby all over Cimarron for soccer practice."

"Like I said, what makes you think—"

"Eew!" Both Nikki and Dani interrupted in unison.

"There's a visual I could have done without," Nikki finally said.

He laughed. "Seriously, I know my sisters are a royal pain with their nagging, but I worry about you, too. What about that guy your neighbor fixed you up with? The one who lost his wife last year. Didn't he take you to that fancy new restaurant on Cooper Street?"

"Number one, he talked about his dead wife all night long. Then he gobbled his food like he hadn't eaten in a week before he went after mine with his fork."

Hector laughed. "Say no more. I know how much you hate for someone to touch your food. Remember when you and Nik were little? She'd inhale her ice cream cone then sneak a big lick of yours. You wouldn't eat it after that, and she ended up getting yours, too. Worked every time."

"She was a brat."

"You both were. Your mother spoiled you rotten." His smile faded. "Back to your love life. What about that guy you met in the grocery store? You seemed excited about going to the movies with him."

"We could have *been* the movie. I saw more action than Bruce Willis. As soon as the lights went down, his hands were all over me like a blind man reading a romance novel."

Hector's brow creased. "Okay, this conversation is over. I'll know better than to ask next time."

Dani stood on her toes and kissed him on the cheek. "No, you won't, but I've learned how to push your buttons. You still see Nik and me as your sweet little angels. I wonder sometimes how you think we ended up with kids. The Immaculate Conception?"

"Stop. You win. Just one more question. How come Tino didn't come today?"

Dani squinted. "You never give up, do you? I've told you a hundred times, Tino and I are just friends. Nothing else, nor will we ever be anything else. I'm godmother to his kids, for pity sakes."

"So where is he today?"

"Said he'd make it if he could. Had some police business at the station. Obviously, he got tied up." Dani sighed. She was relieved he hadn't made it. Between her dad and her two aunts, she couldn't have handled Tino and the pressure.

"He'd make a great father for Abby," Hector said, before turning and sprinting out of the kitchen.

Nikki laughed. "Wouldn't you like to see his face if he knew the truth about the real doctor you met at the bar?"

Dani giggled. "It would serve him right. He'd probably find him and kick his ass, though."

"Oh yeah. You gotta love him."

"Hold that thought, Nik. My phone's vibrating." Dani reached into her pocket and flipped up the receiver.

"Perez."

There was a silence on the other end.

"Is anyone there?"

"Are you the lady looking for information about Apollo?"

Dani stiffened. "Yes. Who is this?"

Another silence. "Remo said you'd pay if I told you what I know."

"Remo was right. When can we meet?"

"At nine. Behind the church on Collins, next to Sonic."

Dani sighed. That area would be deserted on a Sunday night. Plus, she'd promised Tino she'd take him with her when she met this guy.

"I'm sort of tied up right now. It may take a little longer than an hour," she said, hoping for extra time to make sure Tino could get there.

"If you're not here in an hour, I'm gone."

Dani thought for a moment. This could be the break she needed to prove Johnny wasn't on the take. She was trained as a cop. Although she knew her way around a pistol, she'd never done anything like this without backup.

"What's it gonna be, lady?"

She blew out a breath. "I'll be there."

"Bring money."

Visibly shaken, Dani stared at the phone. With a million thoughts swirling around in her head, most of them not good, she forgot Nikki had heard every word.

"Dani, there's no way you're meeting someone by yourself. Don't make me pull the sister card and tell Dad."

"Don't you dare, Nik. I'm calling Tino right now to meet me there. Can Abby stay at your house tonight in case this takes a while?"

"Of course she can, but I don't like this. Are you sure you shouldn't wait right here for Tino?"

Dani glanced at her watch. Fifty-five minutes and the guy would be gone. "Can't." She knew it would take another thirty minutes to say her goodbyes and explain to her dad why she was leaving without arousing his suspicions. Add fifteen minutes driving time, and that only left ten minutes to play with.

She kissed Nikki's cheek. "Thanks, sis. I owe you."

"I think the balance sheet on favors is still tipped in your direction after what you did for me. Do you want me to call Tino?"

"I'll do it from the car so Dad doesn't hear. You know how goofy he'd get if he knew where I was going. Probably want to come with me."

"That might not be a bad idea." Nikki's brow wrinkled with concern. "Promise you'll call me the minute you leave and head home. Otherwise, I'll be forced to tell him."

"Deal." Dani walked into the living room and approached her dad. "I just got a call from Harry. I need to go on an emergency surveillance right now. Abby is spending the night at Nikki's."

"Harry called? I thought he and Marie were going to be out of town today. Something about antiques shopping in Granbury." His eyes drilled into her.

"He is. That's why I have to go." She turned quickly and kissed her daughter, avoiding Hector's scrutiny. "Are you okay hanging out at Aunt Nik's tonight? I have some important spy work to do."

"I'm good, Mom. Casey wants to show me his new train. His other grandfather gave it to him for no good reason." Abby lowered her eyes. "Guess it's because he's sick."

Dani pulled her daughter close. "Hopefully, he won't be for much longer, honey. We're working on that. I promise."

Her eyes lit up as she bought into the hope. "Okay. See you in the morning, Mom. I love you."

"Love you, too." Dani shut the door and bolted to her car. As she predicted, it took a half hour to get past the aunts and her dad and head toward Division Street.

She picked up her cell phone and dialed Tino's number, drumming her fingers on the steering wheel as it rang and rang. When his voice mail picked up, she blurted, "Tino, it's Dani. It's eight-thirty, and I just got the call from the snitch. Says he's got information about Apollo. I'm on my way to meet him at the Baptist church behind the Sonic on Collins. Call me ASAP."

She hung up, feeling discomfort squeeze her insides. She made a quick stop by her house to pick up her gun and the money she had tucked away for emergencies, losing another five minutes in the process. That left her with only a five-minute window, but she felt better knowing she was going in armed.

Turning into the church lot, she glanced at her watch once again. Three minutes left, but there was no sign of anyone in the parking area.

She pulled into a spot and cut the lights, leaving the motor running. Her eyes scanned the darkness, her foot on the gas pedal, ready to get the heck out of Dodge if there was trouble.

Nothing.

She was more than a little nervous about this meeting. A little excited, too. Did this guy have good information, or was he simply going to take her money and spout off a bunch of bullshit? The best case scenario would be if he had proof Johnny wasn't dealing with Apollo. She wasn't ready to accept the possibility the informant might not tell her what she wanted to hear.

A slight movement in front of the car made her jump. She let out her breath when she realized it was only a cat, probably looking for some action. An alley cat in heat.

She'd been there, done that.

Her shoulders tightened, and she shrugged to relax them. Where in the hell was Tino?

She screamed when a man appeared out of the darkness and tapped her window.

Hesitantly, she rolled it down just enough to see the top of his head.

"You got the money?"

CHAPTER EIGHT

Dani rolled down the window a little further, just enough for him to hear her. "I've got the money, but first, tell me what you know. Then I'll decide what it's worth."

The man looked quickly over both shoulders before drawing the hood of his grungy parka tighter around his face. Dani used the few seconds to size him up. He looked to be in his late twenties, his clothes begged for an ironing board, and the few strands of hair peeking out from his hood were in desperate need of shampoo. In the light from the full moon shining high above the darkened lot, his eyes shifted anxiously.

"Lady, I got the goods, all right. Word is your cop friend was set up."

Dani narrowed her eyes to slits. "Whose word?"

"It's from the street."

Disappointed, Dani shook her head. "And you think this information is worth a payout, why?"

"This is an eyewitness account."

Dani huffed, pretending to be uninterested. "I have to have more than that, friend. If you want cash, I need names."

Nervously, the man reached up, squeezed the bottom of his nose and sniffed, all the while stealing furtive glances around the lot. His hands shook noticeably now, probably from too much of something he'd either swallowed, sniffed, or smoked. Dani reached into her jacket and positioned her finger on the trigger of her thirty-eight, wishing she'd waited on Tino.

"Apollo had a cop in his pocket. Someone he trusted. Someone who double-crossed him."

Dani leaned back in the seat, her hopes vanishing. This was old news. Everyone at the Cimarron precinct assumed Johnny was on the take. Even the media had reported the suspicions. Anyone who read a newspaper or watched TV knew as much as this loser.

She pressed for more. "How would you know that?"

He cleared his throat then went into a coughing jag. Finally, he spoke. "The night Apollo died, I went to his crib for another line." He squeezed his nose once again.

Now there's a surprise! Bet the stuff you were supposed to sell went up your own nose.

"Go on," she snapped, her voice harsher than she intended. She wanted to be home in her warm bed, not here with this wigged-out junkie who, so far, had nothing useful to say.

"Apollo was in a big-ass hurry. Didn't argue with me about the fucking drugs like before." He paused and leaned closer to the gap in the window. "He never gave me more shit without knocking me around first."

"And this proves what?"

His voice dropped. "Said he was gonna do a cop."

Dani edged closer to the window. "You actually heard him say those exact words?"

A half-smile crossed the junkie's face. He had her full attention, and he knew it. "Pay up or I'm gone."

Dani cursed herself for losing the upper hand. She reached over the seat and opened the glove compartment. Taking out three twenties, she lowered the window an inch and shoved the bills through.

He snatched the money from her hand and counted it. "This ain't enough."

"It's all I'm paying for what I've heard so far. You want more, give it up."

He stepped backward. "Said the cop had no idea he was walking into a trap. Apollo even offered me a little something if I would help him get rid of the body afterward."

He looked away, mumbling something under his breath, and for a moment, Dani thought he was conversing with the voices in his head. This guy was too strung out to last much longer without a fix.

"Did Apollo say why he was going to kill him?"

"I told you, lady. The cop wanted a bigger cut. He threatened to throw Apollo's ass in jail."

Both Dani and the man jerked around as a police cruiser turned into the parking lot, moving slowly at first, then speeding toward Dani's car. The driver slammed on the brakes and jumped out, his gun pointed at the junkie.

"Don't move, dirt-ball," Tino said as he walked over and yanked back the junkie's hood. "All I need is one good reason to blow you away."

With his face exposed, Dani decided her first impression was way off base. He wasn't a man at all. If he was a day over seventeen, it would surprise her. He wore the toll of his habit and his lifestyle all over his young face. Even so, with his hood off, he could have passed for any one of the college kids walking across the UT Cimarron campus every day.

She opened her door and stepped out. "We're only talking, Tino. You don't need your gun."

Tino glanced at Dani, keeping his weapon leveled on the boy whose eyes were now wide with terror.

"Tino, put the damn gun away," Dani repeated, the pitch of her voice rising.

Slowly, Tino shoved the automatic into his shoulder holster. "What's this scumbag saying?"

"Johnny was set up. Apollo knew he was going to kill him way before you two raided his apartment. You didn't surprise him in the middle of a drug buy like everyone thought," Dani said, annoyed Tino had interrupted her conversation with the doper.

Tino turned to the snitch, whose eyes still reflected his absolute fear. "How do you know this?"

The boy reached up and wiped his nose on his sleeve, his hands shaking violently now. "I made it up."

Dani gasped. "You what?"

"Yeah, it's all a lie."

"Why would you lie about this?"

The kid's eyes held Tino's stare momentarily before he blinked. "Heard there was money for information."

"He's lying through his ass, Dani. You can't believe anything this piece of shit says."

Tino grabbed his shirt front and pulled his face close to his own. "Did she give you money, asswipe?"

The man nodded. It was obvious Tino had scared the hell out of him.

"There are no handouts for bullshit. Where is it?"

The boy reached into the front flap of his windbreaker and pulled out the twenties.

Tino ripped them out of his hand and shoved him. "Get the hell out of here. If I see you around her again, I won't be so charming."

The boy turned, sprinted across the parking lot, and disappeared down the dark alley.

"Damn it, Tino! Why'd you do that?" Dani couldn't believe what had just happened. She sensed the snitch had more to tell, and her money might have bought a new lead.

The hard look on Tino's face softened, and he smiled. He moved a little closer and took Dani's chin in his hand. "The kid had nothing. You should be glad I got your money back. If I hadn't showed up when I did, he'd probably be jerking off with his homeys right now, laughing his ass off."

Dani twisted her head away, her brow creased in anger. "I didn't want my money back. I wanted more information. I believed him when he said Apollo planned Johnny's death. I don't buy that crap about him lying. He only said that because you showed up like a goddamn knight in a shiny, freakin' police car."

She was so furious, she couldn't even look at him. "I keep telling you, Tino, I don't need you to take care of me. I'm going to prove Johnny wasn't a bad cop with or without your help. I know that guy knows more than he told me, and I won't stop until I find answers."

"A two-bit junkie will say anything for a fix. Surely, you haven't been away from the job so long you've forgotten how to read perps, or have you?" He touched her wrist and started a slow trail up her arm.

"Don't." Dani pulled her arm back so quickly, the back of her elbow slammed into the car. "Shit. That hurt." She rubbed the sore spot and glared at him.

His eyes slowly crinkled with amusement. "Serves you right, you ungrateful wench." He stepped closer but didn't touch this time. "Come on, Dani. Think about it. Why would Apollo tell some lowlife anything he was doing much less his plans to kill Johnny?"

"I don't know. Just a gut feeling the snitch told the truth about that."

"I told you how it happened. I'll go to my grave wishing it had been me who led the way into that drug bust instead of Johnny." He paused when his voice cracked.

Dani's anger passed. "You've been a good friend, Tino. Sorry I was such a witch. I want to know the truth so badly, it makes me crazy. I can't let myself believe Johnny was on the take."

"It's like I said, when we walked in, Apollo and some other guy were doing business, and Apollo got off a round before I could even draw my weapon. In the second it took to put a slug between Apollo's eyes, the other guy had already jumped out the window and was long gone. By the time the ambulance got there, it was too late to save Johnny." He lowered his eyes.

Hearing the details again brought back intense feelings of grief and despair, and Dani swallowed hard to keep her emotions in check. As horrible as the story was, the alternative was too heinous to consider. If what the snitch had told her was true, it meant Johnny and Apollo did have some kind of relationship.

She lowered her head, trying to erase that vision. Her Johnny would never partner up with a drug dealer. How many times had she heard him say he would string them all up if he could? He'd hated it when he'd arrest some young prostitute who should have been at home doing her homework instead of prowling the street corners talking dirty to strangers for drug money.

But why would Apollo say that? And what about Johnny's secret bank account? It was all too much to think about.

She opened the door and slid in. "You're probably right. It sounded like it might be a big break for me. A lot of wishful thinking on my part." She sighed. "Gotta go. Maybe there's still time to pick up Abby before she goes to sleep."

She turned on the ignition and eased the car forward. "Thanks, Tino. I owe you big time."

Nate sat propped up in the bed, snacking on a pack of crackers left over from his room-service dinner. The television blared, but he was no longer watching it. With the exception of *Sixty Minutes*, the Sunday night lineup didn't interest him. He liked the noise, a welcome distraction that kept him from thinking about things he'd put off the entire year. Things he knew had to be dealt with.

He was going stir-crazy in the hotel room. He couldn't remember the last time he'd been off for an entire weekend, finding it easier to be at the hospital on call than to be in the house on Janelle's property. But he had some serious decisions to make if he was ever going to get his life back on track.

He reached for the remote and flipped off the TV, then pulled the folder from the overnight stand and spread the pages across the massive bed. The papers were the only thing he had to show for the seven hours he'd spent yesterday with a real estate agent. He'd previewed so many houses, they all ran together in his head. He'd concentrated mainly in North Dallas, far enough away from his Swiss Avenue house, yet not so far that rush hour traffic would be a major problem.

He'd loved being this close to downtown Dallas. Loved that he worked only a few miles from home. That was probably his main reason for taking so long to search for a new location. But staying nearby was no longer an option. The further away he could get from his past life, the better. He needed a clean break.

He turned his attention back to the house hunting and studied each picture carefully, trying to decide which had possibilities and which were unacceptable for one reason or another. His stack of potentials was alarmingly small, considering the grueling amount of time he'd spent checking them out.

Nate glanced at the first sheet on the pile and studied the photo. A three bedroom near the Galleria. He could hop on the Tollway and be at work in under forty-five minutes. A definite possibility. Then his eyes skimmed the page until he found the price. A million and a half.

Sighing, he tossed the flyer on the reject stack, leaving only five others with potential. A quick glance showed all of those to be out of his price range, too.

No way he could afford that kind of house with all that was going on in his life. Janelle had threatened to ruin his practice, something he didn't take lightly. How far would she go to make his life miserable? Had she already started blackballing him at the hospital?

He'd blown an entire day with the realtor for nothing, and now he'd have to do it all over again. This time, he'd insist on properties under a half mil even if that meant moving someplace farther from his job, assuming he still had one after Janelle manipulated the hospital board members.

Nate glanced around the room, thinking how convenient the Marquee would be. The fact that it was only minutes from Grace Memorial and just a stone's throw farther to the Fair Park Clinic made it the perfect place to settle until things calmed down. But the convenience of close proximity to his job and daily maid service didn't come cheap. At three hundred a night, he would soon have to find other arrangements.

His partner had offered his house until Nate found something, but that wasn't an option, either. Although he and Roger had been classmates at Southwestern, they really hadn't cultivated a relationship outside the office. How uncomfortable would that be? He knew very little about Roger's home life other than the feeling that his wife was a control freak. That, in itself, was a deal breaker. As for his other partner, no way he'd stay with Paul.

No, he needed his own place, and the sooner he found one, the faster he could get on with his life. *What life?* How sad that his only good memory of the past year had come with a price tag.

A smile formed at the corners of Nate's mouth at the thought of Sophie, hot and naked in the shower. Slippery, soapy Sophie. Oh so soft Sophie.

He got hard just thinking about it. As pathetic as paying for sex was, he had no regrets. If it hadn't been for Sophie, he'd probably still be living in Janelle's house, still procrastinating about what he should have done a year ago.

Sophie had not only brought the tension between him and Janelle to a head, she'd also awakened emotions he hadn't felt in a long time. For the first time in over two years, he'd begun to think about a life that didn't involve working eighteen hours a day or coming home to a loveless marriage.

Part of him wished he had Sophie's phone number so he could call and thank her for changing his life. He definitely could use another night with her no matter what the price. Feeling her body under his one more time would be worth blowing his budget.

Nate's cell phone rang, jarring him back to the present. He reached across the nightstand to grab it, his eyes squinted in question. Who would be calling this late on a Sunday night? Roger was taking calls the entire weekend so Nate could house hunt.

"Hello."

"Oh, Mister Nate, come quickly. Miss Janelle—Miss Janelle..." The voice on the other end cracked.

"Rosa? Is that you?"

"You must come quickly, Mister Nate. Miss Janelle's not breathing." She choked on a sob, unable to continue.

"You know how soundly she sleeps when she takes a couple of those sleeping pills, Rosa. Put your fingers over her mouth and nose and see if you can feel the air." Nate was already out of bed and pulling his jeans over his hips, scattering the entire stack of real estate flyers in the process.

"No, Mister Nate. Her lips are blue and her skin's like ice." The maid's voice escalated to hysteria.

"Rosa, calm down. Did you call 911?"

"No, only you. I didn't know what else to do."

"Okay, I'm calling them now. I'll be right there."

"Hurry."

Nate flipped the phone shut and quickly reopened to dial the number.

"911. What's your emergency?" a woman's voice asked.

"This is Dr. Nate Randall. I just received a call from my house-keeper who said she found my wife lying in bed unresponsive. Can you send an ambulance to 63808 Swiss Avenue?"

"I have one on the way, sir. Stay on the line. I'll need more information."

"I can't. I'm on my way there myself."

"But sir, I need to know..."

Nate closed the receiver and reached for his car keys. In a sprint, he headed for the door, his mind racing.

Janelle was dead. What was Rosa doing there on a Sunday night?

CHAPTER NINE

By the time Nate pulled into the driveway an ambulance and a police cruiser were already parked in front of his house, their flashing lights illuminating the entire yard in a psychedelic pattern. He slammed on the brakes and ran from the car, sprinting up the steps, only to be met by a young police officer standing guard over the front door.

"Can't go in there, sir. There's been a death."

"You're sure?"

"Yes, sir. My orders are to see that no one enters until the coroner arrives."

"But I'm a doctor. It might not be too late."

The officer's eyes narrowed. "She's been dead a few days. No one can help her now."

Nate halted, shocked. As much as he wanted Janelle out of his life, he hadn't expected to feel any pain. A memory of their early years flashed back to a time when they hadn't been at each other's throats. A time when threats and lies hadn't soured their love.

"I'm her husband."

The officer looked surprised. "You should have said that in the first place." His voice softened. "Go on in. Lieutenant Markle's been asking about you." He opened the door and stepped aside to allow Nate to enter.

"Thanks." Nate rushed to the kitchen after hearing Rosa's cries.

"Mister Nate, I was so scared." She ran to him and threw her arms around his neck.

Nate cradled her as she cried, touching her hair, comforting her. Rosa had been with them more than two years, quite a track record considering Janelle had managed to run off a truckload of housekeepers before her.

"I know you were scared, Rosa. I'm sorry you were the one to find her." He pushed the now-shivering petite woman away from his body and swiped at the tears running down her cheeks. "Stay here while I talk to the policeman." He nudged her toward the table and pulled out the chair. "Sit down. I'll be back in a minute."

He started down the hallway, taking a deep breath as he approached the bedroom. He stopped shy of the open door, gagging as he reached for his handkerchief to cover his mouth and nose. He stood in the doorway, his eyes taking in the activity in the room that had once held happy memories for him. One man was taking pictures of the body while the other wrote furiously in a small notepad. Both wore masks and gloves.

Nate forced himself to look at the bed and was immediately sorry. Janelle lay on top of the comforter, her color almost purple, her eyes frozen in a blank stare, as if she were looking right at him. His breath caught in his throat. Even in death, Janelle was beautiful.

Nate walked closer to the bed. Janelle had on a see-through black teddy that exposed her long legs nearly all the way up to her waist. He reached down to cover her up. A hand stopped him before he could grab the sheet.

"Don't touch her," the officer growled. "We're still processing the scene."

Both policemen glared at him.

"Who the hell are you?" the one with the notepad asked.

Nate rubbed his forehead in an attempt to compose himself.

"I said, who the hell...?"

"Nate Randall." His voice was barely a whisper.

"The husband?"

"Yes. Now, can you at least pull the sheet over her?" Nate asked, wrenching his hand from the grasp.

"Not until the coroner gets here." The policeman grabbed Nate's arm again and pulled him to the back of the room, away from the body. "Lieutenant Kevin Markle, Homicide."

Nate ignored the extended hand. "Homicide?" He couldn't hide the surprise in his voice.

"Everything's a homicide until we prove otherwise."

Markle nudged Nate farther from the bed. "Where were you tonight when your housekeeper found the deceased?"

The deceased. How final that sounded. "I'm staying at the Marquee Hotel downtown."

Lt. Markle's eyebrows lifted. "Problems between the two of you?"

Nate ignored the question. "How did she die?"

"Don't know. There's a small amount of a white substance on the dresser and a little under her nose. My guess is she snorted a tad too much with her brew." He pointed to the half-empty bottle on the nightstand. "Just have to wait for toxicology to tell us." He scribbled something on his pad. "Did you know your wife did drugs, Dr. Randall?"

The question caught Nate off guard. For a few months now, he'd suspected she was taking something, but he'd assumed it was a legal prescription. "No idea," he lied.

Markle's eyes narrowed. "Kinda hard to miss that when you live with someone."

"I haven't lived here for over a year. I stayed in the small house behind the pool. I work long hours at the hospital, so I didn't see much of Janelle."

"Were you getting a divorce?"

"Yes."

Markle opened the notebook, his pen poised. "Who's your lawyer?"

Nate exhaled noisily. "Don't have one yet. I was going to start the process this week. Thought it was time."

The lieutenant smiled. "Why now?"

Nate glanced back at the bed. How could he explain his relationship with Janelle to a perfect stranger? "We both agreed it was over," he lied again.

Janelle would have stopped at nothing to keep him from going through with the divorce. Hadn't she told him that the other night?

"The timing seems a little convenient, don't you think?" Markle asked, the smile gone from his face.

Before Nate could answer, his attention was diverted to a commotion in the hall. Moments later, a husky, football player- type guy rounded the corner and headed straight for them.

"That's the coroner. You'll need to wait in the other room, Randall," Lieutenant Markle said, already shoving him toward the kitchen. "Don't go anywhere. I'll want to talk with you more after Milton checks out the body."

Nate glanced over his shoulder for one last look at Janelle, a sense of sadness filling his heart. She looked so pitiful all alone in the big bed, unable to scream obscenities at the man now probing, measuring, touching her. This wasn't the kind of attention she craved.

A lone tear trickled down Nate's face, and he quickly wiped it away. He made his way to the kitchen and sat down next to Rosa. He couldn't believe Janelle was really dead.

Dani pulled into the garage and lowered the door before climbing out of her car. She was a little more freaked out after her encounter with the snitch than she liked to admit. That guy had definitely been creepy. Walking into a dark, empty house did nothing to calm her already frayed nerves.

She flipped on the kitchen light then walked to the front door, her fingers touching the butt of her gun tucked into her jacket pocket. Switching on the front porch light, she opened the door and waved to Tino, who had insisted on following her home. Normally, she would have put up a fuss, arguing she didn't need a damn watchdog.

But not tonight.

She almost wished she'd agreed to let him sleep on her couch for protection.

From what?

Dani breathed in then slowly exhaled to clear her thoughts. She was being ridiculous, but still, she couldn't shake the uneasiness.

After double-locking the front door, she headed to the kitchen to fix a cup of hot chocolate. Besides the comfort it gave her, it would warm her up. The chilly night air had seeped into her bones through her thin jacket. She hadn't planned on standing in a cold parking lot when she'd dressed for her dad's.

While she waited for the water to heat in the microwave, her mind replayed the earlier events. Why had the kid lied? Her source had reassured her this guy knew something. His story, although shocking, was half-way believable, as much as she hated to think about what that could mean. So why had he suddenly changed his story?

The microwave dinged, scaring the bejesus out of her, and she gasped.

Okay, Perez. You're not a rookie. Get a grip.

She poured the water over the chocolate mixture and stirred, her mind still on the snitch. If what he said was true, there was a real possibility Johnny had some kind of relationship with Apollo. She had to figure it out.

She inhaled sharply and blew out a frustrated breath. She needed a lot of emotional fortitude to force her mind to remember back to the time before Johnny died, after she'd worked so hard to suppress those memories. A sense of disloyalty overwhelmed her, thinking he might have had a dark side.

If Johnny had been on the take, wouldn't there have been some kind of sign? *I was a trained cop, for God's sake.*

If she was going to go down that road, she needed more than hot chocolate to deal with it. She reached into the cupboard for a bottle of Baileys and poured a healthy dollop of the creamy liquor into her cup. Then she turned out the light and made her way up the stairs to her bedroom, carefully balancing the hot drink and the still-unread, Sunday paper. Reading about other people's problems always took her mind off her own.

When she'd finally finished with her nightly routine she lay on the bed and propped the pillows behind her. A long sip of the drink along with the flannel pajamas her dad had given her for Christmas last year had her body temperature almost back to normal in no time.

She spread the front page of the Dallas Daily Tribune across the bed in front of her, but she wasn't reading it. Her mind was back on the rendezvous with the snitch. If Johnny's death wasn't a case of a cop being in the wrong place at the right time like she'd convinced herself, then what did it all mean?

She sat up straight as the thought came to her, spilling the drink on her comforter with the sudden movement. It was a set up. She was sure of it. But that meant Johnny had been in bed with Apollo. The pain in her heart forced her to lie back on the pillows.

Not her Johnny. Oh God, not him. He was the only person she'd never doubted in her life. The only man besides her father she'd ever completely trusted.

But if she trusted her instincts that the snitch was telling the truth, she had to at least consider the possibility that just maybe there was a connection between Johnny and Apollo. She wasn't ready to go there. Wasn't ready to condemn the only man she'd loved since junior high. Not yet. It would take a lot more to convince her.

But for the first time since his death two years ago, she was no longer one hundred percent sure of his innocence. She searched her brain, trying to remember if he's acted differently in the last few months before he died, the last hours before he was gunned down. How could he have known he was about to shake down a dangerous felon like Apollo without some anxiety?

Nothing had been different about his behavior that night. Right before he'd left the house for his shift with Tino, he'd said he was going to catch a bad guy. But he always said that before he went to work. Always kissed her, patted her fanny, and reminded her to keep his side of the bed warm until he returned.

Life was good then. They'd dreamed about traveling, even talked about taking Abby to Hawaii. Dani still had the brochures Johnny had picked up at the travel agency.

Both knew it was a pipe dream. They had too many other demands on their money. But it'd been fun thinking about it. They'd called it the "honeymoon they never had", then had laughingly added, "with a precocious eight-year old as a chaperone."

Dani smiled. God, she'd loved that man from the minute he'd moved into their neighborhood when she'd just turned fourteen. Johnny Perez had quickly became the popular kid on the block. Always had all the pretty girls falling all over him. Dani had thought a tomboy like her didn't stand a chance against the cheerleaders and prissy girls. But she'd been wrong.

Two years older, he'd never seemed to notice her until that hot Fourth of July day, right after the makeshift carnival closed down on their street and the kids got together for a softball game. To the dismay of all the boys in the neighborhood, he'd called her name first for his team.

She hadn't disappointed him, playing her heart out to prove to the other boys who'd complained about a girl on their team. Two home runs and a double-play later, Johnny had smiled his thanks.

That smile could melt an iceberg. As long as she lived, she'd never forget how he could light up a room with it.

Later that night, at the big shindig the firemen had planned, he'd made sure he sat next to her on the grass in the dark. She remembered thinking the fireworks display didn't hold a candle to his eyes when she caught him looking at her several times that night.

By the end of her Sophomore year, she and Johnny were inseparable. When he graduated and left for college in Austin, Dani thought her heart would break, knowing he'd meet a sophisticated college girl and leave her behind.

But that hadn't happened. They'd married the summer after he graduated, right before he entered the police academy. Dani's father had insisted they move in with him and Nikki, at least until Dani finished college herself.

She smiled at the thought. Those were the good old days when she and Johnny couldn't keep their hands off each other. When they would sneak up to her old bedroom in the middle of the afternoon and lock the door. They'd giggle so hard, trying unsuccessfully to be quiet. Finally, she'd gotten this brilliant idea to turn on the clothes dryer in the laundry room across the hall from the bedroom to cover the telltale, squeaking bed frame and the moans.

Her dad never questioned why that old machine was on nearly every afternoon after Johnny got home at four. At least he never let on like he knew. Nikki still called it the permanent-body-press cycle.

When Abby was born a few months after Dani graduated from college, Johnny had actually cried holding his daughter for the first time. How could a man with that much love for his little girl be a part of the dangerous drug culture that could one day harm her?

Dani exhaled slowly, fighting the despair bubbling in her throat. She'd find that snitch and force the truth out of him, one word at a time. Her gut told her he'd lied because he'd been terrified when Tino charged across the lot as if she were some goddamn damsel in distress.

Damsel in distress, my butt!

The next time she talked to the snitch, she'd go without him. He had a way of intimidating people, and she didn't need that. It would be just her and her trusty gun.

Dani climbed out of bed and made her way downstairs. The spiked hot chocolate had begun to warm her insides. One more swig of Baileys should do the trick.

Finally settled back into her bed, sipping the hot liquid once again, she turned on the TV hoping to catch the sports. The Cowboys had beaten the Eagles earlier with a last minute field goal, and she was anxious to hear the chatter about the game.

She turned to the local news where a trailer crawled across the bottom of the screen with breaking news. Even without an address, Dani recognized the mansion immediately.

"Oh, my God!" she whispered, as she watched the paramedics roll out a gurney holding a sheet-covered body. She turned up the volume, her eyes riveted to the unfolding drama.

"We are at the scene in an upscale neighborhood on Swiss Avenue where a woman was found dead just hours ago. Police are investigating the apparent drug overdose of Dallas socialite Janelle Randall, daughter of the late pharmaceutical giant, Gregory St. Clair. No further details are available as the police await the results of an autopsy. Stay tuned to Channel Six News for more on this developing story."

Dani slapped her hand over her mouth, not believing what she'd just heard. Nate's wife was dead?

Convinced she had heard wrong, she flipped the channel. The death of Janelle Randall was the lead story on every local station.

Dani stayed with ABC and watched as the camera panned across the mansion grounds. The voice of the newscaster described the elaborate house in detail. For a split second, she caught a glimpse of Nate Randall on the front porch watching as his wife's body was placed in the ambulance, his arm around a sobbing young woman.

Dani didn't know why, but for some reason, an overwhelming sense of grief hit her. She hadn't even met Janelle, yet she was saddened by the woman's tragic death. She watched, mesmerized as cameras zoomed in on Nate and the other woman, described as the housekeeper who had found the body. His eyes looked blank as he comforted her.

She reached for the alcohol-laced chocolate drink and drained the cup. For the first time since the night she'd spent with Dr. Nathan Randall, she experienced an intense feeling of remorse. She wished she could comfort him, tell him she knew what it felt like to lose someone you cared about.

But she could only watch, helpless. Silently, she prayed Janelle Randall's death had nothing to do with her sinful night at the Marquee.

CHAPTER TEN

Nate waited at the small deli for his ham and cheese sandwich before heading to the office. Today was his first day back at work since Janelle's funeral on Wednesday.

What a fiasco that had been. Everybody who was anybody in Dallas showed up to pay last respects to the daughter of a man once viewed as one of the most powerful entrepreneurs in the city. Pretending he and Janelle were not estranged had proven to be harder than Nate expected.

Only his partner Roger knew they had been living apart and respectfully, he'd kept that information to himself. No matter how miserable Janelle had made Nate's life, she didn't deserve to have the world privy to her personal affairs.

"Want chips with that, Dr. Randall?"

"What? Oh. No thanks, Lucy. Just a black coffee, please."

Nate smiled at the older woman. She'd been running the deli since Nate and his partners moved their practice to the Schaffer Building last year. On Thursdays, the only day Nate was in the office, he'd pick up a bite to eat before settling in with paperwork. Lucy looked surprised to see him on a Friday.

"Here you go."

He grabbed the bag and handed her a ten. "Keep the change."

Her smile always made the day brighter, and he needed every little boost he could get today. He felt strange, as if his identity had changed. He was a widower. He'd been so absorbed in arranging Janelle's funeral, he hadn't given it much thought.

Until now.

Since Janelle had been the only child of Gregory and Rachel St. Clair, both of whom had been killed several years before, the job had naturally fallen to him to make the funeral arrangements. Janelle had no other family.

Two days after her funeral, Nate moved back into the small house behind the garage to oversee the endless details necessary for the up-keep of the property. A temporary move, he hoped, that wouldn't involve too much of his time. It took all he had to force himself to enter her house when it became absolutely necessary, and even then, he did what had to be done and got the hell out. The air inside seemed chilly and stale, the smell of death still apparent. Even the walls echoed his imagined guilt.

Feeling so much remorse surprised Nate. He wondered if things might have ended differently if he'd given it another chance. His common sense told him it wouldn't have. Still, he felt her presence in the house, her cold eyes accusing him of not trying hard enough.

Inner torment gnawed at him. Life with Janelle hadn't always been so hard, but he had a difficult time remembering the good times when there were so many bad memories to offset them. When he and Janelle had decided to marry after a three-month whirl-wind, sexually-charged courtship, he'd been a resident with no money and no social life. But she'd convinced him they wouldn't need much. Only each other.

That lasted until the elaborate wedding, and they'd moved into the small house on the back side of the St. Clair property, a gift from her parents. How ironic that he'd lived there by himself for the past year.

After the St. Clairs were killed in a freak private plane crash over the Colorado Mountains, nothing was ever the same. About that time, Nate set up his private practice, and he and Janelle moved into the big house. But his feelings didn't change. Like a lot of other people with marital problems, he'd made the mistake of thinking a child could fix things.

All those months had been a lie. The tears, bogus.

The intercom buzzed, pushing the bad memories out of his mind. "Yes?"

"There's a Lieutenant Markle here to see you, Nate. Said it's urgent."

What the hell do the police want with me?

"Thank you, Gina. Send him in."

The door opened and the burly policeman who had first interrogated him at Janelle's house the night Rosa found her dead sauntered in. Walking directly to his desk, he laid an official-looking paper in front of Nate.

"What's this?"

"Search warrant." Markle smiled. "My men are at your house with a similar one right now, and they're checking your car downstairs."

"What are you looking for?" Nate's eyebrows creased.

The lieutenant ignored the question and stepped aside to allow two of his officers to enter the room. Donning gloves, they searched behind the books on his shelves, pulling out drawers in his cabinet.

"The files in that cabinet are confidential," Nate protested. "They're protected by HIPAA."

"We're not interested in patient records, Dr. Randall. No one's reading anything."

"What are you looking for?" Nate repeated.

"Do you keep any drugs in your office?"

Nate looked confused. "There's a bottle of Tylenol in the second drawer." He reached down to open it.

"Don't," Markle commanded. "Sit over there until my men finish." He directed Nate to the couch. "Shouldn't take too long."

Markle opened the drawer and pulled out the half-empty bottle of Tylenol. After bagging it, he asked. "Any other drugs?"

Nate thought for a moment. "A few samples over there." He pointed to the cabinet in the corner. "What's this all about?"

"We think your wife may have taken a drug that killed her."

"I thought that was a given. I was told the toxicology report was positive for cocaine."

Markle smiled. "That's true, but it wasn't enough to kill her."

"A person can die with their first hit."

"True again, but we don't think that's what happened to your wife."

"I presume you plan on sharing your reasons with me, or are you just going to keep me in the dark while your men tear up my office?"

Markle's eyes grew cold. "Remember that small amount of white residue on the dresser?"

When Nate nodded, the lieutenant continued. "Found a little under Mrs. Randall's nose, and the lab took a second look. Seems there were traces of another drug along with the blow."

"What kind of drug?"

"Vecuronium bromide. Familiar with that, Randall?" Markle lifted his eyes to meet Nate's.

"That isn't possible." Nate couldn't hide his surprise. Vecuronium bromide was a drug used routinely on surgical patients. A potent, skeletal muscle relaxer that paralyzed the lungs. Having an endotrachial tube in place was crucial for the patient to breathe whenever it was used. "What in the hell was Janelle doing with Vecuronium bromide?"

"You tell me."

Nate shook his head. "Wait a minute. You think I gave her the drug?" When Markle didn't respond, Nate continued. "I wasn't anywhere near Janelle that day."

Markle returned Nate's stare. "You sure about that?"

"Look, I hadn't been inside the house in over a year. I told you that on Sunday. I have no idea where Janelle got the Vecuronium, but if, in fact, she did, I had nothing to do with it. Maybe her drug dealer used it to cut the coke."

Markle's eyebrows arched. "You gotta name for her dealer?"

"Hell no. I'm just saying maybe that's what happened."

"Maybe. Or maybe someone who has access to the drug every day slipped a little into her blow and watched as she struggled to breathe. Or maybe someone gave it to her and waited till she decided to party. Maybe that someone knew he would be nowhere near her when she did. A perfect alibi, don't you think?"

Nate jumped to his feet. "Are you accusing me of something, Markle?"

One of the other officers stepped between the two men. "Take it easy, Doc, unless you want us to haul your ass downtown for assaulting a police officer." He pushed Nate down on the couch.

Despite the smirk on Markle's face, his eyes remained cold. "I'm not accusing you of anything, Randall. At least not right now. I'm simply looking for answers. Vecuronium is not a drug that's readily available to the general public."

"And your point is?"

"It's used to put people to sleep. Last time I checked, that's what you get paid to do." Markle moved closer, leaning down until his face nearly touched Nate's. "Here's where it gets good. Seems Mrs. Randall didn't change her will even though you were about to divorce her. Looks like you're the one in line to collect her fortune."

"What?"

Markle laughed out loud. "If I didn't know any better, I might actually believe you really didn't know you were the lone beneficiary named in Janelle's will. You get everything, Dr. Randall." He backed away and smiled. "And you have access to the drug that killed her."

Nate sighed. The only reason Janelle hadn't changed the will was because she truly thought they would work things out. If he was guilty of anything, it was for allowing her to hold on to that false hope.

"Did she threaten to cut you out of the will if you divorced her?"

Nate didn't bother to respond. Markle couldn't understand his relationship with Janelle. Hell, he didn't understand it himself. Why hadn't he started divorce proceedings a year ago when he'd first moved out? And what could he possibly have been thinking when he had agreed to move into the house on her property?

He remained silent while the policemen went through his personal things, feeling victimized himself. But hearing Markle's suspicions, he decided that was the least of his worries.

"Should I call a lawyer?"

A shadow of doubt crossed Markle's face. "Your prerogative. I'm only asking questions right now."

The lieutenant turned his back. "The coroner estimated the time of death as early as noon Thursday or as late as six that night." He faced Nate. "Can you account for your whereabouts during that time period, Dr. Randall?"

"Thursday mornings, I'm in surgery at County General. I'm always at the office by noon for catch-up paperwork unless I have an emergency at the hospital. About five-thirty, I head to the Guadalupe Mission Clinic on the corner of Pike and Martin Luther King. I end up at the Marquee usually around ten, depending on what's happening at the clinic. Some nights, I have a drink or two in the bar before heading to my room." Nate looked away from Markle's glare. Lately, that drink or two was more like three or four. Occasionally, they were doubles.

"Every Thursday?"

"Yes."

"Kinda convenient, don't you think"?" Markle wrote something in his notebook. "Can anyone verify this?"

Nate thought for a minute before getting up and walking over to his desk. After a quick glance, he remembered last Thursday was the day he'd left the hospital around eleven. He remembered because he'd been called in at three that morning for an emergency spleenectomy on a young girl who'd been in a car accident on the freeway. Things had gone from bad to worse, and three hours later, they'd called off surgery and wheeled her to the morgue. He'd ended up in the surgeons' lounge trying to catch a few winks before his scheduled surgery at seven.

"Got to the office around noon. The secretary's off on Thursday afternoon, and Roger–Roger McMillan–my partner, was still at the hospital when I arrived. Paul Gerard, my other partner, has Thursday afternoons off. You'll just have to take my word on this one."

"No offense, Dr. Randall, but I wouldn't take my own mother's word. You're sure there's no one who saw you here that afternoon?"

"Positive. Like I said, Roger didn't get to the office until after two."

Markle sneezed, then reached for a handkerchief from his back pocket and blew his nose. "Allergies. Sorry." He reopened his notebook and walked closer to Nate. "No cleaning lady, no mail room person?"

"The cleaning service comes at night. Mail's in the morning."

"What about lunch? Did you go out?"

Nate's brow creased in deep thought. Lunch. That was it. "I always order from Lucy's Deli on the ground floor. She'll remember." Nate was visibly excited as he handed Markle the phone. "The deli's programmed in. Number eight."

He stepped back to give Lieutenant Markle room to make the call. Thank God for Lucy. Things had started to go south with the direction of the new line of questioning.

"No, not today. Last Thursday. Do you remember Dr. Randall stopping by for lunch?" Markle's voice grew impatient as he spoke into the phone.

Nate stood silently by, hoping this would clear things up once and for all.

"I see. And you're sure?" Markle turned slightly to make eye contact with Nate. "Thank you, Lucy. I'll send one of my men down to get a signed statement from you." He hung up the phone and turned to Nate without speaking.

"So, do you believe me now?"

"Your friend Lucy said you ordered a sandwich but never picked it up. She remembered because she ended up eating it herself after she waited for over an hour. Said that rarely happened and when it did, you usually came down and paid for it anyway. Lucy doesn't remember seeing you at all last Thursday."

Shit. He'd forgotten how exhausted he'd been, how he'd fallen asleep after his all-nighter in surgery.

His hope vanished. "Forgot about that. I spent half the night in the OR and crashed on the couch after I ordered the sandwich. Didn't wake up until after the deli had closed." He'd meant to explain to Lucy and pay as usual, but Friday had been another hectic day, and he didn't make it to the office until five.

Nate cringed at the look that passed between Markle and one of the men ransacking his office. "This wasn't the first time I've forgotten to pick up my lunch. Did Lucy tell you that?"

Markle walked behind the desk and stared out the window. The view of downtown Dallas from that window was breathtaking, but the expression on the lieutenant's face never changed. This wasn't good.

"Was there an attendant on duty in the basement when you parked your car?"

"No."

The silence maddened Nate as the lieutenant paced the room.

"So, no one can prove you didn't leave the office at any time on Thursday afternoon?"

"Just one freaking minute, Markle. I've already told you I had nothing to do with Janelle's death. Unless you want to take me downtown and book me, I'd suggest you get the hell out of my office. Looks like your men have finished tearing it apart."

Markle sneezed again. "Allergies," he explained for the second time before he shoved the notebook into his jacket pocket. "We're leaving for now, but I'm sure we'll want to talk to you again. Don't take any out-of-town trips in the next few weeks without calling my office first." He headed for the door.

He made it halfway out of Nate's office when the elevator door opened, and an excited police officer ran up to him, waving a plastic baggie.

"Found this in his car."

Markle reached for the bag and held it up to the light, twisting it for a better look. "Well, well, well. What do we have here?"

Nate stretched to see what was in the bag, but he couldn't make it out. "What?"

Markle laughed. "Unfortunately for you, Dr. Randall, it's a rubber stopper from a medicine vial, and damn, if it doesn't have a little bit of white residue on it. I've got a twenty in my wallet that says our lab boys will find out this is Vecuronium bromide."

He pointed to one of his officers. "Cuff him."

They twisted Nate's arms behind his back as Markle stepped in front of him. "You have the right to remain silent. Anything you say can and will be used against you in a court of law..."

Nate tuned the detective out as a thought ran through his head. Even dead, Janelle had made his life miserable.

CHAPTER ELEVEN

"Give me one good reason why I should pay for bullshit?" Dani asked.

"It isn't bullshit."

She flopped down on the couch. It pissed her off when some idiot tried to pull a fast one on her simply because she had ovaries. "Look, I'm not interested. One trip to a dark parking lot was enough for me, thank you. If you're looking for another handout, you're talking to the wrong person. I'm done."

"I didn't lie the last time," the snitch said, his voice louder. "And I got more, but it ain't free."

"Quit jerking me around. How stupid do you think I am?"

After a few moments of silence, he cleared his throat. "It's your fault I said I lied. You shoulda came by yourself like you said. I freaked out when the other cop showed up." He stopped to cough.

One cough turned into three, then four in a row, the croupy hacking of a homeless person with tuberculosis sleeping under a bridge.

Dani jerked the phone away from her face as if the germs could reach her. When the coughing jag ended, she swiped her sleeve over the receiver as an added precaution, feeling a little stupid for doing it. "Bottom line. Unless you convince me you're not talking out of your ass, this conversation is over."

"I do that, and I never see any money."

"It's been nice talking to you, kid. Do yourself a favor and invest in a bottle of cough medicine." She pulled the cell phone away from her ear, praying her bluff would work. She believed this guy really did have information, but she wasn't about to let him know how badly she wanted it. She'd made that mistake the last time.

"Wait!" he yelled. Then he lowered his voice. "Apollo said his name when he walked in. Called him Johnny."

Dani gasped. Hearing this lowlife say her husband's name in the same breath as Apollo's unnerved her. "That's hardly a news flash. Johnny's name was splattered all over the TV."

"I saw it go down."

"What?" Dani sprang from the couch and pulled on her jacket. "You were there when Apollo shot Johnny?"

"I was in the head when the two cops walked in. When bullets started flying, I got the hell out."

Dani inhaled sharply. This new piece of information matched Tino's account of that night. "What did you see?"

His laughter set off another round of coughing. "Yes or no, lady. I can't stand outside all fucking night."

Dani needed no time to consider. This was the opportunity she had been waiting for, a chance to talk to the snitch without Tino around. "I'll meet you at the same place in about an hour. Before I part with my cash, I get to decide if it's worth it."

"It's worth it all right." He paused. "And bring the money your cop friend took from me the other night, or the deal's off. I want that up front, or I clam up."

Dani hung up the phone, her hands literally shaking. Was she dumb enough to meet some hopped-up druggie in a secluded spot with no back-up, knowing the man had already lied to her once?

She sighed. Unfortunately, the answer was yes. She had to find out what he knew. She'd come too far to stop now.

She dialed her sister. "Hey, Nik, can I bring Abby over for a few hours?"

"Why?" Nikki didn't even try to hide her disapproval. "You're not going off on some half-assed, wild goose chase again, are you?"

Dani hesitated. Her sister knew her too well. No need for her to lie. "I have to, Nik. This guy said he was there when Johnny was killed. I'll never forgive myself if I don't at least hear him out."

"Is Tino going with you?"

"No, and don't you dare tell him where I am if he calls. He scared the crap out of the kid last time."

"Dani, what have you been smoking? There's no way I'm letting you go by yourself. Dad would have my head if something happened to you, and he found out I knew and didn't tell him."

"I used to be a cop, remember? I can handle a seventeen year-old kid. Besides, I'll have my weapon. Please, Nik, I need this one favor."

When Nikki hesitated, Dani switched tactics. "You said there was no way you could ever pay me back for my hooker thing with Randall. Well, this will make us even."

"Don't try to guilt me. You're forgetting we went to the same Catholic schools."

"Come on, Nik. I told the guy I'd be there in an hour. I've already wasted ten minutes."

Nikki huffed. "It's against my better judgment, but okay. Promise me it's the last time you'll do this. I've got enough to worry about with Casey. Promise?"

"I promise," Dani said. "We'll see you shortly."

"Yeah, yeah. You'd better not get hurt, or Dad will kill me."

"Wow, I can feel that love all the way over here," Dani teased. "I'll see you in about ten minutes."

Dani pocketed her cell phone and headed to the kitchen to search behind the cake mixes in the pantry. She pulled out the little tin that once held gummy bears and popped it open. Every cent she and Abby had saved for emergencies was in this little box. She took two hundred in twenties and shoved them into her pocket. She swore she'd never do this, but it was kind of an emergency. Abby would understand.

She walked to the bottom of the stairs and called her daughter's name. When Abby appeared, Dani said. "I need to take you to Aunt Nik's for about two hours, Abs. You can use my laptop to finish the rest of your homework."

"Where are you going?"

"It's business, honey. I promise I'll pick you up before ten."

"What kind of business?"

Dani sighed. No use lying to her daughter, either. Everyone who knew her well could read her like a damn book. Thank God she didn't play poker. "It's about clearing Dad's name. I have to use some of our emergency money."

Abby's eyes lit up. "You can use the money from the potty mouth jar, too, Mom. I'll get it."

Dani grabbed her daughter's arm before she turned and bolted up the stairs. "I have enough, honey. I made an executive decision not to use the money in your jar. Hawaii is way more important than some silly old emergency, don't you think?"

Abby lowered her head at the mention of their dream vacation– hers, Abby's, and Johnny's.

"Which reminds me," Dani continued. "I probably need to throw in another fifty bucks for this week."

Abby looked up, her eyes squinted in deep thought. "And that's just counting the cuss words you fess up to." She pursed her lips and sighed. "Okay, I'll go to Aunt Nik's without giving you a hard time, but I get to stay up till ten every night next week." She grinned, unable to hide the sparkle in her eyes.

Dani sniffed a laugh. "You are your mother's daughter." She grabbed the keys from the hall table. "Deal. Now come on. I'm already late."

The ride to her sister's took another ten minutes, leaving Dani barely enough time to run in and say hello. Seeing her nephew brought tears to her eyes, and she fought to hold them in. Not only had his color worsened, but he had noticeable bruises on his arms, the result of his low platelet count. That in itself was a brutal reminder that his bone marrow was failing miserably.

Casey and his parents were scheduled to leave for Minnesota to see the specialist at the Mayo Clinic in a month, but Dani worried that might not be soon enough. As she kissed him on the forehead, she vowed to try one more time with Nate Randall. As cold-hearted as that sounded since he'd only buried his wife a few days before, time was running out for her nephew. If she got through tonight in one piece, that would be her next big project. She smiled at the thought. How sick was that?

She waved goodbye and headed for her car, her smile replaced with a scowl. She was more than a little rattled at how much Casey's condition had deteriorated since she'd last seen him.

In record time she turned into the church lot behind the Sonic, easing her car into the same spot as before. Leaving the motor running, she waited. Wasn't long before the snitch appeared, the familiar parka tied tightly around his face.

Dani lowered the window about two inches. "Let me get this straight. Are you saying you saw the murder?"

The kid coughed twice before sniffing. "You bring the money?"

A whiff of foul body odor reached her nostrils as he swung his arm around to wipe his mouth and nose with his dirty sleeve.

She raised the window a half inch. "Yes." She pulled out five twenties and placed them up to the window. "First, you have to make it worth my while."

The kid's eyes lit up at the sight of the cash. No doubt he was way overdo for a fix.

She repeated the question. "You saw the shooting?"

He coughed violently several times then wiped his mouth again with the sleeve of his filthy jacket. "I'm not saying nothing else until I get my money from the other night."

"I'll give you half, but I'm not convinced you're not blowing smoke again." She lowered the window a little more and shoved two twenties out.

The snitch grabbed the money before she could push them all the way through, leaving another rotten whiff of B.O. in the process. He jammed the bills into his parka, his eyes constantly darting from side to side.

Suddenly, he jerked his head to the right, and his eyes opened wide. "You hear something?"

Dani shook her head.

"Your cop friend ain't gonna show up again, is he?" The fear in his voice was unmistakable.

"I already told you I'm alone. Quit stalling."

He moved closer to the car, and Dani automatically leaned toward the passenger side.

"Apollo told him he was ready to deal. I opened the bathroom door and heard the cop holler, 'On your feet, Apollo.' Next thing I know, shots are flying. I slammed the door and hauled ass out the window. Damn near broke my fucking ankle in the fall."

Dani's heart raced. If this kid was telling the truth, Johnny had been involved with the drug dealer. Why else would Apollo talk about making a deal?

An overwhelming sense of defeat pulsed through her body, and she exhaled in frustration. How would she ever explain to Abby that maybe the cops had it right all along? That maybe her father was not the man they'd thought he was. She didn't want to believe that. Couldn't let herself believe. It went against everything Johnny stood for, everything he was. The snitch had to be mistaken.

"So, Apollo was expecting Johnny to bring drugs that night?" she asked, hoping his answer would be different this time. That he would wipe away the doubts his earlier statement had raised.

"You don't get it, lady. Johnny didn't bring drugs. He wasn't..."

The sound of a gun shot pierced the quiet night. Dani watched almost in slow motion as the kid fell backwards, a gaping hole between his eyes.

"Jesus!" she screamed.

Instinctively, she crouched in the seat, knowing full well she was a sitting duck for the shooter, and he was one helluva marksman.

Dani quickly pulled out her own gun and cocked it, listening for anything that would tell her the location of the killer. The night went deadly quiet except for the chirping of crickets.

Suddenly, the screeching of tires pierced the silence as a car pulled away somewhere behind her on the right. She jerked in that direction, but the car was gone before she could see anything. Unsure if the gunman was still out there, she sank lower in the seat so her head wasn't visible above the headrest and reached into her jacket for the cell phone. Automatically, her fingers moved across the buttons, punching numbers in the dark.

"911. What's your emergency?"

"There's been a shooting in the parking lot of the Baptist church behind the Sonic on Collins. One man is down, probably dead, and the shooter may still be out there."

"I've dispatched an ambulance and the police to the site. Stay on the line until they arrive."

"Okay."

"Are you in any danger?"

"I'm not sure. A car pulled away a few minutes ago, but I don't know if it was the shooter." Dani wished she felt as calm as the voice on the other end of the phone.

"Are you in a safe place?"

"My car. If he's still out there, I–" Dani stopped when she heard the sirens. "The police are here now. Thank you." Her hand shook as she disconnected and waited.

First one, then two more police cars sped into the lot and headed toward her, their lights illuminating the dark lot like a disco ball on prom night. Within seconds, she was surrounded.

"Get out of the car with your hands elevated," a voice commanded.

Dani opened the door and slowly slid out, careful not to step on the body. She resisted the urge to lower her arms and wrap them around her shoulders as chilly autumn air seeped through her thin jacket. Squinting into the glare of the headlights, she waited, motionless, knowing even the slightest movement might set off an overly cautious rookie with his finger on the trigger.

"Dani, is that you?" a familiar voice asked.

"Yes."

The cop walked around the car and started toward her. "What the fuck are you doing out here?"

"Spig?" She relaxed a little when she finally recognized the cop she'd partnered with for over two years. She lowered her arms but immediately shot them back into the air when Spig stopped dead in his tracks.

"Whoa, Dani. You know the drill. Until we check you out, don't make any quick moves. Keep your hands up. We had a near disaster last month during a routine traffic stop. No one's taking anything for granted anymore."

He walked closer to her and smiled before bending to check the snitch's pulse. "Dead," he shouted to his fellow officers who were now moving closer.

He turned back to Dani. "You know I gotta frisk you. Can't say I'm gonna hate it."

A twinkle of mischief flashed in his eyes before she turned and placed her hands on the car. She felt safe with Spig around. She loved this man and still met him for an occasional beer or two. "If just one of your fingers touches my boobs, you're dead meat. I'll call Joanne so fast, your head will spin."

He laughed as he moved his hands up her body, "What I have to do in the line of duty," he joked, but his voice quickly turned serious when his hands rested on the pocket of her jacket. "Gun," he called out.

Immediately, a young cop stood beside them with a plastic bag.

"Gotta take this, Dani. I can tell it hasn't been fired, but ballistics will still have to check it out." He dropped it into the bag then turned her around. "You can lower your arms now and tell me how the hell you got yourself into this mess?" He pointed to the dead body. "Who is this guy?"

"One of Apollo's junkies. He called and said he had information about Johnny's death. He was right in the middle of telling me when a single shot came from somewhere over there." She pointed to an area behind her car shadowed by several huge oak trees. "At least that's where I think it came from. A car peeled out from that direction right after the shot was fired."

"Jackson, take two guys and check out the area beyond those trees over there. Dani thinks that's where the shooter hid." He pointed to the trees before turning back to Dani. "You don't know this guy's name or anything else about him?"

Dani lowered her eyes and shook her head, too embarrassed to make eye contact with Spig. Her story sounded so stupid actually hearing it.

"Jesus, Dani. Are you fucking nuts? Why didn't you call me or Tino to go with you?"

She finally met his outraged glare. "He would only meet me if I came alone. He's just a kid, for God's sake. Give me some credit, Spig. I can handle a teenager."

"Maybe so, but you're no match for a perp hiding in the trees waiting to put one of his incredibly accurate bullets between your eyes, too."

She shook her head, knowing he was right. "It was stupid, I know, but I had to find out about Johnny."

"What possible information could he have about Johnny?"

Both she and Spig turned. Tino stood directly in front of them.

Dani flung herself into his arms and hugged him. "Tino, I was so scared."

"No shit. You should have been. Who knows how many creeps this kid has seriously pissed off? You should have your ass kicked, Dani, and you know it." He held her away from his body and looked into her eyes. "So did he tell you anything more?"

She glanced from him to Spig. How could she admit to them the snitch had confirmed her worst fears that Johnny may have had a relationship with Apollo. "Not really," she lied instead.

"And did he screw you out of your money like last time?"

"Last time?" Spig moved closer. "This wasn't your first meeting with this scum, Dani?"

"I met him two weeks ago. Same place, but Tino showed up and scared the crap out of him. I thought I could get more info if I came alone." She pulled away from Tino's grasp and faced Spig. "You can call me every name in the book, but I can't help it. I told you I'd die before I give up on proving Johnny was innocent." She lowered her eyes, hoping to hide the doubt.

"You almost did," Tino said sarcastically. "Why in the hell didn't you call me?"

"Because last time you came racing over here to play big brother to poor little old me. You and your freakin' big gun. I wanted a shot with him alone. Thought he would open up if you weren't here scaring the crap out of him."

Tino snorted. "Good thing I went by your house tonight to talk to you. When I heard the report there was a shooting here and a woman was involved, I figured you were just dumb enough to try something like this." He bent down beside the body. "Jesus. Wonder if this kid's had a bath in the last century." He raised up and walked around the body. "Looks like a thirty-eight. Somebody wasn't playing."

"Damn good shot, too," Spig added.

"So have you finally had enough, Dani?"

"What do you mean, Tino?"

"This crusade you're on. Do you really want to see Abby lose both her parents?" His eyes were hard.

Dani blew out a slow breath, defeated. "No," she whispered. "I'm done. Guess I'll have to live with the fact I'll never be able to prove Johnny was set up, even though in my heart, I know he was."

Spig put his arm around her shoulder. "I'll never buy that story about him being a bad cop, either." He led her away from the action as crime scene investigators swarmed the body. "Come on. You can sit in my car until they release you. We'll talk about old times."

She shrugged in mock resignation. "Oh, great. A few hours with you, and I'll be talking like a sailor again." She followed him to his car and hopped into the front seat. Tino got in the back.

An hour or so later, they released her. After saying her goodbyes to all the cops she knew from her days on the force, she headed home, suddenly remembering Abby was at her sister's. She dialed the number, noticing she had seven voice mail messages.

"Dammit, Dani, why haven't you answered your phone? I was just about to call Dad." Nikki was dangerously close to hysteria.

"Sorry, Nik. It's a long story. I had my phone on vibrate. I'm on my way there now. Make a pitcher of margaritas because I've got one heck of a story to tell."

"Are you okay?" Nikki's voice softened.

"Yeah, but it's been an interesting night, and my nerves are shot."

"Blender's ready to go. Hurry and get over here. I have some pretty radical news myself."

"Oh, please. Can't it wait until tomorrow? I don't think I can handle any more drama tonight."

"Randall's been arrested."

Dani's eyes widened, and she nearly missed the red light around the corner from her sister's house. "Are you serious? Why, Nik?"

"They think he killed his wife."

CHAPTER TWELVE

Nate rolled onto his side, groaning as he twisted his back. An old injury from his medical school days when he'd been rear-ended by a pickup truck, and the unbearably hard surface he'd slept on had kept him tossing and turning all night.

He glanced at his wrist before remembering his watch had been confiscated along with his other personal effects when they'd booked him yesterday. Since breakfast hadn't arrived yet, he figured it was still early. Noon couldn't come fast enough. That was the scheduled time for his bail hearing, and he was anxious to get out of this hellhole.

Actually, if he forgot about the slab of concrete covered with a half inch mattress and sheets reeking of Clorox and rough enough to file his nails, this place hadn't been as bad as he'd expected. Never having been anywhere near a jail before last night, he'd assumed the worst, his imagination working overtime about becoming the wet dream of some toothless good old boy.

Jeez. He had to quit watching those B prison movies.

Last night's dinner was as good as most hospital cafeteria food, although he hadn't had much of an appetite. He'd expected to post bail and go home yesterday then pay some high dollar lawyer to work things out. Unfortunately, he'd learned the hard way that wasn't how the system worked. The process was slower than cold molasses, he'd been told, and the court wouldn't even hear his plea until today.

They hadn't been so damn slow when they'd accused him of murdering Janelle and slapped his ass in jail. The mug shots and the whole fingerprint thing had been humiliating, but not nearly as much as the two-hour interrogation that had turned ugly before he finally demanded to see his lawyer.

His lawyer? The only one he knew was the guy who'd read the St. Clair will after Janelle's parents were killed. A lot of good an estate lawyer would be dealing with the murder rap hanging over his head. Then there were the three guys whose names he'd highlighted in the phone book a few weeks ago when he'd finally decided seeing a divorce lawyer was long overdue.

In desperation, he'd called Jake Deleon, his friend and roommate from medical school. Why he thought Jake might know a good defense attorney was still a mystery to him, but his old buddy had come through big time. One of Jake's patients was a well-respected criminal lawyer, and Jake had given him a call yesterday. Since everything was on hold until the bail hearing, the guy hadn't bothered to show up at the station yet, and that had pissed Nate off royally. How in the hell would the guy prove he was innocent if he couldn't find five minutes to talk to him? He hoped Jake hadn't botched the attorney's hip replacement, or worse, and this guy was looking to settle a score with Jake's friend behind bars.

"Breakfast, Randall." The guard deposited the tray on the slide-in rack on the door of his cell. "Eat up. You've got a big day today."

"Thanks." Nate lifted the metal lid and inspected the food before raising his eyes. "Any idea when my lawyer will show up?"

"Nope. Sometimes your first meeting happens when you walk into the court room."

Great. Nate reached for a strip of bacon and took a bite, then quickly dropped it. Bacon should be hot and crisp, and this was neither. He pushed the tray aside, figuring if the bacon was cold, chances were the eggs were nowhere near edible. He could still hear his mother's voice calling up the stairs for him to come to breakfast. "Nothing worse than cold eggs," she'd said religiously every morning. Nate had to disagree. Rotting in a cell because they said you killed your wife was far worse.

He reached for the orange juice, hoping it was as cold as the rest of the food. No such luck. Giving up, he pushed the tray back through the bars and paced the small cell, his mind racing. He hoped Roger had taken care of his schedule this morning. He'd had an unusually busy day planned, with no let-up until well after lunch. Hopefully, someone else had been available to step in. The thought of leaving all those people high and dry without an anesthesiologist bothered him.

"Nate Randall?"

Nate stopped mid-pace and stared at a young guy in a dark suit, accompanied by the same guard who had brought his breakfast. This couldn't be his lawyer. At about five-six and probably one-hundred-forty pounds soaking wet, he didn't look old enough to be out of junior college, much less law school.

At least he hadn't had a hip replacement. One less thing to worry about.

"That's me," Nate answered.

A smile crossed the man's face. "Thomas Prescott. Your friend Jake DeLeon called last night and said you had a problem."

The guard picked up his barely-touched breakfast tray and retreated, leaving Nate alone with the lawyer whose hand was now extended.

Nate shook his hand and sat on the bed. "What are you, like seventeen?"

Prescott stared, his face hard. "Is that a problem?" When Nate didn't respond, he laughed. "They tell me one day I'll appreciate this baby face. I'm still waiting." He rubbed an imaginary beard.

"Actually, I've found it to be an added benefit at times," he continued, "particularly when some older lawyer seriously underestimates my ability because of it." He sat beside Nate. "I've been in solo practice for two years. Before that, three years in the DA's office. I know my way around a court room, Dr. Randall, but if you can't get past that, I'll be glad to recommend a colleague who might be better suited for your personality."

Nate studied the boyish-man. "You ever defend a murder case?"

Prescott snorted. "More than I care to admit. Prosecuted a few as well. Dallas isn't Small Town, USA, Dr. Randall. The crime rate is right up there with the rest of the big cities across the country."

"And your record?"

"Let's just say every lawyer who has gone up against me the first time treats me like a grown up the next time he faces me in the courtroom."

Cocky little bastard. Nate liked that. He squinted. "What'd Jake do for you?"

"Cleaned up a botched ACL repair." Prescott smiled, looking even more like a teen than before. "Tore up my knee in college. I owe him."

"You played football?" Nate couldn't hide the grin at something so obviously a stretch.

"Flag." The lawyer laughed again. "I like your sense of humor, Randall. Now let's cut the chatter and get down to business. Make a decision. I can have another defense lawyer here in an hour."

Nate didn't hesitate. Something about the guy oozed confidence, and he found his spirits already lifted. "I'm good with you." It was that simple. In less than ten minutes, he'd turned his entire defense over to this Doogie Howser look-alike. Make that his entire *life*.

Prescott smiled again. "Smart choice. Now let's get started. Any logical reason why they found a bottle of Vecuronium bromide under the front seat of your car? Other than the obvious one, of course."

"Not a clue. It's not a medicine I use outside the operating room, not even at the clinic."

"Hmm. What about your alibi at the time of the murder? Do you—"

"They're one-hundred percent sure Janelle was murdered?"

"Yes. Not many people would have that drug available to mix with cocaine. That leaves us with someone with access who knew what would happen. Then we're back to the empty bottle in your car. Coincidence?"

Nate got up and slammed his fist into the wall then quickly re-coiled his arm in pain. "Shit."

The last thing he needed was to break a bone. He turned, cradling the injured hand in his other hand. "How much will this end up costing me?" He cussed himself for asking such a stupid question. Like it mattered. He wasn't about to bargain hunt with his life on the line.

"I won't lie. I don't come cheap. Plus, I'll insist you hire a private investigator to work behind the scenes if you sign on. That's not free, either. Your wife's assets were frozen when you were arrested yesterday, and your friend put up the cash for my retainer. At a discounted rate, I might add."

Nate sighed with relief. Good old Jake had come through when he needed him most. At least someone out there believed he was innocent.

He stared at the lawyer. "So what's next?"

"The bail hearing. Hopefully, the judge will keep that figure low, given this is your first trip to the city jail and the fact that you're an upstanding citizen and gainfully employed. With a little luck, he'll see you as a low flight risk, and you can fall sleep in your own bed tonight instead of this nasty one." Prescott patted the mattress. "Not much of the enormous annual budget for this place goes into comfort items, apparently."

"Then what?" Nate wanted to hear it all, good or bad. It was easier to deal with things knowing all the facts.

"Then you sit and wait while I do what you pay me the big bucks to do. Sometimes it takes as long as a year to go to trial, sometimes half that time. Depends on the evidence and the court docket. The DA doesn't want to get started until they're reasonably sure they can nail you."

"I've never been very good at waiting."

"You will by the time this is over. In the meantime, you'll work with a private investigator to find someone who saw something that day or who can testify you really were asleep on the couch in your office at the time Janelle was murdered. Best scenario, we'll find someone else with a motive for killing her. Even a long shot would help me put a hole in the 'beyond a reasonable doubt' theory." He paused. "Ever watch reruns of *Boston Legal*, Randall? They call it Plan B."

He stood and called for the guard. "I've got to run. I'll see you in court."

"You didn't ask if I killed her."

Prescott turned back and grinned. "Doesn't matter. You're paying me to convince twelve people you didn't."

The guard unlocked the cell door, and the lawyer walked through. Halfway down the corridor, he turned and sauntered back to Nate's cell. "Forgot to give you this. It's a list of the top three private investigators in the area. In my opinion, the first guy is the best. He's also the most expensive. His office is in Cimarron, far enough away from the police investigation for him to keep an open mind, but close enough that he can still call in a few favors from his cop friends in Dallas. He's an ex-cop himself, actually." He slipped the paper through the bars. "Don't look so worried, Dr. Randall. You've hired the best."

As Prescott walked off down the hall and disappeared out the door, Nate prayed that what he'd said was true. He would need the best to get him out of this jam. After a few minutes, his eyes fell on the piece of paper in his hand. One of the investigators was in Cimarron and the other two were in Plano, all about the same distance from Janelle's house. When he was released, he'd call the one Prescott had recommended.

He studied the name at the top of the list, the one in Cimarron. Harry Fielding.

CHAPTER THIRTEEN

Dani took a deep breath in an attempt to slow her breathing. The hospital parking lot had been overflowing, and the only available spots were in another zip code. Even with flat shoes, the run had left her winded.

As soon as the elevator door opened, she spied her dad huddled next to his sisters, both unusually quiet, a bad sign. Dani braced herself.

Hector Ramirez stood immediately and hugged his daughter. "You got here quick. You must have been flying," he scolded.

Dani avoided her father's accusation. "How's Casey?" She'd driven like a crazy woman, but she wasn't about to admit that to her dad. By the look in his eyes, brimming with tears, he probably couldn't handle much more right now.

"Not so good, honey. Bobby and Nik are in with him now, waiting for the doctor. They poked him with a bunch of needles, and the little guy never even cried." This time Hector couldn't stop the tears from streaking a path to his chin. "They finally got his temperature down to a hundred and two."

"What happened, Dad? I was over there last night until after midnight. Nikki never said a word about Casey having a fever. When she called this morning, I was in West Fort Worth running surveillance."

"West Fort Worth? You obviously broke a few laws getting here." Hector's eyes softened. "Casey woke up with a bad headache, and by ten, his temp had jumped to a hundred and five. Nikki called the pediatrician, and he told her to bring him to the emergency room. They took one look and admitted him."

"Is he going to be all right?" Dani covered her eyes with her fingers in an unsuccessful attempt to stop her own tears.

Hector moved closer and massaged her shoulder. "We don't know."

"Can I see him?"

He shook his head. "Only parents right now. ICU rules. They'll come out and fill us in after they talk to the doctor. I thought I saw him in the hall about ten minutes ago."

"Here, sweetie." Aunt Carmella handed Dani a tissue. "Come sit by Sophie and me. There's nothing we can do but wait." She sat on the couch and scooted over, patting the seat between her and her sister. "Wait and pray," she added.

Dani dabbed her eyes and settled between them. Aunt Carm was right about waiting. She felt so helpless. The doctor had warned them children with Fanconi's could develop something called aplastic anemia. The little bit Dani understood about it was that the bone marrow flooded the blood with immature white cells, crowding out the red ones, the platelets, and the healthy white ones. It didn't take a medical genius to know white blood cells were necessary to fight off infection.

She leaned forward on the couch and covered her face with her hands. Was this why Casey had spiked a fever? Was he starting to show signs of aplastic anemia?

Oh, God, please don't let it be that.

That would mean the anemia was progressing at a much faster rate than they'd expected. She didn't even want to go there.

She jerked forward as the ICU door swung open and Nikki walked through, her eyes red and swollen. Dani sprang from the couch and ran to her, enclosing her in her arms. Hector came up from behind and completed the circle with his own massive arms, as if in doing so, he could protect his two little girls from all the evils in the world.

Sniffling, Nikki pulled away and faced them. "The pediatrician thinks Casey has a raging sinus infection that has spread to both ears. He's running tests to rule out a whole bunch of other stuff, but that's his best guess right now."

"A sinus infection?" Dani allowed her hopes to mount. "So, all he needs are antibiotics and decongestants?" she asked, remembering the last time her sinuses were messed up.

Nikki sighed. "I wish. Medicines will take care of the infection for now, but he also has a bigger problem."

"Oh no, Nik. What?"

"The doctor noticed all the bruises on Casey's arms and legs, and he's concerned the Fanconi's is escalating." She caught her breath in an attempt to choke back a cry. It didn't work. She took a deep breath before exhaling slowly. "He wants us to call the Mayo Clinic and see if we can get Casey's appointment moved up. Said it would be a good idea to start thinking seriously about a bone marrow transplant."

"I thought we already did that, Nicole," Aunt Sophie said in between sucks of oxygen.

"We did, Aunt Soph, and no one matched." She turned and met Dani's eyes. "We have one or two other options before we resort to the Bone Marrow Registry."

Dani knew exactly what those other options were. "Has Casey's fever broken?"

"Yeah. He's already had one dose of an IV antibiotic, and the Tylenol brought his temp down to under one hundred and one. The kid's amazing. Sick as he is, he smiles at every one who comes in, even the lab people who have stuck him more times than I would ever let anyone poke me."

Dani lifted her eyes to her sister's. "This will be okay, Nik. I promise. Whatever I have to do, I will." The promise was one only the two of them fully understood. Here in the Pediatric ICU waiting room, Dani vowed to stop at nothing to keep that promise.

The door swung open, startling her back to reality. Bobby walked out, a big grin covering his face, slitting his eyes, also red and swollen. "The nurse brought him a milkshake. He's sitting up watching cartoons."

"That's my angel," Nikki said. She kissed her dad then turned to Dani. "Go. Abby will be home from school soon. No sense in all of us staying, although I can't tell you how much it means to have my entire family here." She smiled at their two spinster aunts who beamed at the recognition.

"The nurse said, barring any further temperature spikes, Casey should go down to the pediatric unit this afternoon. They'll put him in a room all by himself because of his white count." Bobby reached for his wife's hand. "He's going to be okay, honey."

"That's great news," Hector said. "Now go back in there and make sure they give my grandson anything he wants."

Dani breathed a sigh of relief as Nikki and Bobby walked back through the ICU doors. Last night when she and Nikki had downed the margaritas and a gallon of ice cream discussing the killing in the parking lot and Randall's arrest, everything had seemed fine with Casey. Ending up at the hospital today had been the last thing on either of their minds.

Oh, Lord!

She'd forgotten about last night. She hadn't had time to look at the newspaper today, but chances were pretty good it contained an article about the shooting. The murder of a drug dealer would definitely get front page coverage in the Cimarron newspaper. That meant her name would be there, also, and her dad would flip out. Since he probably hadn't read it yet, it would be in her best interest if she told him about it first. Either way he found out, he was going to throttle her.

"Dad." Dani tugged at his sleeve and lowered her voice. "I need to talk to you." She glanced at her aunts, both straining to hear, and pushed her dad back a few inches. "Can we go somewhere a little more private?"

Hector's face said it all. It was a no-please-I-can't-handle-any-more-today look. He turned to his sisters. "Dani and I are going for a coffee run. Either of you want anything?"

"I'll have a coffee with cream and two sugars, please," Carmella requested. "And maybe a honey bun, if they have one." She turned to her sister when Sophie clucked her tongue. "I didn't have a big breakfast like someone I know."

"Would have been healthier," Sophie scolded. "Make mine black," she said, turning back to Dani and her father. "No, make that a hot chocolate. It's too late in the day for that much caffeine. I need my beauty sleep."

Hector rolled his eyes and led Dani toward the elevator. As soon as the door closed, he turned to her. "What's on your mind, honey?"

She flipped her head in the direction of the young couple standing behind them, a subtle hint that she wanted to delay this conversation.

"I don't give a damn about them. Tell me what's wrong."

She threw up her hands. There was no arguing with him when he was like this. "Did you read today's paper yet?"

The elevator stopped and the young people reluctantly exited to the lobby, glancing back as if they were waiting for an invitation to stay and hear the story. As soon as the door snapped shut, Dani continued, "I'm talking about the *Cimarron Gazette*."

He stared at her, his eyes questioning. "No, not yet. I met a friend at IHOP. You remember Joe, the old evidence room guy?" When Dani nodded, he kept going, "Anyway, it was after ten before I got home. That's when I got Nikki's call about Casey." He paused, his eyes narrowing. "Why are you asking?"

"I'll tell you when we get the drinks." She needed more time before the confession that would automatically be followed by a long lecture, or worse. At least he couldn't ground her.

They exited in the basement and walked to the cafeteria. Once they were seated at a far corner table, she gathered her courage and plunged ahead. "A drug dealer was killed last night in the parking lot of the Baptist church on Collins."

"So? That's always been a problem area."

Dani licked her dry lips before she took a sip of the hot coffee. "There was a witness."

"Cut it out, Dani. Since you were a little girl, you've had a way of turning a story into a ninety-minute, made for TV movie. Usually when you were in trouble. Just blurt it out, dammit."

"I was the witness."

His face turned crimson. "You *what*? Why in the hell were you in a parking lot with a drug dealer?"

"Don't get bent out of shape, Dad. I used to be a cop, remember?"

"You're not anymore."

"He said he had information about Johnny's death. I had to go."

"Oh, Christ, Dani. As much as you loved Johnny, you have to give that up. Get on with your life. You could have been killed." His voice broke.

"I know." She patted his arm. "I also know it was incredibly stupid. I'm only telling you because I don't want you to have a heart attack when you read about it."

"Why didn't you take Tino with you?"

There was no way she could tell him that. She'd have to confess this was her second encounter with the snitch. Talk about blowing a gasket...

"I thought I'd be okay. I had my gun if things went bad."

Hector shook his head. "Thirty years chasing criminals and not so much as a bloody nose, but you girls surely will be the death of me." He tilted the cup and drained it. "So did you find out anything new?"

She'd been prepared to lie to him like she'd done with Tino and Spig last night, but she couldn't. "He said Apollo planned the killing. The guy was in the bathroom when Johnny and Tino walked in, and he heard Apollo tell Johnny he was ready to deal." She lowered her eyes. She hated knowing this. Hated what it could mean.

"Never met a drug dealer who didn't lie through their teeth, Dani."

"I know, but for some weird reason, I believed him."

"Is that all he said?"

"I think he knew more, but the bullet between his eyes ended our conversation."

"Jesus, Dani. You're going to give me a heart attack. What did you do?"

"Called 911. The cops were there in a flash. The shooter was already gone by then. They think it was a hit. Maybe a rival gang. Who knows?" She shook her head. "Anyway, I'm through trying to find out about Johnny. No one will ever believe he wasn't dirty, so why keep trying? Besides, I don't like the things I'm finding out."

"You and I both know Johnny wasn't on the take. Abby does, too. That's all that matters."

"Guess so." Dani picked up their empty cups and carried them to the trash. "Come on. Your sisters are probably imagining I told you I'm getting married or something. They'll probably grill you all the way home. You get Aunt Carm's coffee and honey bun. I'll get the hot chocolate."

Later that night, as Dani tossed and turned in bed, her mind was in overdrive, wondering how she was going to keep her promise to Nikki. Dr. Randall's arrest had been the lead story on every local news channel the entire day. That definitely put a wrench in her quest for his body fluids, unless they allowed conjugal visits from hookers.

Doubtful.

Unfortunately, her only option seemed to be to face the man and tell the truth. *I'm really not a hooker. I tricked you into having unbelievable sex with me. Oh, and by the way—you have a son, and he's dying. Any chance we can get a tiny bit more of your sperm?*

Yeah, that should work.

He'd probably have her committed.

Chapter Fourteen

Nate glanced at his watch as he pulled out of the underground parking garage and headed west. He hoped I-30 traffic was better than usual, or he'd never make his appointment. He'd allowed forty-five minutes to get from downtown Dallas to Cimarron, but even that might not be enough on a bad traffic day.

He'd rushed all morning playing catch up on the last two weeks worth of paperwork. Like it was so damn urgent all of a sudden. According to Prescott, he'd have a lot of free time over the next six to twelve months. Thanks to his lawyer, at least he had free time to complain about. Prescott had earned his retainer fee many times over when he'd persuaded the judge to reduce Nate's bond from the million dollars the DA wanted to a manageable two hundred and fifty thousand.

With Janelle's estate in limbo, Nate had been forced to liquidate most of his savings, and even that hadn't been enough. Jake DeLeon had come through once again. He owed that guy big time. But his financial situation wasn't going to get better any time soon, since he no longer had an income-producing job.

Yesterday, before his first scheduled surgery, Nate had been called to the medical director's office at Grace Memorial, his biggest contract. Although he'd never been good friends with the director, they'd served on a few committees together.

Nate knew things weren't good the minute he walked in. Without making eye contact, the man explained the hospital board had held an emergency meeting the night before. In light of his arrest, they'd decided it would be best if Nate refrained from further surgeries at the hospital until his legal problems were resolved. Given the fact Nate was accused of murdering his wife with a drug he would be using on actual patients, the board had delivered a unanimous vote.

So much for innocent until proven guilty.

Nate's first reaction had been anger, but after giving it some thought, he didn't blame the hospital for taking that precaution. The first time one of his cases went bad on the table, the media would go ballistic. He could visualize the headlines now.

Accused Murderer with Free Rein over Lethal Drugs Kills Again.

Maybe that was a little extreme, but Nate understood the logic behind the board's decision. People were uncomfortable around him. Some he considered friends, like the medical director, couldn't even look him in the eye. A few went out of their way to avoid him. Most stammered.

What did he expect? What does one say to a suspected murderer? "Hey, Nate. Killed anyone lately?" Maybe taking a few months off until this whole mess was straightened out wasn't such a bad idea.

But what would he do with all his free time? It wasn't like he had close family around. He had no one, hadn't for most of his adult life. His dad had disappeared with his mistress one night after leaving a bar south of town. Even though Nate had only been thirteen at the time, he could still visualize the look on his mother's face when the police officer had delivered the news.

She'd never been the same. As an adolescent on the verge of morphing into adulthood, Nate hadn't known what to make of her sudden anger, a lot of which was directed toward him. As if she'd blamed him for his father's infidelities. Pretty soon, he'd accepted that guilt himself, ridiculous as it now seemed.

When his mother remarried many years later and moved to Oklahoma, Nate was already on scholarship at Southern Methodist University in Dallas. Other than an occasional phone call, they didn't have much contact. He spent holidays with various girlfriends and worked during summer vacations to maintain his off campus apartment.

Wasn't until he was in his third year of medical school that he finally came to terms with his mother's rejection. By then, she'd already divorced her second husband, having taken the brunt of his anger for five years. That same year, she'd been diagnosed with stage four ovarian cancer and begged him to come for a visit. Nate was glad he had, because seeing her again forced him to deal with his own demons once and for all.

He'd searched for his father to tell him about his mother's cancer but discovered the man was somewhere up north and wanted nothing to do with his past life. On his last visit before his mother passed away, Nate was able to forgive her, to let go of the adolescent guilt that somehow, he had been responsible for his father's choices in life.

He'd grown up lonely, constantly searching for his mother's love. When it never came, he'd had to learn how to live without it.

At first, he'd sought out a string of women to soothe his inner child, but that feeling never lasted very long, and he'd look to the next one. Wasn't until he met Janelle and her family that he'd come to terms with his issues.

Gregory St. Clair became the father he never had. Nate had been devastated when he died, feeling a sorrow deeper than when his own father had abandoned him.

Over the last few weeks, those repressed feelings had surfaced with a vengeance. In the past, he'd used his work to fill up the holes in his otherwise empty life.

Now even that was gone. Although the two smaller hospitals where Nate practiced hadn't officially shut him out, it was only a matter of time.

He made a mental note to call the free clinic and schedule extra hours there for awhile. Although that wouldn't solve his financial problems, it would eat up a lot of time.

Nate glanced at his watch. Time wise, he was still okay; his appointment was only fifteen minutes away. Fortunately, traffic on the interstate wasn't a total parking lot at ten in the morning, despite the construction. He exited at Green Oaks Boulevard and followed his GPS to a three-story office building located just south of the interstate.

His stomach churned as he pulled into the parking lot. He'd never used a private investigator before. Never had a reason to. The fact that he needed one now unnerved and shamed him.

Guilty.

That one word would end his career and life as he knew it. No wonder he felt on edge. He was about to share the most intricate details of his life with a man he'd never heard of until three days ago.

Sharing intimacies was something he hadn't even done with Janelle. Explaining his relationship with her to a perfect stranger would be difficult, but if he held out any hope of freedom, he had to do it. Maybe somewhere in the sordid little details, Fielding would pick up something that might prove useful.

Nate got out of his car and walked to the building, taking a deep breath before opening the door. The directory in the small atrium listed the office on the third floor. The elevator ride up took mere seconds before he exited and followed the signs down the hall.

FIELDING INVESTIGATIONS, painted across the door, glared as he hesitated before going in. He hated this, but hated the possibility of spending the rest of his life in prison even more. Right now, lethal injection sounded better than that.

He took a deep breath and pushed through the door. "Nate Randall. I have an appointment with Harry Fielding at ten-thirty." He smiled when the young girl behind the desk glanced up.

She returned the smile. "He's expecting you, Dr. Randall." She punched the intercom and announced his arrival. "His office is the first door on the left. Go right in."

Nate started down the hall, the knot in his stomach unrelenting.

Why hadn't he eaten at least a half a bagel this morning?

Because he was too frickin' nervous. Still was.

He knocked on the door. "Mr. Fielding?"

A booming voice answered, "Come in, Dr. Randall. I just finished rereading your file."

After a quick scan of the office, Nate's first impression was that it seemed oddly quiet and unusually organized, not like he'd imagined. Of course, his only knowledge of a PI's office had come from television where the desk was always overflowing with stacks of records and dirty ashtrays. Fielding's office had neither.

Nate shook the man's hand when the investigator stood, noticing his strong grip. The guy looked like he could play tackle for the Cowboys. Broad shouldered, Harry Fielding appeared to be in his late fifties, early sixties. From his handshake and a quick assessment, Nate would bet the house this guy still worked out regularly.

"Have a seat while we get the preliminary stuff out of the way."

Nate sat in one of two chairs facing Fielding's desk, his gaze darting to the numerous pictures on the wall. Mixed in with a number of photos of the investigator with important looking people, most of whom Nate didn't recognize, was one of him with two teenage girls who both looked vaguely familiar.

"Is there anything new you can add to the original police report, Dr. Randall?"

"Call me Nate. You're probably going to know more about me before this is over than my own mother did, Mr. Fielding."

"Only if you'll call me Harry. Everyone does." The big guy smiled. "Anything new, Nate?"

Nate thought for a moment. "Other than the fact I had nothing to do with my wife's death, contrary to what the Dallas Police Department thinks, there is nothing." His lawyer had faxed him a copy of the original police report yesterday, and after reading it, it was obvious why he was their number one suspect.

"I just got off the phone with Tom." He paused when Nate's forehead creased. "Your lawyer," he explained. "He finally got the results of the tests done on the rubber stopper they found in your car."

Nate straightened and leaned closer to the desk. "And?"

"It's a good news, bad news thing. The bad news is the stopper tested positive for Vecuronium bromide."

"Shit!" Nate exclaimed, and then exhaled noisily. "And the good news?"

"They didn't find your fingerprints on it."

Nate's shoulders relaxed, and he sat back in the chair. "Does that mean I'm no longer a suspect?"

Harry's eyes held Nate's stare, as he rubbed both cheeks with his thumb and forefinger. "Unfortunately, they weren't able to lift any prints. The bottle had been wiped clean."

"So it's back on me again?"

"Afraid so, but at least they can't directly connect the bottle to you. Of course, finding the drug that killed your wife under the seat of your car with the stopper wiped clean won't exactly have the jury ready to acquit. It's my job to find a way to persuade them to do that. Let's get started."

He punched the intercom button. "Margie, did Dani get here yet?"

"No, Harry. She called earlier to say she's running a little late. Abby had an orthodontist appointment before school. She should be here any minute."

"Send her in as soon as she gets here," Harry barked before turning back to Nate. "Dani's my best investigator." He grinned. "She's also my goddaughter, an ex-cop like me and tough as nails. She has a way of getting details out of people when no one else can. I want her in on this from the get-go. If anyone can spot a weak link in a police report, it's Dani."

He stood and walked to the counter against the wall. "Coffee?"

He opened the cabinet to reveal a spotless kitchenette. Definitely was not what Nate expected to see in a private investigator's office. Fielding was a neat freak.

"Make mine black, thanks." Nate smiled for the first time in several days. Something about the big guy gave him renewed hope this might not turn into the nightmare he had anticipated. He sipped the hot coffee, enjoying the time before they would have to get to the sordid details of his dysfunctional life.

Both Nate and Harry turned toward the door at the sound of a soft knock. No one could have prepared Nate for the woman who walked in. His eyes widened as he stared at the familiar face. Despite the fact she had on little makeup, jeans, and a T-shirt, and had her hair pulled back in a ponytail, there was no mistaking those chocolate eyes.

She gasped when she saw him, and he was more shaken than he cared to admit. Why did Sophie need an investigator?

"Oh, good. You made it." Harry smiled at the young woman, whose eyes were still on Nate. "This is Dani, the investigator I mentioned. I want her working with you day and night to find a break in your case."

The young woman finally looked at the older man. "I don't think that's a good idea, Harry."

"Why not?" Harry looked confused.

"It's personal."

Finally over the initial shock at seeing the woman whose body he had ravaged, Nate extended his hand, unable to conceal the unbridled anger in his voice. "Hello, Dani. It's nice to meet you." Was it a co-incidence that the hooker from the Marquee had turned out to be a private investigator? Had Janelle hired her?

He held her hand too long before he released it and turned back to Harry, trying hard to stay in control of his feelings.

"If Dani can get past her objections to me, I'd like to get started here. Can you do that, Dani?" He looked directly into her eyes. One way or another, he would find out if this woman had been paid to seduce him.

She hesitated only briefly before plopping into the chair opposite him. "Where's the police record? Let's start there."

CHAPTER FIFTEEN

Dani took her time reading the police report, hoping to get a grip on her nerves before facing Randall again. Talk about having a bomb dropped on your head.

She had to hand it to the man, though. If he recognized her, he wasn't letting on. Despite his silence, his intense, anger filled stare burned into her. What kind of game was he playing? How had he found her?

Finally, she took a deep breath and glanced at her boss, careful not to look at the man who had seen more of her than a business relationship allowed. "Looks pretty cut and dried, Harry. The warrant's good. They Mirandized him. Finding a flaw with this will be tough."

Harry stared at her, and his brows crinkled. "Read it again, Dani. You always find a glitch, no matter how perfect it seems at first."

Dani exhaled. "There is one thing. We might be able to get them on their chain of custody procedure with the rubber stopper they found in his car," she said, speaking to Harry as if the good doctor wasn't sitting next to her. "The young cop bagged it then rode up in the elevator with it by himself. It's a minor technicality, but right now, looks like that's all we've got."

She turned to Randall, finally acknowledging him. "Sorry."

He held her eyes as if trying to figure it all out. It must be mind-boggling, she thought, to find out the hooker he'd bought was now the investigator holding his life in her hands.

Randall attempted a smile but couldn't quite pull it off. "Harry tells me you're his best investigator, Dani. Says if anyone can pull this off, it's you. I believe him. I think you could probably pull off anything you set your mind to."

The innuendo stung, and Dani glanced at Harry to see if he'd picked up on it. The confused look on his face told her he hadn't.

She ignored the comment. "Can you get your cop friend down in Dallas to nose around a little and see if he can find out anything more, Harry?"

"Yeah. I'll get right on it. In the meantime, take Nate to your office and go over the details with a fine-toothed comb. I'll have Margie order a couple burgers so you can work straight through lunch without interruption."

"What's the rush?"

"His lawyer has nothing. The sooner we give him something to work with, the better."

Harry stood up and extended his hand toward Randall. "I've got a meeting with the local cops about another investigation, Nate. Dani will take good care of you."

Funny how something said so innocently could take on an entirely different meaning. The irony of it all tickled Dani, and she smiled before she could stop herself. Quickly, she coughed, hoping Randall hadn't noticed. A glance his way proved this was not going to be her lucky day.

His piercing blue eyes held hers as his lips tilted in a half smile. "I'll just bet she can." He turned back to Harry. "Thanks for getting me in so quickly. I know how busy you are. I'm confident your agency is a good fit for me. What do you need in the way of money?"

Harry opened the door. "Talk to Margie. She'll work out the details." He walked over to Dani and bent to kiss her cheek. Halfway out the door, he turned back, his eyes on Nate. "Oh, I almost forgot. Tom also said the police are still looking for the woman who spent the night with you the week before at the Marquee. Care to enlighten us about that?"

Dani lowered her head. *Here's where I get outed.* Without glancing up, she felt Nate's stare.

"She was a hooker."

"A hooker? Why does a guy like you need a hooker?" Harry asked then shrugged. "I'm sorry, Nate. That sounded judgmental. I only asked because if the police find her before we have a chance to talk to her, they'll want to know. Guys like you usually have their pick of the ladies without laying out cash. That's all I meant."

"Janelle and I'd been separated for over a year. Up until that night, there had been no one else. The girl walked in, took my breath away, and I paid her for sex. End of story. I never saw her again, and I only know her first name."

"What was it?" Harry asked. "That might help us find her."

Dani held her breath.

"Desiree." He glanced at Dani as he recited the name he'd told her suited her more than Sophie that night.

She let the air escape her lips and finally found the courage to look up, her eyes on Harry. If Nate was going to give her up, he would have already done it. He had no reason not to do it. That night had happened long before the murder.

Unless he was trying to protect her.

That was it. He thought the hooker thing was her naughty, extra cash job on the side. Or that she actually lived out her sexual fantasies. Either way, her secret was safe.

At least for the time being.

"Dani, get on that, will you? Check out the girls on Harry Hines Boulevard and see if any of them know a Desiree." He walked through the open door. "This time I really have to go. We'll be in touch, Nate," he said, over his shoulder as he walked to the elevator.

Alone in Harry's office with Randall, Dani's cheeks grew warm. If there was any doubt he didn't recognize her, his conversation with Harry had put that to rest.

How would she explain how a hooker is suddenly transformed into a private investigator? And why hadn't he sold her out and said something to Harry? Surely he couldn't feel comfortable with her as the lead investigator.

Nate broke the silence. "Look, Dani. Or Sophie. Or whatever the hell your name really is. I don't know why you cruise downtown. I'm guessing my wife paid you to come on to me. I hope it was worth the cash."

She struggled to hide her confusion. "Why would you think that? I've never even spoken to your wife."

"Frankly, I don't give a damn." His eyes narrowed as if he were trying to figure out if she was lying. Finally his shoulders relaxed slightly, and he took a deep breath. "I just need to know you can do your job. Otherwise, I'll simply tell Harry I'm more comfortable with a different agency. No big deal."

She looked up, surprised. "You seriously think you can work with me after what happened?"

He stared until finally she looked away. "If you're as good as Harry claims you are, I'd be foolish to allow your occasional moon-lighting or whatever you call it to jeopardize my chances of proving I'm not a murderer."

At the reference to the dead woman, Dani's police instincts kicked in. "Any clue who might have killed your wife?"

Randall exhaled and shook his head. "Unfortunately, I have no idea what went on in Janelle's life. We'd been separated for over a year." He paused. "I didn't know for sure she shoved drugs up her nose until the police told me. I had my suspicions sometimes, especially when she'd erupt in a rage during one of our many arguments."

"How often was that?"

"Only when I wouldn't give in to her pleas for me to move back into the house and pretend nothing was wrong between us."

"Why didn't you get a divorce?"

Randall laughed. "Now there's a question I've been asked a dozen times since her death. The truth is, I'm lazy. I kept thinking she'd file the paper work. I only made the decision to hire a lawyer the week she was killed."

"Why the sudden urgency?" Dani studied his face. Usually, she had no problems deciding if someone was lying just by watching their eyes. His were unreadable.

"No reason." He stood and walked to the window overlooking the parking lot before turning back. "That's not entirely true. After that night with you at the Marquee, she confronted me. Apparently, she'd been paying someone at the hotel to watch me and report back to her."

"She knew about me?" Dani interrupted, suddenly understanding why he thought she was on his wife's payroll.

"Not you, specifically. She only knew I took a hooker up to my room." He paused and shrugged. "Sorry."

Dani never flinched. Having him believe she was a hooker was way better than having him find out the real reason she had sex with him that night.

"Was she angry?"

He snorted. "Major understatement. At first she tried to use it to get me to go back to the way we used to be. When that didn't work, she threatened to blacklist me and ruin my career."

Not a good scenario for a man paying her to find proof he didn't kill his wife. Clearly, he had motive.

"Could she do that?" Dani asked, tentatively.

"She owned the building and sat on the board of the three largest hospitals in Dallas. So yes, she definitely could have made life difficult for me."

Margie walked in and deposited two bags on the desk. "Brought you burgers and fries. Hope you like mustard." She started out the door and turned back. "What about drinks, Dani?"

Dani stood and grabbed the bags. "We're going into my office, Margie. Harry would have a hissy if we got mustard on anything on his desk. I have sodas there. Thanks." She walked to the door then turned her head. "You coming?"

Her face burned. She'd have to be careful with her words.

They walked in silence to her office, two doors down the hall. She shoved the mound of files covering her desk aside to make room for the bags.

"I only have water and Diet Pepsi." She walked to a small built-in refrigerator.

"Either's fine." Randall reached for the bag and pulled out one of the burgers.

Dani sat the canned drink in front of him and watched as he attacked the sandwich. Good Lord, the man was inhaling it. She unwrapped hers and sat down. They ate the rest of the meal without further conversation. Randall polished off his burger long before she even made a dent in hers.

She opened the bottom drawer of her desk and pulled out a half-empty box of Twinkies. "Here. I keep these on hand for late afternoon hunger attacks." She tossed the box at him. "There aren't many left," she said, embarrassed.

Lately, she'd been having almost daily eat-everything-in-sight cravings in the afternoons. The Twinkies had become a godsend.

Randall smiled. "I haven't had one of these since I was a kid. They were my mother's favorite."

Dani thought she detected a catch in Nate's voice, and she wondered if he was carrying baggage about his mother. She forced herself not to ask as she tossed the remnants of their lunch in the trash. "Okay, Dr. Randall, let's get back to this police report."

"Call me Nate. I think you know me a little better than your average private investigator does, don't you think?

Dani blushed again.

Dammit. She wouldn't be able to work with him with that night hanging over their heads.

"Okay, Nate, let's put it out there. I was lonely and went to a bar. Apparently, you were lonely, too. We had sex. That's it."

"Damn hot sex," he added.

She blew out a noisy breath. "Can we get past that?"

He leaned back in the chair and studied her face. "You left the money on the dresser."

She met his stare. "Obviously, I'm not very good at what I do."

"Oh, yes. You are definitely good. When I woke up the next morning alone, I looked to see if you'd left a number or at least your name so I could get the money to you." He laughed. "Guess a name wouldn't have helped."

He lowered his eyes. "Unfortunately, I'm no longer in a position to give it back to you. If you can wait it out, you'll get it with interest."

Dani was surprised by his sudden embarrassment. She guessed most of his money was tied up in his defense.

"Fair enough. Now, can we get back to the questions? I have to pick up my daughter at—" She stopped. The last thing she wanted to do was give him any personal information about her life.

What if he decided to blackmail her?

"Abby, right?"

She gasped. "How do you know that?"

"Margie told Harry you took her to the orthodontist this morning. How old is she?"

Dani breathed a sigh of relief. For a minute, she imagined he was a stalker. "Ten. Now back to you. According to the police report, you claim you were asleep on the couch in your office around the time your wife was murdered. Is that correct?"

"Yes."

"And no one can verify this? Not your partner or your secretary?"

His eyes turned defiant. "I've already gone over this a dozen times with the cops. Don't you think I would tell you if there was?"

Dani ignored the anger. "And that was on Thursday, September thirteenth, between the hours of ten and two, right?"

"Correct. I'd been in surgery most of the night and crashed on the couch." His voice had softened. "Sorry about the outburst."

Dani glanced at the calendar that doubled as her desk pad. The thirteenth of September was the day she'd followed Joe Hamilton and his big-busted secretary to that slimy motel. The same day she'd made Ellen Hamilton a happy woman with the photographs she took, nailing the cheating husband.

She gasped.

"What?" Nate asked.

The thirteenth was also the day she'd followed Nate from his office to his house and waited outside for him to finish what she'd imagined was an afternoon tryst with his wife.

Dani walked over to the cabinet and flipped through the folders until she found the one she wanted. She'd hidden the pictures from Harry that day and stored them with the info she'd accumulated over several weeks in D.N. Romeo's file. With Romeo, of course, being her code name for Randall.

Reaching in, she turned so her back obliterated Nate's view of the folder. She glanced at the images of him leaving the driveway of Janelle's house, of him passing her on Swiss Avenue, and her eyes focused on the date stamp on the right edge of the pictures. September 13. One forty-five p.m.

She stared at the file, unsure how to proceed. Finally, she took a deep breath and turned back to Randall. "You never left the office at all that afternoon?"

"No," he replied without hesitation.

She walked to her desk and sat down. Silently she stared at the man who, in all probability, had killed his wife. Although his eyes didn't give him up, Dani held the proof in her hand.

Nate Randall was lying.

CHAPTER SIXTEEN

When Dani was halfway out the door, the phone rang. She walked back to her desk and glanced at caller ID. This was one call she didn't want to miss.

"Hey, Spig, what's up?" She sat in the chair and propped her feet on the desk. She adored this man.

"Staying out of trouble, Dani?"

She laughed. "Never. You should know me better than that." She paused. "Is this an official call or an invite for a brew?"

"Both, actually. Your gun cleared ballistics. You can pick it up anytime."

"Great. I was just leaving the office when you called. I'll swing by the station on my way home. Unless you want to hang out and talk about old times with a full slab of ribs and a cold Corona."

"No can do tonight. Joanne's dragging my sorry ass to some kind of concert with our new neighbors. Next week will work, though."

"Whoa! Back up. You at a concert? You must have really screwed up big time." Dani chuckled. "What'd you do?"

He snorted. "Shee-it! We were supposed to have dinner with her folks at our house Thursday night. You remember Thursday Night Happy Hour at Pete's?"

Dani laughed so hard she coughed, anticipating his tale of what had happened. "Keep going."

"I may have been a little late getting home. Maybe had a few too many beers at Pete's. Mom and Dad weren't impressed. So now Joanne's milking it for all it's worth."

"When will you guys ever learn?"

"I know. I know. But Joanne's laying it on pretty thick dragging me to some damn hillbilly concert at Billy Bob's, don't ya think? You know how I hate country music. I'd rather put my balls in a fucking vise grip."

"Think what a great country song that would make." She hummed before singing, "I stayed too late with my homeboys, now she has my real boys in a vise grip." Dani couldn't continue because she was laughing too hard.

Everyone knew Spig was whipped, despite his macho attitude. The running joke at the station was that he worked every extra job that came along, not only to keep up with his wife's spending habits but also to give him some relief from her nagging.

"Dammit, Dani, that ain't funny." He paused. "I guess it could be worse. She could make me spend more time with her parents."

"Trust me, big boy, you're getting off easy." She paused. "Hey, Spig, anything new on the druggie who was killed the other night?"

"Nah. Autopsy showed he was hopped up on meth. No surprise there. It's going down as a rival gang killing. Doesn't take much to get bangers shooting at each other. My gut says this won't be the last dead kid we see."

"No doubt," Dani replied. "But I've never seen one who could shoot like that. The guy must have been at least a hundred yards away and still hit the kid dead on between his eyes."

"You don't know where he was, Dani," Spig said, his tone suddenly serious. "He could have been on the other side of your car. You're damn lucky he wasn't trying to nail you."

Dani shuddered at the thought. Spig was right. The shooter could have been that close to her. She'd been so intent on hearing every word the kid had to say, an elephant could have walked by unnoticed.

Maybe Tino was right. Maybe she had lost a step since she'd resigned from the force.

She cleared her throat. "Believe me, I do know." She stood up and glanced at her watch. "Gotta run if I'm going to get that gun tonight. Tell Joanne I said hello and enjoy the concert." She giggled. "Or not. Call me next week so we can grab that beer."

"Sounds good. I'll tell Sarge you're coming."

Dani held the phone long after Spig disconnected, thinking about what he had said. The gunman really might have been closer than she had originally thought. She'd have to be more careful, maybe take Tino with her next time.

What next time? She had no other leads. Even the snitch who'd set up the initial meeting with the dead kid wasn't returning her calls. Her investigation into Johnny's murder was at an absolute dead-end for the first time in two years. She had to be missing something.

But what?

She grabbed her purse and turned out the light, suddenly grateful Spig couldn't make it for a beer tonight. She'd spent the entire day with Randall, and she was exhausted. She'd tried several times to trip him up about his alibi, but he'd stuck to his story about not leaving the office all day. At one point, she'd even contemplated showing him the photos but decided to hold off until she had time to dig deeper into his personal life.

Well, that and the fact that she'd have to admit why she'd been following him that day in the first place. She wasn't ready to do that yet.

Actually, the six or seven hours she'd spent with Randall in her office had not been unpleasant. His sense of humor had kept her laughing more than once as he described his life at the hospital. He'd even gotten a little flirty.

What had she expected? The man had carnal knowledge of her. She had no intention of following through on the flirtation, though. Number one, she was working for him now, but even more importantly, she didn't want him getting too close to her family—especially Casey.

Under different circumstances, Nate Randall was a guy she might even learn to like. That's if she could get past the fact he was probably a cold-blooded killer. She shivered at the thought of Casey carrying his genes. Sweet, innocent Casey who was getting ready for his trip to Minnesota next week with his parents.

Since his release from the hospital, his blood counts had finally started coming back up again. Nikki had finagled an earlier appointment with Dr. Juliana, the Fanconi expert at the Mayo Clinic who had initially diagnosed Casey's disease. If he agreed with the local pediatrician that Casey was showing signs of aplastic anemia and escalation of the Fanconi's, the search for a bone marrow donor would intensify.

Flirting with Randall might prove useful if another shot at getting the specimen became necessary. With that on her mind earlier, she'd found herself glancing at him when he wasn't looking and remembering bits and pieces about the night in the hotel. She wouldn't complain too much if the situation warranted another roll in the hay with the man.

Jeez, woman. Are you out of your freakin' mind?

She shook her head in an unsuccessful attempt to erase those thoughts. Thank heavens the stitches on her forehead were out and the headaches had finally gone away.

She was acting like some horny teenager.

She smiled. That's what Johnny used to say when she was ovulating and turned into a raging nympho. How he'd loved those hormone jumps.

Johnny. She wouldn't believe he might not be the man she'd thought he was. The man with whom she'd fallen in love that Fourth of July so many years ago. She had to keep looking.

She pulled into the parking lot at the police station and turned off the engine. Blowing out a slow breath, she stared at the building, dreading what she had to do. Other than when she'd picked up her last paycheck, she hadn't been back since resigning.

Apprehension gripped her insides. This might be harder than she thought. She got out of the car and walked across the lot, pausing at the massive door separating her from the world she'd loved for so many years.

The door swung open as she reached for the handle. Two young cops emerged, barely noticing her as they chatted. Thankfully, she didn't recognize either one of them. She walked in and strolled up to the desk.

The cop looked up then smiled. "Hey, Dani. Long time no see. Spig mentioned you'd be coming by tonight." He paused. "You look good."

"Thanks, Sarge. You do, too." She stole a glance around the room, hoping no one else was here who might recognize her. She wasn't in the mood for awkward moments when her former colleagues struggled for something to say.

She turned back to Sarge. "Got my gun?"

He reached under the counter then placed a large envelope on the desk. "Ballistics proved it hasn't been fired in a long time." As if to reassure her, he added, "Not that anybody really thought you killed that lowlife."

Dani smiled. Sarge had always been one of her favorite people at the house. "I understand why Spig had to take it. After all, I was the only other person at the scene besides the dead guy when the cops got there."

"Apollo got what he deserved."

Something about the way he said it made Dani look up. "You knew Apollo, Sarge?"

He hesitated for a moment. "Who didn't?"

"I didn't, at least not until he killed Johnny. From what the kid said in the parking lot, I would have to agree he was evil."

"Your dad know about you being there that night?"

She nodded. "Please—if you're fixing to read me the riot act, save it. He did a pretty good job already."

Sarge laughed. "Good. Saves me from having to hear myself." He shoved the envelope across the desk. "Any progress on Johnny's case?"

"No, I've run out of leads." Dani sighed. "Guess we'll never really know the truth, as much as I hate to admit it."

"Yeah, I heard IAB is in the same fix. Heard they were closing the file if nothing more turned up by the end of the year."

Dani perked up. "Really? That would mean Abby and I can finally collect Johnny's death benefits from the department."

"Money's still tight?"

"Always. You'd think a guy on the take would have a few grand stashed away somewhere for emergencies." As soon as the words left her mouth, Dani froze.

That's exactly what Johnny had done. She'd forgotten about the five thousand dollars in the secret bank account. She glanced up to see if the older man caught that. His eyes said he had.

"Well, I'd better go. Hope your family is good. See you, Sarge." She picked up the envelope and walked toward the door, her mind racing.

As long as Johnny had the bank account, she and Abby might as well use it to help out with the expenses. Her new pickup had cost more than the insurance company's reimbursement check for the one she'd totaled, and the car payments were putting a crimp in their cash flow.

She walked away from the station, her head high. No matter what the evidence showed, she had nothing to be ashamed about. Tomorrow, she'd go down to the bank and get the money. If she and Abby were going to live under a cloud of suspicion, at least they should have some kind of perk.

Dani had arranged to be out of the office for most of the next day. She had an appointment at one-thirty with Nate and his partner to go over more details, hoping to catch something the police may have missed.

She dropped Abby off at school and headed to Starbucks for her morning jolt of caffeine. She needed all the help she could get if she intended to march into the bank and make that withdrawal. Taking money that may have been part of a payoff from a drug dealer felt like an admission of guilt, though.

Still, she couldn't think of it that way. Couldn't let herself believe it.

Suddenly, she made a U-turn and headed back home. Quickly, she ran into the house and grabbed a picture of Johnny in his police uniform. Sadness overwhelmed her as she placed it on the seat beside her. A lot of men were made for uniforms. Johnny had been one of them.

Her heart ached as she forced her eyes back to the road, and a flash of loneliness stabbed at her. Maybe because of all that had happened over the past few weeks. She also found herself growing tearful at the least little thing. She'd never been an ice queen, but this was getting ridiculous.

She pulled around to the Starbucks drive-through and ordered her usual Venti White Chocolate Mocha fix then decided she deserved a blueberry scone, too. By the time she arrived at State National Bank in south Cimarron, it had just opened for business. She sat in the car, sipping her drink while she watched several people enter and exit.

Finally, she felt composed enough to do what she'd come to do. Her nerves threatened to ambush her as she walked inside and looked around. This wasn't the bank she and Johnny had used for their checking account, and she was unfamiliar with the employees. She walked up to the only teller who wasn't assisting a customer.

Dani smiled. "I'm interested in closing a savings account. Can you help me with that?"

The girl smiled back, and Dani noticed for the first time how attractive she was. "Do you have your savings book with you?"

Oh, crap!

How could she have been stupid enough to think they would hand her the money without it? Her name wasn't even on the account, and she had no clue what Johnny had done with the book. Despite a thorough search of the house after the police had discovered the secret account, the whereabouts of the book was still a mystery.

She sighed. "I left it at home. Do I need to go back and get it, Sandy?" she asked, after a quick glance at the girl's name badge.

"No, I'll get a withdrawal form for you to sign, but I'll need a picture ID and a credit card."

"No problem," Dani responded. "The account is under my husband's name, Johnny Perez."

If the girl recognized the name, she didn't let on as she scanned the computer. After a few minutes, she looked up again. "I'm sorry, Mrs. Perez. That account is frozen."

"Frozen? Does it say why?" Dani had been worried this might happen, but actually hearing it made her stomach lurch.

"No, I'm sorry. Let me call the bank manager. He'll be able to tell you what the problem is."

"No, that's okay," Dani answered quickly. "I'll do some investigating myself and find out what's going on. I appreciate your help." She turned and started for the door.

Do it, Dani. It's now or never.

She walked back to the counter. "How long have you worked here, Sandy?"

"Four years. Why?"

"May I ask you a quick question?"

"Sure, Mrs. Perez. How can I help you?"

Dani reached into her purse and pulled out Johnny's picture, unable to look at it for fear she would tear up again.

"Two years ago, this man opened an account here. I know you must see a lot of people come and go, but is there any chance you might remember seeing him in here?"

Sandy studied the picture before looking up at Dani. "Is this your husband?"

"Just a client," Dani lied. She reached into her purse and pulled out her PI license.

The girl chewed on her lower lip, her eyes squinted as if she was contemplating whether to answer or not. Finally, she handed the picture back to Dani. "Yeah, I remember him. He was flirting with all the girls here, even asked one of them out for drinks. Never even bothered to hide his wedding ring."

A ton of bricks fell on Dani's chest.

She tried unsuccessfully to hide her reaction and breathe at the same time. *Oh, God.* All this time, she'd been fighting to prove Johnny wasn't a bad cop. Now she'd learned he might have been a cheater, as well.

Dani took another deep breath and shoved the picture back across the counter. "Please take a second look. This is really important to me."

"You working for his wife?"

Dani forced a smile. "Something like that. The photo?" She pointed at the picture.

Sandy stared at it for a full minute before glancing back up, her eyes filled with pity. She'd seen Dani's reaction and wasn't buying her story. "I'm sorry. He's not the kind of guy you forget."

Just then, another teller walked by and Sandy grabbed her arm. "Carolyn, do you remember that cop who came in several years back and asked you out?"

The girl looked surprised by the question. "Sorta, why?"

"This lady is a private investigator asking about him. Did you ever go out with him?"

"Are you kidding?" Carolyn shook her head. I don't do married guys. Bedsides, I was still with Larry then, remember?"

Dani spoke up. "Could you take a look at this picture and tell me if this is the guy?"

"Sure." Carolyn studied the photo only momentarily before she met Dani's eyes. "No doubt about it. That's him." She handed the picture back.

Suddenly lightheaded, Dani leaned into the counter for support. She didn't want to believe that Johnny had run around, but she had trouble discounting two positive identifications.

She laid the picture on the counter and pointed to Johnny. "You're one-hundred percent sure this is the man who asked you out?" Dani braced for the answer she knew would crush every bit of her hope.

"Not that one," Carolyn said. She tapped her finger on the cop standing on the driver's side of the car. "The guy with the shades."

Dani gasped as the words registered. They weren't talking about Johnny. Carolyn had pointed at Tino.

Chapter Seventeen

Nate met her at the elevator door, a broad grin spreading across his face when she smiled. "Hope this means you have good news for me."

Dani wrinkled her nose and shook her head, allowing him to lead the way to his office. "Unfortunately, no. I was thinking about other news I got today."

A faint scent tickled his nostrils as she passed, and he inhaled deeply. She was wearing the same perfume she had on that night at the Marquee. Mental pictures of her writhing in pleasure flooded his mind before he turned away, out of range of the killer scent. The last thing he needed was to obsess about that night, especially now that he needed her focused on his case. It was critical that he focus, too.

"Care to share the news?"

She looked embarrassed. "Sorry, it's personal." She opened her briefcase and spread the contents of a file across his desk. "Let's get started. We need to make sure we go over every detail before I pick up Abby after soccer practice."

A little disappointed she didn't want to share her personal life with him, Nate broke his stare and walked around his desk to sit beside her. "Where do you want to start?"

He scooted his chair slightly to the right, a little farther from her.

This was going to be harder than he'd thought. Every time he looked at her, he envisioned her raising her hips for him to slip off the black lacy undies. Remembered her soft moans as he'd moved inside her.

He jerked his head away, forcing those thoughts out of his mind and trying to concentrate on something ordinary, like his shift at the clinic last night. He thought about the little old woman who had fallen and broken her wrist three days before and sat for seven hours in the emergency room at County Hospital before she finally gave up and left in disgust. He wondered if the clinic would open one or two extra nights if he offered to put in more hours.

Wondered if Dani would consent to work extra hours with him.

Shit!

With her sitting so close, he found it impossible to concentrate on anything but that night.

Who was he kidding? Even if she did agree to another night, he had no money to pay her. She definitely didn't seem like a credit card kind of girl.

"Nate, are you listening?" Dani's insistent voice broke through his sub-conscious.

"What? Sorry. I was thinking about the clinic last night."

Okay, partly true.

"I asked if you had read over the police report. Sometimes, a small detail you didn't consider important will jog your memory."

"I read it three times." Nate stared into her eyes. He'd forgotten how dark they were. How they sparkled in the light. "Nothing popped up. I was asleep on the couch. When I woke up, Roger was already in his office."

"Roger?"

"My partner."

Dani jumped up, visibly excited. "He can swear you were asleep."

Nate shook his head. "The police have already questioned him. He went straight to his office and closed the door. He only saw me about an hour after he got to the office, a few hours after the police say Janelle died."

"I'll need to talk to him myself. Is he here?"

"Not yet, but he should be out of surgery soon. I'll page him and ask him to come straight to the office afterward. I'm pretty sure you won't get any new information out of him, though."

Dani turned to face him. For a split second, Nate studied her dark chocolate eyes. Then it hit him. "You don't believe me, do you?"

"What does it matter?" She looked surprised by the question. "I'm hired to find reasonable doubt one way or another."

Her disbelief shouldn't matter, but it did. He hated that she doubted his word. "I didn't kill my wife, Dani. I wanted out of the marriage, yeah. But I was nowhere near her that day."

She lowered her eyes. He had to find a way to make her believe him. He picked up the phone and dialed Roger's cell phone. When his partner's voice mail picked up, he left a message for him to come to the office as soon as he was out of surgery. Then he sat back down and reached for the police report. Silently, he read it again, sighing before he glanced back up at Dani.

"I really don't see anything in here that makes me change my story."

"And the lady at the café downstairs doesn't remember seeing you at all that day?"

"No."

"What about the parking attendant? Did he see you leave or return during that time frame?"

For a second, Nate allowed a sliver of hope to excite him before it was dashed. "There's only card access."

Dani jumped up. "That's it. We can get the computerized printout from that day."

"The card reader's been broken for a couple of weeks now. They've had so many complaints, they're keeping the arm raised until they can get it fixed. Anyone can come and go at will."

Doubt reappeared in her eyes, and an odd twinge of disappointment slid through him. "That would have proved my innocence, I know. My car never left underground parking that afternoon."

The shrill ring of the phone startled him, and he automatically reached across the desk to pick up the receiver.

Dani studied Nate's face as he spoke into the mouthpiece. He was lying about his car never leaving the garage, but she couldn't tell him she knew that. Not if she wanted to keep him out of jail to save her nephew.

Nate hung up the phone, a confused look on his face. "That was our accountant. He called to remind us to let him know when we wanted the audit rescheduled. First I've heard of an audit." He sat in the chair, his eyes squinted. "We were just audited less than a year ago. We shouldn't need another one until sometime in January."

"I see." Dani dug into her purse for her notebook. "What accounting firm do you use?"

"McLaughlin and Tate. They're on the second floor."

"It's probably nothing, but I'll chat with them. Possibly a screw up on the date."

"He said someone from the lawyer's office called and cancelled right after Janelle's funeral." Nate paused to rub his forehead. "That's odd. Wonder how they would know about it in the first place."

"I don't know, but I'll check it out." Dani scribbled once again in her notebook.

Both Dani and Nate turned when a knock rattled the door. An attractive man in hospital scrubs walked in. When Dani stood up, he scanned every inch of her.

"Hey, Nate. What's up?" Before Nate had a chance to respond, the man turned to Dani, his hand extended. "Paul Gerard. Nate's partner. And you are?"

Dani's eyes met Nate's. "I thought you said your partner's name was Roger."

Nate moved out from behind his desk and stood beside Dani, a scowl on his face. "I did. Three of us work in this office." He glared at his partner. "Paul, this is Dani Perez. I've hired her agency to investigate Janelle's murder."

Paul held Dani's hand way too long for her comfort level. From the way Nate frowned, it was way too long for him, too. He waited until his partner finally released her hand.

"You didn't tell me she was gorgeous." Paul smiled at Dani, letting his eyes move over her again, this time undressing her.

Jeez! The guy had on a wedding ring. Now she knew how those women at State National Bank had felt. Getting hit on by a married man was not the greatest compliment.

Suddenly embarrassed, Dani shifted her weight to lean away from him. Had Nate shared the intimate details of their night at the Marquee with his partner? She searched Nate's face for any hint this was true. A knowing smile? A wink between them? No. He only looked halfway pissed. She wondered why.

"What's going on, Nate?"

All three turned as another man strode into Nate's office.

Dani sized up the newcomer, his starched shirt and creased slacks in direct contrast with Paul's scrubs. Although he wasn't bad looking, the other two were definitely the lookers of the group.

"Dani, this is Roger McMillan."

Dani shook his hand, then dove right in. "We've been going over the details of the day Janelle was murdered. I've read your account in the police report, Roger." She glanced toward Paul.

"Any chance either of you can recall anything else about that day?"

"I wasn't here," Paul said, still smiling at her. "Thursdays, I play golf."

Roger walked to a chair and sat down, his eyes on Nate. "Like I told the cops, I got back here sometime after one. Went straight to my office and closed the door. I was swamped with paperwork. Didn't even know Nate was here until he stopped by later that afternoon to ask me about a patient."

"Do you always go straight to your office without saying hello to Nate?" Dani asked.

Roger seemed annoyed by the question. "What difference does that make?"

Dani held his stare. "It might be useful in Nate's defense. If Nate thought there was a chance you might stop in to say hello, it stands to reason he wouldn't risk you telling the cops he wasn't in his office. He would have come up with a better alibi."

"Why does he even need an alibi? He said he didn't kill her. I believe him," Roger asked, obviously angered by the statement.

Nate stood. "My wife's dead, Roger. The whole world knows I wanted out of the marriage. That's why I need an alibi." He walked to the window and stared. Finally, he turned back. "Then there's the little detail about the cops finding the stopper from a Vecuronium vial under my front seat. A solid alibi would be really helpful about now."

"We're anesthesiologists, for God's sake." Paul's voice climbed an octave. "We use Vecuronium bromide every day."

"Do you bring it home from the hospital every day?" Dani asked.

Paul turned and met her gaze. Something about the way he smiled convinced her Nate had confided in him about the sex. That pissed her off.

"No," he answered finally.

Dani turned her back to him. "How does the hospital deal with the drug, Nate? Do you have to sign for it?"

"No. Every operating suite has a cart containing all the drugs we may need during surgery. Vecuronium is one of those drugs. The cart's unlocked every morning before the first surgery."

"Who unlocks it?"

"The nurses. They use our anesthesia report to input the charges. The patients are billed by the vial."

"Do you always use the entire vial?"

"Usually, but not always. Any unused portion is discarded."

Dani frowned. "That's not good. Anyone could take it out of the operating room trash then?"

"Pretty much, but it's already been reconstituted. It's liquid. The drug they say killed Janelle was still in powder form."

Dani paused, thinking. "Hmm. So, let me see if I got this right. If the nurses are the ones who charge the patient, do they make sure the supply is replenished?"

"Yes, they reorder from the pharmacy at the end of the day." Nate eyed her closely. "Where are you going with this, Dani?"

She rubbed her chin, mindlessly ignoring his question. "If a person wanted to walk away with a bottle or two, it wouldn't be that difficult?"

Paul laughed. "Hell, no. Everybody in the operating room has access to it, including the unit secretaries who pick it up at the pharmacy and restock it." He shrugged. "And what about the times we drop it?" He looked down at his beeper as it went off.

Dani faced Nate. "Has that happened recently?"

"Damn." Nate slapped his head. "Several weeks ago, I knocked over the entire tray, and all the drugs splattered."

"Did anyone document that?"

"One of the nurses, I'm sure," Nate said, a touch of defeat in his voice.

Dani thought for a moment. "My guess is it won't be long before the police find out."

"What's to find out? They can't pin this on Nate just because he was clumsy one time," Paul interrupted.

Dani ignored him and concentrated on Nate. "They can and they will, unless we find someone who swears you didn't leave the office the day Janelle was killed. They could say you pocketed the drug and then knocked the tray over to make it look like it had been destroyed."

Nate sighed. "Back to square one."

Paul headed for the door then stopped directly in front of Dani. "As much as I've enjoyed meeting you, Miss Perez, I'm wanted in OR." He reached for her hand.

"It's Mrs. Perez," Dani answered. She glanced at Nate in time to see his eyes dropping to her ringless left hand before he nailed her with a questioning stare.

Dani cursed under her breath. If only she hadn't taken her ring off last week after another one of Tino's lectures about getting on with her life. "I hope you'll be available if I have any further questions, Dr. Gerard."

Paul's smile returned, and again, he held her hand too long. "Anytime, Mrs. Perez," he said, emphasizing the Mrs. "Catch you later, Nate. Roger." He released Dani's hand and walked out the door.

"I could say I saw him sleeping on the couch when I got here."

Both Dani and Nate whirled to face Roger.

"Why in the hell would you do that?" Nate's voice had escalated. "No one's asking you to perjure yourself."

"Okay." Dani had heard enough. "Let's move on. Temporarily, we're at a dead end. We'll have to come up with something else."

"Did you know we were getting audited this week, Roger?" Nate asked, suddenly changing the subject.

Nate's partner did a 180 degree turn. "Who ordered that? It's usually done at the first of the year."

"I know," Nate replied, shaking his head. "But I just got a call reminding me to let them know when we want to reschedule. I can't figure out why."

"Neither can I. Probably just got their dates confused." He shrugged. "I've got to scoot, too. I have a ton of paperwork to finish before I head out." He glanced one last time at Dani. "Nate didn't kill his wife, Mrs. Perez. We're counting on you to prove it."

For a few seconds, neither Dani nor Nate spoke after Roger left. Finally, Nate broke the awkward silence. "Are you married?"

She hesitated, wondering if it was wise giving him personal information about her life. "I was. My husband was killed on the job two years ago."

He studied her face before turning away.

"Obviously, Roger won't be much help," Dani said, directing the conversation away from herself. "We'll have to work on another angle."

Nate blew out a breath. "Looks like I'm running out of angles, doesn't it?"

CHAPTER EIGHTEEN

"Tino, we need to talk." Dani pulled him from the couch where he was wedged between her two aunts. "In private."

He bent down and kissed Aunt Carmella's forehead. "Sorry to leave you lovely ladies, but when Dani says jump, I ask how high." He winked at the pair and followed Dani into the kitchen.

"What's up? Did you bring me in here because you can't keep your hands off me?" he joked after she closed the door.

"Shut up, Tino. This is important."

"Okay." He tried to look serious, but his eyes still sparkled with mischief. "What's up?"

Dani met his gaze, wondering how she could do this without setting him off. She decided the only way was to come right out and say it. "Have you ever been in State National Bank off Division Street?"

Tino's smile faded, the playfulness gone. "Why would you ask me that? I've been in a lot of banks on the job."

She hesitated, staring at him. "That's where they found the account in Johnny's name."

"Remember me, Dani? I was Johnny's partner. Of course I know that. But what's that got to do with me? Alana and I did our banking at Western State down the street."

Dani studied his face, searching for a sign he was lying. Anything.

She plunged ahead, knowing she was about to really push his hot buttons. "I stopped by there Friday and talked with a few of the employees. Two of the tellers recognized you from the picture I showed them."

He squinted. "What in the fuck were you doing showing them a picture of me?"

His voice had grown threatening. Surprised by his outburst, Dani stepped back. She'd expected anger, but his angry words were way out of character.

"I wanted to find out if any of them recognized Johnny. I was running late and grabbed the first picture I found of him in uniform. You were in it, too." She paused and moved closer, her voice barely a whisper now. "Neither woman recognized Johnny, but both picked you out."

"They're mistaken," Tino said, taking her statement in stride like any trained cop would do.

She held his gaze. "They said you hit on them. Said you even asked one of them out."

He glared at her for a second, anger flashing in his eyes before he eased back into a smile. "Sounds like wishful thinking to me."

"Dammit, Tino, I'm serious. Were you there when Johnny opened that account?"

"Jeez, Dani, I've never set foot in that bank. If Johnny opened an account there, it wasn't with me. I was just as surprised as everyone else when they found it. Someone's jacking you around."

"Why would they do that?"

"Who knows? I'm telling you, it wasn't me. I never cheated on Alana." He moved closer and pulled her to his chest, his voice growing softer. "Ah, Dani, when are you going to give up this stupid investigation? It's ancient history. Even IAB is ready to close the book on it."

"Closing the investigation doesn't clear Johnny's name. People still believe he was dirty." She pulled away to face him. "I'm close, Tino. I can feel it."

His brow creased and he shook his head. "You damn near got yourself killed last week, and what did you find out? Squat. Nothing out there, Dani. Let it go."

"I can't." She lowered her head. "I owe it to Johnny."

"That's bullshit," he snapped. "You owe it to Abby and your family to stay alive. You owe it to me, damn it!"

"You?"

His expression softened. "Haven't I made my feelings perfectly clear?"

"I thought I made mine clear, too." She swallowed the lump in her throat, trying to think of a way to gently say what had to be said. "I love you like a brother, Tino. Nothing more."

They both turned as Abby walked through the door. "Come on, Uncle Tino. Aunt Sophie's starting to freak out. Something about her blood sugar."

Both Tino and Dani laughed, a welcome respite from their serious conversation. Aunt Sophie made no bones about wanting to eat exactly on time. You could set a watch by her eating habits.

"Come on, princess. You can sit between Tino and me." Dani put her arm around her daughter and guided her into the living room, sensing Tino's intense stare following her out. He always sat next to her at the dinner table, but today, she needed space.

Just as everyone was seated, the doorbell rang. Dani jumped up. "I'll get it."

She rushed through the hallway, wondering who it could be, knowing they weren't expecting anyone else. When she opened the door, she stared, tongue-tied for a moment.

"Nate! What are you doing here?"

"Is Harry here?"

"Why?"

"I've been poring over my finances all weekend, and I found something weird. He gave me this address when I talked to him this morning. Told me to drop off these books. I didn't know you'd be here." Nate smiled.

"Who is it, Dani?" Nikki hollered from the dining room.

Her sister's question jolted Dani, spreading panic through her body.

She didn't want Randall anywhere near Casey.

She grabbed the file from his hands. "I'll take it to him, Nate. Thanks for bringing it by. One of us will call you in the morning." She opened the door and stood aside to allow him to pass when Harry rounded the corner.

"Thought it might be you, Nate." He glanced at Dani. "I acted on a hunch after you told me about the cancelled audit. I asked Nate to do some digging. When he called this morning to say he'd found some inconsistencies, I told him to swing by and bring the books so you and I could go over them after dinner."

"It's probably nothing," Nate said, still grinning at Dani.

God, he has a great smile.

"Maybe not, but if it caught your attention, I want to look at it." Harry reached for the file in Dani's hand.

Aunt Carmella appeared in the hallway. "Come on you two. Dinner's getting—" She broke off in midsentence, and a smile tipped the corners of her mouth when she saw Nate, obviously liking what she saw. Apparently the old girl still had a smoldering flame in her furnace. "And who is this nice young man, Harry?"

Dani answered quickly. "This is Dr. Randall, Aunt Carm. Harry and I are working with him on a case. He brought something for us to look at, and he's just leaving." She opened the door a little wider.

"You're the doctor who murdered his wife?"

"Aunt Carm," Dani scolded, outraged by her aunt's bluntness.

Nate seemed unfazed and shot her one of his killer smiles. The kind that probably had panties dropping all over Dallas. "Yes, ma'am, I'm the doctor accused of that, but I didn't kill her. Harry and Dani are working to find out who did."

Dani watched, fascinated, while Nate bewitched her aunt. Carmella blushed like a teenager.

The older woman grabbed his hand and pulled him toward the dining room. "Come with me. I want you to meet my sister."

Dani grabbed his other arm and pulled him back. "That's not a good idea, Aunt Carm. I'm sure Nate has somewhere he has to be right now." Her eyes begged him to agree.

"Actually, I don't." He looked confused by Dani's behavior before finally turning back to Carmella. "I'd love to meet your sister. If she's anything like you, I'm in for a real treat."

Holy Mother of God! Nate Randall was about to get his first look at his son, and Bobby and Nikki were about to meet the man who'd fathered their child.

And Dani couldn't do a damn thing to prevent it.

Walking into the dining room behind Nate and her aunt, Dani glanced at her sister, who looked horrified. Dani shrugged, praying for enough strength for the three of them to get through this awkward moment. Praying that Nate would meet her family and go home before anyone got suspicious or picked up on their reaction to the man.

"Sophie, this nice young man is Dr. Nate Randall."

Nate turned sharply toward Dani, hearing a name he was familiar with, a name he probably thought had come from out of the blue at the Marquee.

Before she finished, Sophie interrupted, "Are you the neurosurgeon from Fort Worth that Dani mentioned?"

Dani groaned. She always knew one day her tales of imaginary dates would come back to bite her in the butt. This day was going south faster than Canadian geese in winter. She lowered her eyes the minute Nate turned to her.

"I'm not a neurosurgeon. I only put people to sleep." He paused, glancing at Dani for a second before continuing. "Sophie. That's a beautiful name. I'm glad to meet you."

Harry stood at Nate's side. "Sorry about this, guys. Nate's a client. He found something pertaining to his case that couldn't wait until morning."

Abby stood and extended her hand, just like Dani had taught her. "I'm Abby. It's nice to meet you, Dr. Randall."

Not to be outdone by his older cousin, Casey stood. "I'm Casey."

When Nikki gasped, Dani mouthed, *I'm so sorry.*

Then Harry took his cue from the kids. One by one, he introduced Nate to everyone at the table. Dani stole a glance at her dad and discovered he'd shifted into police mode, shaking Nate's hand while sizing him up. Something he did before every interrogation.

Nodding briefly, Tino didn't bother to stand when the introductions were made. All the women at the table, with the exception of Nikki and Dani, looked at Nate as if they'd just been introduced to Dani's new boyfriend. Even Marie, Harry's wife, who was usually a little more reserved than the spinster aunts.

Then Aunt Sophie invited Nate to stay for dinner.

Dani's sudden sharp intake of breath turned into a momentary coughing jag. Nate glanced at her, his eyes questioning.

Say no, hers pleaded.

He turned to Aunt Sophie, his lips parted in a dazzling display of straight, white teeth. "As lovely as that sounds, I wouldn't want to impose on your family meal. Besides, I have a few more errands to run before I leave Cimarron."

The sigh of relief from both Dani and Nikki was nearly audible over the swooshing of Aunt Sophie's oxygen machine.

"Nonsense!" Carmella said, her voice rising. "Errands can wait, especially on a gorgeous Sunday afternoon like this. Sophie and I cooked enough to feed an army."

Nate shifted uncomfortably, meeting Dani's stare for a second time. "Thanks, but I'll have to take a rain check. It's been my pleasure meeting all of you." He turned to Harry. "You'll call later?"

"Just as soon as Dani and I have a look at what you brought."

"Abigail, come sit by me so the doctor can squeeze in between your mother and Tino." Aunt Carmella patted the chair next to hers. "We'll put Sophie's oxygen on the floor."

An awkward silence hung over them as Abby walked around the table to the chair between her two great-aunts.

Hector was the first to speak. "Obviously, my sister won't take no for an answer, Dr. Randall. Unless you really do have pressing issues, please have a seat and join us for dinner. We were just about to say grace."

Nate glanced at Dani again. This time, she shrugged. The damage was already done. He'd met Casey. Hopefully, he hadn't made a connection.

Why would he? The man had no idea what had happened with his semen sample so many years ago at the fertility clinic.

Nate held out Dani's chair out, and she sat next to him. She hesitated after making the sign of the cross before reaching for his outstretched hand when they said the prayer. Surprisingly, his hand was warm and dry, despite the pressure from her aunts. An image of those same hands moving over her body flashed through her mind just before the *Amen.*

What kind of Catholic girl am I?

A flame crept up Dani's cheeks, and she bowed her head even lower.

Despite the prayer's end, Nate held her hand a second or two longer, a gesture not missed by Tino, whose face hadn't lost the scowl since Nate claimed the chair between him and Dani.

The tightness in Dani's shoulders eased slightly as everyone passed the food around the table and filled their plates. There was nothing more she could do. Only three people at the table knew how complicated the meal would get if Nate took a good look at Casey and noticed his shortness of breath. As a doctor, he'd be curious.

What if, unlike her and her sister, he knew he carried the Fanconi gene? Was he smart enough to put two and two together, or was that an incredible stretch for even a doctor? Fanconi's was so rare, what if he asked questions?

Dani stole a glance at her sister and Bobby as the aunts monopolized Nate's attention. She knew Nikki well enough to know the crinkle in her forehead meant she was worried. Had she noticed the same thing Dani had when Randall had first walked into the room? Was she thinking there was more than a little resemblance between Nate and his son sitting directly across the table besides their bright blue eyes?

Dani sighed, drawing Nate's curious look. She managed a weak smile. Maybe he wasn't as observant as she'd feared.

Surprisingly, the rest of the dinner went well. Nate charmed even Harry's wife, a born skeptic who was extremely protective when it came to Dani and Nikki. Not like Carmella and Sophie, who would sell her off to the first rich guy with the least little bit of interest.

Finally, the last of Aunt Sophie's famous chocolate cake was served and inhaled, and Dani got up to gather the dirty dishes.

"Let me help," Nate said, pushing away from the table and reaching for her plate.

Before Dani could protest, his arms were full, and he was on his way to the kitchen. Given no other choice, she followed with both Nikki and Bobby at her heels. No doubt they wanted a closer look at Casey's father.

Once in the kitchen, Nikki positioned herself directly between Nate and the dishwasher, daring him to ask her about Casey.

"If you'll rinse these off, I'll load the dishwasher," she said finally, never breaking eye contact with him.

For a brief moment, Nate studied her before he finally walked to the sink and turned on the faucet.

Dani glanced toward Nikki and almost lost her cool. She knew from the look on her sister's face that she was about to tell Nate the truth. Frantically, she tried to get her attention to stop her. Now was not the time or the place.

Just as quickly, Nikki lowered her eyes, apparently deciding against it. She and Bobby were taking Casey to the Mayo Clinic on Tuesday. If the news was even the least bit hopeful, they would have no reason for Nate to know about the consequences of the fertility clinic screw up.

As the two sisters made idle conversation, carefully choosing their words, Bobby and Nate engaged in lively banter. Before long, they were laughing about something that had happened earlier when the Cowboys beat the Redskins. Dani wondered what Bobby must be feeling, standing face to face with the man who could definitely complicate their lives.

And save his son.

Occasionally, Dani studied Nate when he wasn't looking and noticed her sister doing the same thing. Under different circumstances, he was someone she'd enjoy having as a friend.

That's if she could forget he was Casey's father, or that he might very well have killed his wife.

How easily she had forgotten the case while he charmed everyone over dinner. Okay, maybe not everyone. Hector never took his eyes off Nate during the entire meal. Dani expected to get an earful of his opinions later.

And Tino. He'd acted like a teenage boy ready to kick Nate's ass. Tino was getting annoying. What would she have to do to convince him she really wasn't interested?

Finally, the table was cleared, the dishes stacked and ready to be cleaned, and Nate had said his goodbyes to the aunts and Marie. Dani walked him to the door and held it open.

"Goodbye, Nate."

Halfway through, he turned back. "I know this must have been uncomfortable for you, but I appreciate the opportunity to see what a normal family does on a Sunday afternoon."

Dani snorted. "You're kidding, right? This family is anything but normal."

He laughed with her. "Anything's better than mine. You gotta love your aunts. They never missed an opportunity to tell me what a great catch you are."

Dani's cheeks burned. "Honestly, since my husband's death, they've tried to hook me up with anything in pants. It's embarrassing."

This time he laughed out loud. "Thanks for bursting my ego bubble. Anything in pants, huh?" His smile faded as he held her eyes. "Does that include Tino?"

Her eyes met his, and she couldn't help herself. She grinned back. He was flirting again, and if she was being totally honest, she'd have to admit she'd enjoyed it.

"What can I say? They're shameless. They're on a mission to find a father for Abby."

"She's a great kid. So is Casey."

Dani looked away. She could tell he wanted to ask about the boy. Hopefully, he was too polite to ask personal questions about the child's condition.

He reached for her hand. "I can't remember when I've had a nicer Sunday afternoon. Good food, great company, and an earlier Cowboys' victory. Who could ask for anything better? Thanks again." He released her hand and walked out the door.

Dani stood on the porch for a few minutes after his car was out of sight. Okay, if she'd had her druthers, today would never have happened, but it really hadn't been too bad. What could have been an absolute disaster had turned out civil. Unless she counted the sarcastic remarks Tino made every time Nate opened his mouth.

All in all, it had been a great day. She'd even flirted with him a little. She told herself it was a strategy just in case Casey's trip on Tuesday didn't turn out as they hoped, and she and Nikki had to go to

Plan B and get Nate back into Dani's bed. She walked into the house, remembering his hands all over her body.

Not a bad idea.

She really wasn't a nice Catholic girl after all.

CHAPTER NINETEEN

Nikki pounced on Dani as soon as she walked through the door, pushed her toward the stairs, and nudged her up the steps, away from the rest of the family. "Come on."

Once they were behind closed doors in Dani's old bedroom, Nikki finally spoke. "Holy guacamole! I didn't know he looked like that. No wonder you acted like a love starved teenager."

A warm glow spread through Dani's body at the mention of her night with Nate. "I tried to tell you."

"Man! All this time, I've been racking my brain to come up with a really great way to repay you for what you did. Girl, you owe me."

Dani threw back her head and laughed. "Let's not get too carried away, Nik. I didn't just walk into a dark room, hop in the sack, and let him tease me into carnal bliss, you know. Don't forget that one little detail about getting naked in front of a prefect stranger."

Nikki bit her lip. Dani knew she was trying to look serious.

"Like it wasn't worth every little goose bump." She put her fingers to her lips. "Shh," she whispered, leaning against the door for a second before turning back to Dani. "Thought I heard someone coming."

"We can't stay long. With Tino's performance downstairs, he's liable to find Nate and haul him off to jail if he thinks I'm still out on the porch with him."

"What's up with that? I thought you told Tino how you feel. Or better yet, how you *don't* feel."

"I did." Dani smirked. "He ignored me. Maybe he thinks I'll come around." She shook her head. "Fat chance! Guess I'll have to distance myself from him for a while. At least until he hones in on another unsuspecting female."

"Tino always was a player," Nikki said.

Dani caught herself before mentioning the women at the bank. What did it all mean, anyway? Probably a case of mistaken identity like he'd said.

Nikki plopped onto the bed. "Did Nate really kill his wife?"

Dani slammed her mouth shut before she mentioned the photo that proved he had been with Janelle at the time she was murdered. If Casey's condition worsened and she found it necessary to try for Nate's specimen one more time, Nikki would never allow her anywhere near him if she knew that.

"He swore to Harry and me that he didn't, but the police have a boatload of compelling circumstantial evidence that suggests otherwise."

"Hmm," Nikki mused. "I don't know, Dani. He doesn't strike me as the kind of guy who could do something like that. Doesn't have the look."

Dani snorted as she sat on the edge of the bed. "The look? Would you think I was the kind of girl who could walk into a bar and have sex with a total stranger?"

Nikki wrinkled her nose. "As much as I want to say yes, we both know you aren't."

"My point exactly. People do unbelievable things when they're up against a wall. That's all I'm saying."

"I hope you're wrong. While you were helping Casey with his dinner plate, I heard both Aunt Soph and Aunt Carm tell him you hadn't had sex in over two years."

Dani gasped. "Are you freakin' kidding me?"

Nikki laughed so hard she nearly rolled off the bed. "Gotcha," she said between giggles.

Dani slapped her sister's leg. "Payback is hell, sis." She jumped up. "Come on. We need to get back before Dad sends out the SWAT team."

"Look at this, Dani." Harry pointed out a highlighted entry later that night. "Twenty grand. Wonder why Nate thought this was significant?" He flipped the pages. "He's marked the same entry every month."

Dani leaned in closer. "Where's the money going?"

"Looks like the Southwestern Medical Insurance Group. Too much for regular health insurance, though."

"Malpractice insurance maybe?"

Harry rubbed his chin, his eyes pensive. "That's what I'm thinking. But why would Nate find that unusual?" He grabbed his cell phone and tossed it to Dani. "Call him and find out. His number's on my caller ID log. I've gotta hit the head before I embarrass myself."

Dani dialed the number and waited through four rings. Expecting the call to roll to voice mail, she was surprised when he answered.

"Randall."

"Hey, Nate, it's Dani. Harry and I have a question about your books."

"I'm glad you called. I was just thinking about you." His voice was soft and low.

Dani froze. Was he flirting again? Glancing around the room, she was relieved to be alone. Nikki and Bobby had left about an hour before because Casey was so tired. Tino had gone home earlier, mentioning something about a stakeout. The two aunts were also gone, since Aunt Carmella hated to drive in the dark. Good thing, because her night vision sucked. Abby was watching a movie with her grandfather and Marie.

"I wanted to tell you how much I enjoyed meeting your family," he continued. "My social calendar hasn't exactly been full lately, so dinner today was especially nice."

"They all liked you," she blurted, then mentally groaned for admitting that to Nate. It sounded like something a teenage girl would say after introducing her pimply-faced boyfriend to her folks. "I mean, everyone thought you were nice."

"That's good." He sighed his approval. "I don't always make a great first impression. What did you want to ask me?"

"Oh," she stammered, forgetting she had called *him*. "You've marked a monthly expense to an insurance company, and we can't figure out why you think that's strange."

He took a deep breath. "Here's the thing. Our medical malpractice is paid quarterly, not monthly. And trust me, the amount of money showing up on the books each month doesn't even begin to make a dent in our premiums."

"Why do you think the extra money was paid then? Is it possible your secretary is paying it out this way instead?"

"Doubtful, but still a possibility. But like I said, it's nowhere near as much as we actually pay out."

"Can't you look at the cancelled checks?"

"They're kept on file at the bank. We only get a hard copy at the end of the year for our records. Unless we have a problem, we simply use the stubs to record the checks."

Harry walked back into the dining room. "You talking to Randall?"

Dani nodded and waved a hand for him to sit down. "I'll need to stop by the bank tomorrow and look at them to figure this out. Will you call first thing tomorrow morning and fax them a release?"

"As soon as they open." He paused. "Let me know what you find, okay?"

"Yeah. Thanks, Nate."

"Dani?"

"Yes?" She turned her back to Harry. She had no idea why.

"Sleep tight." His voice had dropped to almost a whisper and felt very much like a caress.

She was glad Harry couldn't see her face. "Good night, Nate." She closed the receiver and handed the phone to him. Quickly, she repeated their conversation.

"Hmm. That's strange." Harry studied the pages of Nate's book again before glancing up at Dani. "You'll check this out on the way to the office?"

When she nodded, he grabbed his coat and headed for the living room. "Gotta run. Tonight's the season finale of *Desperate Housewives*."

Dani smiled. "Why am I not surprised you watch that show?"

"Sexy women, outrageous story lines, and an ex-cop right in the middle of it. What's not to like?" He bent and kissed her forehead. "See you tomorrow, kiddo."

Dani slammed the book shut and followed him out to the living room. After kissing Marie goodnight, she pulled on her jacket.

"Come on, Abs. It's getting late."

Abby turned her angelic face up to her mother. "Can I stay with Gramps tonight, Mom? There's no school tomorrow." Abby shook her head and smiled when Dani looked confused. "Teachers' meeting, remember? Please, Mom? We're right in the middle of this movie."

Dani looked at her dad, whose grin had spread from ear to ear. He loved it when Abby wanted to spend time with him.

"If it's okay with your grandfather." When he nodded, she continued, "I'll come home early tomorrow, and maybe the three of us can run over to the Cheesecake House for some dinner."

Abby's eyes lit up. "Yeah."

Dani swooped down and kissed her daughter. "You get to bed before midnight, you hear?"

No way was that was going to happen, and everyone in the room knew it. Still, Dani felt like a better mother if she said it every time.

Abby's eyes connected with her grandfather's, and he winked. "Okay, Mom. See you tomorrow."

Dani kissed her dad on her way out the door and ran to her car. The October nights were getting colder, and her light jacket didn't offer much protection. She started her pickup and headed home.

All she could think about on the ride home was sitting next to Nate at the dinner table. The way his hand had held hers during the prayer. The way their bodies had touched as he reached for the salt shaker.

She slammed her hand on the steering wheel when she realized she was smiling.

"Damn it!" she said aloud.

What in the world was the matter with her? Maybe Tino was right. Maybe it was time she had some fun. But Tino wasn't the guy she wanted to do that with.

She thought about all the men she knew, some she'd only met after Johnny's death. She couldn't think of a single one she wanted to spend time with. She wanted a man who made her feel young again. Who knew how much she'd loved her husband and didn't demand she forget him.

Oh, and he'd definitely have to be a good lover. She and Johnny had always had a good sex life, and she wouldn't settle for mediocre. She couldn't.

The ideal man would have to be tender and romantic and make her feel as if she were the most important person in his life. And he'd have to love Abby. Anything less was a deal breaker.

And when Mr. Perfect looked at her, she had to see raw desire in his eyes no matter where they were. In short, she wanted a man who loved her unconditionally, was good in bed and loved her family.

A man like Nate.

She slammed her hand on the steering wheel again.

Tell me I really didn't just think that.

Shaking her bruised, tingling hand, she thought about Nate Randall. He was a man she could have fun with. He liked her family and Abby. And there was no mistaking the sexual interest she saw in his eyes every time he flirted with her.

Nate was Mr. Perfect.

Except for one thing. Chances were good he was a wife killer.

He hid in the bushes across the street from her house. Waiting. He wasn't happy it had come to this, but he had no choice. She was getting too close. He'd thought when he punctured her brake line that would scare her enough to get her off his case.

It hadn't.

Too much was at stake to allow her to jeopardize it. Despite the fact he'd fed her clues he thought were a dead end, she'd managed to find bits of potentially damning information. She wasn't stupid. Sooner or later, she'd figure it out.

Yes, she had to be eliminated. Damn shame, too. A waste of a perfectly good piece of ass.

He could have broken down her resistance with a little more persuasion. She was like every other female he knew—ready to hop into the sack with the first guy who said, "I love you."

He would have said it if it had come down to it, but she had never given him the opportunity. That pissed him off even more than her meddling. She acted like some kind of prima donna, turning her nose up at him. She was gorgeous, but he'd seen better.

He'd *had* better.

He got horny just thinking about those long legs wrapped around his neck, his mouth on her, his tongue inside her making her scream his name. He'd show her who really had control.

He knelt on one knee as the car rounded the corner and cocked the thirty-eight in his hand. For an instant, a touch of remorse slid through him.

Damn shame.

Dani's mind raced as she turned down her street. A flash from a neighbor's yard caught her attention, and she twisted her head for a better look. The yard was empty, the house dark. *Must have been my imagination.* She pulled her car into the garage and lowered the door.

Normally, entering an empty house didn't bother her, but for some reason, her nerves were on edge. The eerie silence didn't help, and for a moment, she wished she hadn't allowed Abby to spend the night with her dad. When she turned on the kitchen light, the ice maker dropped its load, and she screamed.

Sheesh, Dani. What's up with you?

She flipped on the lights in the living room before she walked through. Her cop instincts came alive, and she scanned the room. She had no idea what she was looking for, only that something was wrong.

Then she eyed the picture window. The edge of the curtain was caught under the glass. A sudden shiver made a slow path down her body, and she froze in her tracks.

The window had been opened.

She moved quickly to the front door to double-check the dead-bolt. It was in place. Then she crossed the room to the window and opened it, freeing the curtain.

Her mind raced. Should she call the police?

And tell them what? Her curtain was flapping in the wind? They'd look at her like she was a nut case. At best, they'd think she was being paranoid.

She took a deep breath. Abby had probably opened the window before they'd left to go to her grandfather's. She was just being silly.

As she bent to free the drape, a bullet pierced the glass, barely missing her. She dove for the floor and crawled away from the window. Her breath came in short fast bursts, and she prayed she wouldn't get lightheaded.

She was too vulnerable. She knew it, and whoever was out there knew it, too. Her thirty-eight was in her purse in the kitchen, and her Glock was locked in the nightstand upstairs. She had no easy way to get to either one.

Crouching low to the floor, she made her way across the living room to the end table, forcing herself to take slow, deep breaths. The smell of dried ketchup from the carpet wrinkled her nose. Just as she reached for the phone, a second shot whizzed above her head, and she flattened her body against the carpet.

Jesus! Someone was really trying to kill her.

With one swift move, she grabbed the phone and huddled beside the couch. For the second time in two weeks, she dialed 911.

Then she waited, using the sofa as her cover and keeping her eyes glued to the front door. She fully expected whoever was out there to break it down any minute.

She desperately needed her gun.

Her breathing slowed when the faint echo of sirens finally wailed in the distance, but she stayed on the floor until the police cars halted outside her house.

Crawling to the front door, she raised up to pull it open, halfway expecting it to be a trap. Relief flowed through her when she stared at the two young cops.

After they'd heard her version of the story, they did a thorough check of the house but were unable to turn up any evidence of forced entry. Apparently the shooter was long gone, leaving no telltale clues behind.

Two hours later, when the police were finally convinced it was safe, Dani climbed back into her car and headed out. She couldn't stay home now, despite the fact the two officers in the police cruiser would be parked out front all night.

Alone in the car, once the reality of the situation hit her, Dani allowed tears to stream down her face. Why would someone want her injured? Or worse, dead?

She found the puzzle too much to think about at the moment. All she wanted was to climb into bed next to her daughter and shut out the rest of the world. At least for a night.

She parked the car in her dad's driveway and ran to the door, pounding on it with her fists.

"Hurry up. Hurry up," she said aloud, glancing over her shoulder every few seconds. When the door finally opened, she fell into her father's arms.

"Dani?" His face registered his surprise. "What's the matter?"

"Somebody tried to kill me."

CHAPTER TWENTY

"What's the matter, Mom?" Abby asked, her voice breaking. "Why are you here?"

Dani opened her eyes then slammed them shut when the light from the opened drapes blinded her. "That sun is killing me." She squinted until Abby crossed the room and closed the drapes. In the dim light, she opened her eyes wide and met her daughter's questioning stare. "Nothing's wrong, honey. I just wanted to sleep with you last night, okay?"

"I hate it when you lie to me." Abby frowned.

Dani grinned back. "You're going to make a great secret agent one of these days." A few months before, Abby had announced her latest career goal after seeing a rerun of *Spy Kids*.

"What's wrong?" Abby repeated.

Dani stared at her precocious daughter. She'd always been honest with her, even about Johnny and the allegations that he had been a dirty cop. She knew chances were good one of Abby's friends at school would have told her if she hadn't. Kids nowadays seemed to know everything.

"Someone fired a gun into our house last night after I got home."

"Mom!" Abby eyes grew as big as soccer balls. "Were you hurt?"

"No. Sit." Dani patted the mattress. After Abby was beside her, she continued, choosing her words carefully. No sense in scaring her. "Probably some stupid kid playing with a gun."

Abby didn't move, and her eyes stayed fixed on her mother. "That's twice now someone's fired a gun close to you. And you're not even a cop anymore."

Dani forced a smile. It was hard to argue with the ten-year-old's logic. "I know, honey, but I promise it's just a coincidence." She paused. "Just to be on the safe side, though, we're going to stay here until the police complete their investigation. I'll run by the house later today and pick up a few things for us."

At the thought of spending more time at her grandfather's house, Abby eyes lit up. "Can Casey stay here, too?"

Dani's smile faded. "Casey's going to Minnesota tomorrow to see the specialist."

"Oh yeah. I forgot." Abby lowered her head.

"But guess what?" Dani hated that sad look and was willing to do anything to wipe it off her face. "Maybe Gramps can take you to a movie this afternoon."

Abby jumped off the bed. "Cool! I'm dying to see the new Harry Potter one."

"We'll ask him at breakfast. Now, come on. I have to get to work, and you have to suck up to your grandfather." Dani hopped out of bed. "Beat you to the showers."

Abby turned and bolted to the bathroom. "Not in this lifetime."

Pleased with herself, Dani broadened her smile. Amazing the way a little psychology worked on a kid. She wished it worked that way on adults.

When Abby finally emerged, her long silky hair bouncing when she walked, Dani remembered the curtains. "Hey, Abs, did you, by chance, open the living room window any time lately?"

Abby shook her head. "Why would I do that? It weighs a ton."

Dani shrugged. "No reason." She waved her hand. "Now get moving. I have a super busy day ahead."

When Dani was dressed, she headed for the kitchen. Abby and her grandfather were already attacking a stack of pancakes and a platter of sausage links.

"Hurry up, Mom. Gramps' blueberry pecan pancakes are awesome."

Dani started for the table when a rush of nausea stopped her cold. She covered her mouth, ran to the bathroom, and threw up what little was on her stomach before dry heaving several times.

"Dani, are you all right?" Her dad sounded worried, reminding her of the many times she and Nik had come home with a virus from school. First one, and then the other would be sick. Without their mother to help, he'd been the one to stay up all night, worrying when the fever rose too high.

"I'm okay, Dad. Guess last night affected me more than I thought." She wiped a sheen of perspiration from her forehead. "Or maybe I'm coming down with something."

"Do you want some breakfast?"

The thought of walking back into the kitchen and smelling the greasy sausages made her queasy all over again. She brought her hand back up to her mouth and swallowed. "No thanks. I'll just grab a piece of toast and head out. You okay with keeping the munchkin today?"

"We've already planned out the entire day, and—" Hector broke off and lowered his voice. "Dani?"

"Yeah," she replied between slow breaths.

"Don't even think about going near your house without me or Tino with you. At least until my friend down at the station calls back with the inside scoop about last night."

"Don't worry. I'm stubborn, not stupid. Still, I think it was some kid out for a thrill. Probably hopped up on drugs."

"Maybe so, but you need to stay on your toes until we find out something definite." He paused. "Stay there. I'll get that toast for you."

Dani glanced around the lobby of Metro National Bank, searching for the manager's office. Not finding it, she walked to the first room with an open door.

"Excuse me."

When the woman behind the desk looked up, Dani smiled. "I'm Dani Perez. I believe Dr. Nathan Randall faxed over a release authorizing me to review his bank statements and cancelled checks. Can you help me with that?"

The woman extended her hand. "Celia Wimberley. I'm the assistant loan officer." After shaking Dani's hand, she opened a notepad and scribbled a few things before she reached for the phone. When she'd relayed the information, she hung up and motioned for Dani to be seated.

"The bank manager did speak with Dr. Randall this morning. He said to give you whatever you need. His secretary is pulling that information now, and she'll bring it here when she gets it together. That should take about five to ten minutes. You can use my office for as long as you need." Celia stood, and for the first time, Dani noticed her maternity top. "I've got to run to the break room for a minute. I'm out of crackers."

Dani grinned. "The mornings are the worst."

The woman smiled back. "I was never sick a day with my first one. This time, I can't even look at food until mid-morning." She walked around the desk. "Can I get you anything? Coffee? Someone usually brings doughnuts on Monday. Would you like one?"

Dani swallowed hard at the mention of greasy doughnuts. "I'm fine, thanks."

Alone in the office, Dani thought about the night before. Her dad had flipped out as expected when she'd told him about the gunshots. He'd held her in his arms and comforted her while she cried, before asking point blank if there was more to the story than she had told him.

He already knew about the young junkie's death in the parking lot and that she hadn't given up on clearing Johnny's name. But he knew nothing about Nate Randall's connection to Casey. That was Nikki's story to tell, not hers.

So she'd lied. Told him everything was okay.

She glanced up as an attractive young woman walked into the office carrying several files. "You can review these here, Mrs. Perez. We shred the canceled checks after two months and only keep a digital copy. I've included the printout of the earlier months in the file." She laid them on the desk. "Let me know when you're through, and I'll pick them up."

"Thanks." After she left, Dani scooted her chair closer to the desk and opened the first folder. It contained the bank statements from Nate's business account, starting with January. A careful review verified they were identical to the ones recorded in the company's checkbook.

She reached for the second file. Canceled checks from the last two months had been bundled together with a rubber band. Copies of both the fronts and backs of the checks from the other months was included, and Dani studied them first. Oddly, the twenty-thousand-dollar payment to Southwestern Medical Insurance Group hadn't started until February.

She made a mental note to call the insurance company to see if their premiums had increased around that time. Maybe they were changing to monthly billing instead of quarterly. But Nate had been sure the twenty grand a month didn't come close to what they actually paid for coverage.

She grabbed the canceled checks next, hoping to get a better feel for Nate's finances. As she flipped through them, nothing jumped out until she spied a five-thousand dollar payment to a Randy Brown, also in February. Curious, she tracked the entry in Nate's business checkbook. The stub read Brown's Janitorial Service.

Sheesh! Her paycheck didn't come close to that. She was in the wrong business.

What was weird was that the check to Mr. Brown had been paid out from March to June, and then had abruptly stopped. She searched the remaining months again to make sure she hadn't overlooked any more checks to the man. She hadn't.

Even more odd was that the twenty-thousand-dollar payment to the insurance company had also stopped in June. She scratched her head, something she always did when she was in deep concentration mode.

She was missing something, but she had no clue what. Why would both of those expenses stop in the same month? She reached for the canceled checks made out to Southwestern Medical Insurance Group and to Brown's Janitorial Service and studied the stamped endorsement.

Nate Randall.

Nate stepped off the elevator, his mind on his last patient at the clinic that morning. A young mother had brought her eleven-year-old son in with a huge lump on his lower leg. If Nate's suspicions were correct, the boy would lose that leg to an osteosarcoma.

The saddest part was that if the young mother had brought him in earlier, most likely the amputation would not have been necessary. But she was a single mother with a lousy paying job that offered no health coverage. She'd assumed her child had been hurt on the playground, and that the swelling would go away.

God! He hated the unfairness of life sometimes.

The receptionist greeted him with a smile. "Afternoon, Nate. There's a Mrs. Perez waiting in your office." She handed him a bundle of mail. "Here are today's offerings."

"Thanks, Gina." He grabbed the stack from her hand. "How long has she been waiting?"

"About fifteen minutes."

Damn. In his determination to get the child over to Children's Hospital for an MRI of his leg, he'd forgotten about Dani's visit. She'd called earlier from the bank to set up this meeting to discuss her findings. She'd sounded excited about something.

Nate's pulse picked up as soon as he turned and hastened down the hall to his office. Something about seeing her again elevated his mood all of a sudden. He opened the door and found her standing by the window, her back to him as she stared out at the city beyond.

"Sorry I'm late, Dani."

When she turned he saw the tears in her eyes, despite her obvious attempt to hide them.

He was beside her in three strides. "What's wrong?"

She took a deep breath and shook her head, before turning away from him. "It's nothing. You have a great view of downtown Dallas. I got a little sentimental looking at it. That's all."

"Sentimental?" He wondered if she was thinking about her extracurricular activities in the city. Why would she be sentimental about that?

She swiped at her tears. "I can't believe I'm crying. It's just..."

He touched her shoulder and turned her around to face him. With his thumb, he wiped a stray tear that had escaped down her cheek. "Just what?" He dropped his voice to a whisper.

She swallowed hard. "My husband loved downtown Dallas."

She tried to lower her head, but he held her chin steady with one hand. Without thinking, he leaned in and brushed her lips with his own, gently nudging her body into his. He'd forgotten how soft her lips were. How soft she was.

"Nate." Her voice turned him on more. "We can't do this."

Her lips were so close her warm breath skated across his skin. "Why not?"

"You know why not."

He moved closer. This time he kissed her more deeply. Sensing her response, he explored her lips with his tongue before plunging inside to taste all of her mouth. Passion rose in his loins like a ball of fire merging with a burst of oxygen. He wanted her. Wanted to be inside her. Wanted to possess her.

But it was more than that. He wanted all of her, not just her body. He wanted to make mad passionate love to her and wake up spooned to her in the morning.

Then, like a Mac truck, it hit him, nearly knocking him off balance. He had developed feelings for this woman. And that thought literally scared the hell out of him.

As quickly as the accidental embrace had started, it ended. He pulled away, leaving her standing alone, her eyes questioning. She wanted him, too. He could see it all over her face. But he couldn't let her know how he felt. Too much was at stake. He had too much to lose.

He cleared his throat and sat in the chair behind his desk. "What did you find out at the bank?"

Confusion clouded her eyes, and he cursed himself. When had his feelings changed? It was one thing to flirt with her, but he had to make sure it didn't go any further.

Dani stared at him for a moment before breaking eye contact, then sat in a chair opposite the desk and pulled out her notes. The desire that had flashed in her eyes moments before had been replaced with a business glare.

"The payment to Southwestern, your malpractice carrier, started in February. Twenty grand was paid out every month until June." She pointed to the entry.

"That makes no sense. Are you sure?" he interrupted.

She flipped through the pages. "The last payment was May fifteenth. Your signature is on every check."

Her intense stare burned into him as if she could read his mind. He hoped it wasn't true because if she could, she'd know he had to fight with himself to keep from dragging her over to the couch and kissing his way up her body.

Like he'd done the last time.

He shook his head to get that image out of his brain. "Gina makes out the checks, sends them to either Roger or me to look over, then stamps them."

"Wouldn't you have noticed a twenty-thousand-dollar check all of a sudden?"

He puffed his cheeks and blew out a breath. "Frankly, my mind hasn't been a hundred percent on business lately. I'm sure I okayed it without looking."

"And you trust Gina?"

"Implicitly," he said without hesitation. "She's been with us ever since we opened this office three years ago. She's like family." Hearing the words saddened him. How pathetic that an employee was the only person he thought of as family.

Dani ran her fingers through her hair, making him wish he were running his fingers through the silky black strands. "I guess the next step would be to call the insurance company and see if they can shed any light on this."

Nate leaned forward and punched the intercom button. "Gina, can you get Southwestern Medical Group on the phone?"

"Sure, Nate. Is something wrong?"

He laughed. That woman had never really understood the concept of employer-employee relationships. "Do you know anything about the extra payment to Southwestern from February to June?"

"Yes," she answered quickly. "They upped the yearly premium by eighty-thousand dollars in January right after I'd made the quarterly payment. I spoke with Roger about this as soon as I received the notice. Didn't he tell you?"

"No." Nate was annoyed and a little embarrassed Dani had heard the exchange with Gina, further indicating just how far he'd had his head up his ass.

"He said to pay it out over a four month period so it wouldn't be one big chunk all at once." She coughed. "I'm sorry, Nate. I thought you knew."

Of course she thought he knew. He'd obviously sent the checks back with his approval. "No problem, Gina."

"Do you still need me to get Southwestern on the phone?"

"Thanks, but that won't be necessary. We've solved the mystery. Isn't it about time for you to head out?" On Mondays, she usually left early to take her kid to Tae Kwan Do lessons.

"Yeah. I'm closing things down now. I'll put the phone on voice mail. See you in the morning, Nate."

Nate sat back in his chair, his hands behind his head, a slight grin on his face. "Okay, I'm an idiot. I should have known about that. Could have saved you a lot of time."

Dani glanced down at her notes. "That explains the insurance checks, but there's one other thing."

"What's that?"

"A five-thousand-dollar check going out every month to Brown's Janitorial Service starting in March. Then all of a sudden, it stops in June just like the Southwestern checks. Why did you suddenly stop paying for a cleaning service?"

Nate sat straight up in his chair. Now she had his undivided attention. "You sure about that?"

She scanned the sheets in front of her and pulled one out. "Again, it's your signature on the checks." She shoved the paper across the desk.

Her eyes drilled into him until he picked up the photocopy of the canceled checks and read it. How had he missed this when he'd examined the check stubs?

Finally, he looked up to meet her eyes. "Our monthly rental for this office space came with a free nightly cleaning crew."

He watched as the meaning reflected in her eyes. "We don't have a janitorial service."

CHAPTER TWENTY-ONE

As soon as Dani walked into Pete's Bar & Grill, she spotted her ex-partner sitting at the far end of the bar, laughing over something Pete must have said. She strolled toward him, aware of the hushed conversations when she passed. Taking a deep breath she held her head high.

Pete noticed her first and broke into a huge grin. "Well, look-ee here. I thought you moved to Alaska or something. Give old Pete a hug, girl." He leaned across the bar and squeezed Dani's shoulder. "You look great, kid."

"Bring her a Corona, Pete. With a wedge of lime just the way she likes it."

"Shit, Spig, I don't need you to tell me what Dani likes. A good bartender never forgets." He gave him a disgusted look before reaching down to get the beer.

"Who said you were a good bartender?" Spig teased.

Pete ignored the remark and slid the bottle across the bar to Dani. "This one's on the house for the pretty cop."

"Ex-cop," Dani corrected, then rewarded him with a smile. It felt good to be called pretty even though she knew Pete blew so much smoke, he was starting to believe his own bullshit.

She slid onto an empty stool beside Spig and hugged him.

"To the best partner I ever had," she said, clinking her bottle with his.

"You weren't such a slouch yourself." He swallowed the last of his Budweiser and motioned to Pete for another.

"Better go easy on those, hotshot. Need I remind you of the consequences?"

He snorted. "Hell, no! I'd rather have my nails pulled out one by one before I sit through another country music fiasco. That was some of the worst, god-awful shit I ever heard."

They both laughed before Spig's expression turned serious. "Ballistics came back on the bullet that killed the doper in the parking lot behind the Baptist Church." He met her eyes, biting his lower lip.

Oh, crap! That always meant trouble. Dani took a deep breath. "Go on."

"Turns out the gun was used in a similar killing near the Fort Worth county line about a year ago. Another dealer was shot at close range, execution style. The weapon was never found, and the case is still an open investigation. Homicide turned the drug community upside down but didn't come up with anyone who looked good for it."

Dani exhaled. "So it was definitely a drug-related killing?"

Spig took a long drink of his beer. "Probably, but things aren't always the way they seem."

"Okay, Spig, now you're scaring me. Just say what's on your mind. I know that look."

He swiveled on the chair to face her. "That gun is the same one someone used to shoot up your living room window Sunday night."

"Seriously?" Dani brought her hand to her mouth. "Why is a drug dealer shooting at my house?"

"That's the sixty-four-thousand-dollar question. My best guess is that it has something to do with your nosing around into Johnny's death."

"What does that have to do with anything?" Tino asked, coming up behind Dani.

Both Spig and Dani whirled around at the sound of his voice.

"Tino, did you hear about the ballistics report?" Dani asked.

"Yeah, I heard." He put his hand on her shoulder. "Doesn't it worry you even a tad that someone who has already killed two people, and probably more, shot up your house?"

"Of course it does," Dani fired back. "What I can't figure out is why."

"Maybe someone thinks the dead dope dealer told you something." Tino motioned to Pete for his usual.

Dani jerked her shoulder, and Tino's hand fell away. Anger flashed in his eyes when she turned back to face him. "What could he have possibly said that was worth scaring the bejesus out of me?"

"Are you positive he was only trying to scare you?" Spig asked.

She didn't even want to go down that road.

"Come on, Dani," he said. "No one's asking you to throw in the towel. I'm just saying that you should let the police handle Johnny's death."

She shoved the nearly-full Corona toward Pete. For some reason, it tasted like bile. "Can't do that, Spig."

Before he could protest, she got up and threw a five-dollar bill next to the bottle. "Gotta run. I'm picking up Nikki and her family at the airport."

Pete slid the money back across to her. "New rule here. No tips from gorgeous lady cops."

"Ex-cop," she corrected him for the second time, reaching for the money. It would be tomorrow's lunch. "Thanks, Pete."

"Don't wait so long to come back and see me."

She flashed him a smile before kissing Spig on the cheek.

"Quit worrying about me. I'm a big girl." She wished she felt as brave as she hoped she sounded.

"Yeah, I know, but big girls stop a bullet just as easily as the rest of us." Spig turned to Tino. "How about you and I take turns parking in front of her house for the next week or two?"

Dani held up her hand. "That ain't happening. The last thing I need is for either of you to get hurt because you spent the night babysitting me. I need a vacation, not a guilt trip." She brushed Tino's cheek with her lips. "I appreciate the offer, I really do, but I'll shoot you myself if I see you on my street."

Spig laughed. "You always were a cantankerous bitch. I have no idea why I love you." He winked at Tino. "Don't let her catch you out there."

Dani headed for the door, hoping they hadn't picked up on the fear probably written all over her face. Knowing the same gun used in two drug-related killings was the one that had shot up her living room unnerved her. What did it mean?

Did the killer suspect she knew something? She racked her brain trying to remember her conversation with the snotty-nosed kid in the parking lot. Obviously, she'd missed something.

But what?

As soon as she saw her sister's face outside the baggage claim area, Dani knew the news about Casey's condition wasn't good. She pulled the car to the curb and hopped out, giving her best imitation of a smile.

Casey ran into her opened arms. "You look tired, kiddo. Did they wear you out in Minnesota?"

The child tightened his grip on her neck. "I have a new nickname, Aunt Dani," he said. "Dad calls me the human pin cushion."

"Ooh, that sounds painful. You must have been really brave today."

He pulled away and smiled. "I only cried two times, and that was when they couldn't find a place to get my blood. They had to use a great big needle."

Dani tapped his nose with her finger. "You, my child, are way braver than I would have been. I'd probably still be crying." She stole a glance at Nikki and saw pain etched all over her face.

Dani's heart skipped a beat. The news about Casey's disease must be worse than she thought. She opened the front seat of her pickup and helped her nephew climb in. "Come on, pin cushion. Let's get you home so you can get some beauty sleep. Want to ride shotgun?"

"Yippee," he exclaimed, before twisting around. "Mom, can I?"

Nikki smiled at her son. "Anyone as tough as you needs to be up front when Aunt Dani drives. She always gets lost. Maybe you can help her find the way home."

After Bobby threw the luggage into the bed of the truck and everyone belted themselves in, Dani headed to Cimarron. They spent the twenty-minute drive from DFW Airport in mindless chatter, further escalating Dani's fears about what they had learned at the Mayo Clinic.

When she pulled up at the house, Nikki asked, "Can you come in for a minute, Dani?" She attempted to sound calm, though Dani knew she wasn't.

After the day she'd had at the office, a takeout dinner from Taco Loco that threatened to come back up, plus the trip to Pete's, the only thing Dani wanted was to go home for her own beauty sleep. She'd been so tired lately, she'd even started popping a multivitamin every night before she went to bed. But she couldn't ignore the plea in Nikki's voice.

"Sounds good." She cut the motor and got out of the pickup, avoiding eye contact with both Nikki and Bobby. No doubt she would lose it. She'd already teared up three times today over minor stupid things. Whatever Nikki was about to tell her had to be really bad. It was hard to miss the despair all over her face.

Once inside, Bobby took Casey upstairs to his room after Nikki kissed him goodnight. Dani followed her sister into the kitchen and sat at the table while Nikki pulled the iced tea from the refrigerator and poured three glasses. The silence was a killer. Intuitively, Dani knew the ballistics report was not the worst news she would get tonight.

She braced herself. "Come sit, Nik, and tell me everything."

Nikki turned and smiled as she walked to the table with the tea. Dani caught her hand when she placed one on the table in front of her, and for a moment, she gently squeezed. No words passed between them. No words were necessary. Nikki's heart was breaking, and Dani felt helpless.

Nikki pulled her hand away and sat, then took a sip of the cold tea. "Casey's going into aplastic anemia," she said, almost calmly.

"Oh, God." Dani would have killed for her twin, would have taken on the disease herself if only to erase the pain from her sister's eyes. But that was impossible. "What exactly does that mean, Nik?"

"His bone marrow is shutting down. The damage done by Fanconi's has increased at an alarming rate since we last saw the specialist three months ago." She paused when her voice trembled.

Dani was out of her seat in a flash. She wrapped her arms around her sister from behind, bending down to kiss the top of her head the way their dad used to do after a tearful breakup with a boyfriend or some other teenage tragedy.

"Can't they treat that with blood transfusions?

She heard Nikki exhale softly. "Yeah, they can, but it's only a temporary fix. They gave him two units this morning because his counts were so low. That's why his color is so much better."

Dani shook her head. "I don't understand, Nik. Why can't they keep doing that?"

"Eventually, his bone marrow will quit making red and white cells all together. Dr. Juliana said that when that happens, his body won't be able to get the oxygen it needs to survive. Casey will..."

She lowered her head, unable to say the words. After a minute, she looked up again. "If that doesn't kill him, a massive infection will without enough white cells.

Dani fell to one knee at her sister's side. "That's not going to happen, Nik. We won't let it happen."

Nikki patted Dani's head, another of their dad's comfort measures when they were kids. "When they took Casey for a bone scan, Bobby and I had a long talk. We realized we can't keep waiting for a miracle. We asked Dr. Juliana to put him on the transplant waiting list."

"I thought you said the chance of success with a non-related donor transplant was only one in five."

"It is," Nikki said softly. "But one is five looks pretty damn good right now."

"Did you talk about the possibility of using cord blood with the doctor?"

Nikki's brow creased. "That's no longer an option."

"Why not?"

Both sisters looked up as Bobby walked into the kitchen. One look at the agony in his eyes was too much for Dani. She bit her upper lip in a desperate attempt to hold back her own emotions.

Quietly, Bobby walked over to the counter, picked up his glass of tea and carried it to the table. "He's finally asleep. As tired as he was, he fought it. Guess it must feel really good to have his energy back." He sat down and reached across the table for his wife's hand. "Did you tell her?"

"Not yet." She licked her lips before continuing. Dani recognized this as something Nikki always did when she was nervous. "Bobby and I need to talk to you about something."

Dani's stomach lurched. This couldn't be good. She stood and walked back to her chair, her heart filled with dread.

"Like I said, Casey needs a bone marrow transplant, and he needs one soon. I'd have to be on fertility drugs for several months before we could aspirate my eggs and fertilize them with Randall's sperm. We're talking at least three to five months. Add in the nine months to carry a child, and we're already close to a year and a half. Casey doesn't have that kind of time." The total despair in Nikki's voice escalated with each word.

"And that's assuming the procedure goes without a hitch. That we'll find at least one fertilized egg that's a perfect match to Casey," Bobby interrupted. "Then we'd have to wait to see if the in vitro works." He lowered his head. "It's a long shot we can't afford to take."

Dani glanced at her sister and brother-in-law, feeling overwhelmed with guilt. She'd promised them she wouldn't let anything happen to Casey. Promised she'd find a way to fix this.

But she hadn't. She'd failed miserably, and now the feeling of total helplessness consumed her.

"Nik?" Her voice caught. "What can I do?"

Casey's parents exchanged a glance that spoke volumes. Whatever they were about to tell her was not something they'd come up with on the spur of the moment. Dani met Nikki's eyes as she waited for the answer.

"Go with me to tell Randall."

"No!" Dani exclaimed. "Oh, Nik, you don't really want to do that."

"It's our only chance," Bobby answered for his wife.

"I thought you said it was too late to go through with the genetic engineering thing."

"Nikki and I aren't talking about that."

"Then what?" Dani asked, confused.

"We're going to ask him to be tested. If he's a match, we'll beg him to be the donor for his biological son." Nikki stopped to smile at Bobby. "We'll do whatever is necessary to save Casey's life. If that means sharing our child with a stranger, then that's what has to be done."

Dani swallowed the last of her tea. As much as she hated to admit it, Nikki was right. As one wise man had said so long ago, *desperate times called for desperate measures.* To have even the slightest chance of saving Casey's life, she'd help them do whatever it took. Even if that meant going to an accused killer and offering him access to her family.

Despite the fact her doubts about Nate's guilt grew the more she was with him, uneasiness filled her heart. At times, she was one-hundred percent sure he was incapable of murdering his wife, but she knew she couldn't rely on her gut. Should he be guilty, it wouldn't be the first time someone had totally surprised her with out-of-character behavior.

Even Harry believed in Nate's innocence. He would never have taken him on as a client if he didn't. In Dani's opinion, Harry was the best cop she'd even known, bar none, even her own father. He could nail a liar from across the room. He would have seen right through Nate.

But how could she explain away the pictures of Nate leaving the scene at the time of the murder? The photos, safely hidden in the bogus file in the office, were hard to get past. Sooner or later, she'd have to hand that file over to the Dallas Police Department, along with the prints. If she was lucky, they wouldn't throw her ass in jail for concealing evidence or obstructing justice.

The threat of being locked up wasn't enough to make her turn them over, though. If Nate was convicted, being a donor for his son would be nearly impossible.

That was another thing. How would he react upon learning that little secret? And what about her deceit the night at the Marquee? Neither would make his day.

But even that didn't sway her to go public with the pictures. Not yet, anyway. Time was running out for her nephew. The last thing they needed was another obstacle in the countdown to save his life.

No, she'd keep Nate's secret for as long as it took.

She glanced up at her sister. "Come by the office around ten o'clock tomorrow, Nik. I'll set something up with Nate at the hotel for after lunch."

She forced a smile despite the pain in her heart. "We'll tell him together."

CHAPTER TWENTY-TWO

Nate walked out of the bathroom, a towel wrapped around his waist. His mind was on the afternoon meeting with Dani and her sister. What did they want to discuss with him? What was so important to justify a drive into downtown Dallas? If it had something to do with his case, why was Nikki coming?

Puzzled, he walked to the window and opened the drapes. The Marquee sat on a block of real estate smack in the heart of the city, and the view from the fourteenth floor window was unbelievable, even in daylight.

He loved the hotel. So much so, he'd worked out a monthly deal with the manager to stay until after the trial, despite his dwindling finances. Given all he was going through, he deserved the luxury even if it meant signing over the Mercedes as collateral in case he ended up in the state prison at Huntsville.

God! Thinking about that was enough to curdle his blood. Like everyone else in the world, he'd seen enough prison movies to know the nightmare he'd be forced to live. Even appealing a conviction would take years. He wouldn't make it. He'd rather die.

The entire scenario was too depressing to think about. Searching for something to take his mind off it, he glanced around the room. Fresh from the daily cleaning, it smelled faintly of roses.

Nate smiled as a vision of Dani lying naked on a bed of rose petals flashed across his brain. Just like the girl in the HBO movie he'd seen the other night.

Thinking of Dani, he wondered if she would be uncomfortable walking back into his room. Wondered if her sister knew what she did as a sideline.

Now that he'd spent a little time with her, he had a hard time thinking of her as a prostitute. After meeting her family, he could only guess that her extracurricular activities were something she did for extra cash or for kicks.

Who had sex with strange men for kicks? Certainly not someone like Dani. But he was living proof that it had happened.

Maybe he'd been so starved for female attention he'd allowed himself to believe their rendezvous had been about more than just sex. He'd felt an instant connection with her, and judging by her response to the lovemaking, she'd felt it too. But he'd been wrong before.

Waking up the next morning alone should have been his first clue. Clearly, it had been just sex for her. He'd been just another john.

But she hadn't acted like a woman of the night, not that he had any expertise in that area. Still, he remembered how nervous she'd been. At one point in the lobby, he'd even thought she was about to run away. Even the desk clerk had looked at her oddly.

Oh, my God! The desk clerk! If the same guy was on duty right now, there was a good chance he would recognize Dani from that night. Even though she didn't look like the same girl out of that skin-tight dress with the fancy hair style and heavy make up, it was always possible.

He reached for his cell phone and pressed a number. He had her on speed dial. What did that say about him?

He breathed a sigh of relief when she answered after the first ring. "Dani, it's Nate."

"Are we still on for one?"

"Yes, but I'm leaving for the office in a few minutes. Do you think you and Nikki can meet me there instead?" Saturday afternoons the place was dead. Why hadn't he thought of that earlier?

Because when she'd called this morning, he'd heard the urgency in her voice. Since he hadn't planned to go to the office today, the logical step was to have them meet him in his room.

"Sure. Is everything okay?"

"Yeah. It's just that I'm worried the guy at the desk might recognize you." He allowed his words to sink in before he continued. "The police are looking for you to ask some questions."

"Oh, man! I forgot about that," she exclaimed. "Your office is definitely a better idea."

"It's twelve-fifteen right now. I can still make it by one. Can you get there then?"

"Nik and I are just finishing lunch. We'll be on our way in a few minutes. See you there."

"Dani, isn't this something we can discuss over the phone?" Nate couldn't hide the fear in his voice. He was more than a little nervous about this meeting.

"No."

"See you at one then." He closed the phone. What information did she have that had to be revealed face to face? Had she uncovered new evidence? If that were true, it must be really incriminating for her to make the thirty-minute trip downtown. And why bring Nikki? His uneasiness jumped a notch.

Grabbing his car keys, he headed out the door, turning one last time to glance at the bed. This time, the visual was different. Dani wasn't lying on top the rose petals. This time, she sat in the middle of the flowers, a police badge on her uniformed chest, and her fingers on her automatic weapon. She wasn't writhing in pleasure at his touch, her face flushed with lust. This time, she swung a pair of handcuffs over her head, and an eerie smile covered her face.

He slammed the door on the image.

Nate glanced up when Dani and her sister walked into his office. He motioned for them to sit.

Dani prodded Nikki toward a chair, noticing how quiet and withdrawn she'd become the moment they'd stepped into the building. She sat beside her sister and reached for her hand.

"Anything to drink?" Nate asked.

When both of them shook their heads, Nate leaned forward. "Okay, let's have it straight out. What's so important that you braved Dallas traffic?"

Dani met her sister's eyes and smiled, hoping to reassure her. "We have a story to tell you, Nate."

"Is it about Janelle's murder?"

"No," both women answered quickly.

"Then what?" His forehead creased in confusion.

"Did you notice anything about my son when you had dinner with us last Sunday?" Nikki asked, leaning forward.

Nate thought a minute. "He was short of breath. I wondered if he was asthmatic."

Dani squeezed Nikki's hand gently, hoping to send strong vibes through the fingertips.

"He was diagnosed with Fanconi Anemia earlier this year."

Dani focused on Nate as Nikki's words sank in.

His face twisted in thought. "I'm afraid I don't remember much about that from medical school."

"It's a genetic disease that will eventually kill him unless he has a bone marrow transplant," Nikki explained.

The empathy in Nate's eyes was genuine. Dani wondered how he would react to the rest of the news.

"I'm sorry, Nikki. Casey's a great kid." His eyes darted from one sister to the other. "But I'm confused. Why are you telling me this?"

"We need you to get tested." Nikki's voice broke, and she inhaled deeply in an obvious attempt to compose her emotions.

"As a possible donor," Dani said, trying desperately to keep her own voice steady.

"Me? Surely, there are others with a better shot at being a match to the boy. Like family members."

Dani rubbed her forehead, hoping to wipe away the headache that throbbed above her eyes. "Do you have any water, Nate? I need to take a couple of Tylenol before my head explodes."

Her eyes followed him as he walked to the small refrigerator then back. He handed her the cold bottle and stayed by her side. Quickly, she swallowed the pills while he waited. She knew he had to be told. She just wished he wasn't standing so close.

"So far, no one in the family is a match," she finally said, carefully dancing around the real issue.

"Not even Nikki or Bobby?"

A cry escaped Nikki's lips. "Bobby's not Casey's father," she blurted, her voice barely audible.

Nate's face softened as he moved away and sat down. "I'm sorry, Nikki. I didn't know." He paused. "But what about Casey's biological father?"

The silence that followed that simple question could have shattered the earth.

Nikki raised her head to meet his eyes. "You're his biological father, Nate."

The full impact of her words finally registered on Nate's face. First shock, then disbelief. "How can I be the father? I just met you last week."

"Ten years ago, Bobby and I were patients at the Lone Star Fertility Clinic near Baylor," Nikki began.

Nate's response to the name was negligible. Other than a slight wrinkle in his forehead, he didn't acknowledge the familiar clinic.

"Apparently, you and your wife were also patients about that time."

Nate's eyes widened. "How do you know that?"

Nikki ignored his question and continued. "Right after Casey was diagnosed, everyone in the family was tested. That's when we found out there was no way Bobby's sperm could have fertilized my eggs."

Nate's mouth fell open, but no words escaped.

"Dani investigated and discovered a major breach in security precautions at the clinic. Who knows how many other people were affected by the screw up?" She met his stare.

He didn't move.

"You're Casey's biological father," she repeated.

He continued to gape at her. "What makes you so sure?"

"Your DNA matches," Dani interjected.

Nate stood, sending the chair reeling backward. "How in the hell did you get my DNA?"

Dani chewed on her lower lip. She'd never seen Nate this angry. She prayed for courage. "After threatening to expose the scandal, the owners of the clinic finally allowed me to examine their files."

"That still doesn't explain how you got my DNA," Nate interrupted, his voice still angry.

"When I narrowed it down to two possibilities, I followed you for five weeks. Knew everywhere you went, everything you did. One day, I retrieved your discarded cup from Starbucks."

Nate glared at Dani, making her wish there was a hole she could crawl into. He had a right to be pissed. She understood his anger at her deception.

"Will you get tested to see if you're a match?" Nikki asked.

"Hell no. Not until I hear the rest of the story." Nate turned to Dani, his blue eyes dark with rage. "Does she know about your walk on the wild side?"

Dani nodded. "She helped me plan it."

"Plan it?" His voice raised an octave. "How could that possibly help Casey?"

This was the part Dani had dreaded telling Nate, especially now that she'd gotten to know him. Now that she was beginning to like him. Her deceit that night would probably end in him hating her. Forever.

"Casey's doctor at the Mayo Clinic told them about a new procedure that's had surprising success on Fanconi patients." Dani looked away for a second. Nate's penetrating glare unnerved her. She gulped a swallow of water before continuing. "They can fertilize a mother's egg with the father's sperm in a genetics lab. If they find one that is free of the disease and matches the patient, they implant it in the mother's uterus. When the child is born nine months later, the cord blood is used to save the dying sibling."

His face turned somber, and his anger appeared to diminish. He rose and walked to the counter.

"You were going to steal my semen?" he asked, his voice suddenly calm, his back to them as he reached for the Scotch and poured himself a drink. He stared out the window after taking a healthy swig.

"Not *steal*, Nate." Dani's eyes turned defiant. "Nobody twisted your arm. If I remember correctly, you were a more than willing participant."

"Yeah." Nate whirled to face her. "To a night of sex, not to a freaking idiotic scheme to steal my body fluids."

He stopped talking and walked around the desk, standing directly in front of them. "A scheme, that had it worked, might have produced a second child I would know nothing about." He focused his eyes on Nikki. "Would you have told me about Casey if his situation had not become desperate?"

"No," she answered honestly. "Maybe eventually when he was older, but not now. We figured he was already going through more than a nine year-old could handle without finding out the father he loved wasn't really his father at all."

"That's bullshit, Nikki, and you know it. At least be honest with me. I deserve that much, although it would probably be the first time either one of you has told me the truth since I've met you."

Dani lowered her eyes under his glare. His anger was justified. She couldn't treat him the way she had and expect him to take it quietly. But Casey's life hung in the balance. If trying to keep him alive meant someone got hurt in the process, then so be it.

"It was my idea," she said. "It seemed simple at the time. No big deal. A lot of men are sperm donors and have no idea if they have children walking around."

"A lot of men have the option of making the decision to give away their rights," Nate interrupted. "I don't remember you flashing a waiver at me that night when you were squirming on the bed." He swept his angry gaze over her. "Or in the shower."

Dani inhaled sharply. This was not going as she had hoped. She'd known he'd be a little reluctant, but she'd thought he'd soften when it came to saving Casey's life. He was a doctor. He'd taken an oath.

Obviously, she had seriously misjudged him. "Bottom line, Nate. Will you get tested or not?"

"What happened to the sperm you stole? I knew something was funny about that ridiculous-looking condom."

"My brakes failed on the way to the lab the next day, and the specimen sat out in the car too long."

"So you came sniffing around again hoping for a replay?"

She shot him a look. "You found me. There's that little issue of you killing your wife, remember?" She blew out a exasperated breath, "So I'll ask you again. Are you going to get tested or not?"

"Don't you think it's reasonable for me to want a little time to mull this over? After all, I just found out I have a son. I'd say that warrants a few days to get used to, don't you agree?"

"We don't have a lot of time," Dani said, her voice more angry than she intended. "The specialist in Minnesota said Casey is going into aplastic anemia."

Nate closed his eyes. He may not know everything about Fanconi's, but it was obvious he knew the serious consequences of aplastic anemia.

"I'm sorry to hear that," he said sadly. "Now if you don't mind, you've given me a lot to think about." He turned to Nikki. "I'll let you know my decision."

"We need your answer now!" Dani shouted. "How can you even think about making her wait?"

Nate's eyes conveyed his fury. "I thought I knew you, Dani. Obviously, you're more like Janelle than I wanted to believe. She lied about everything, too."

"How dare you!" Dani sprang from the chair, causing the pounding in her head to intensify. She reached into her purse and pulled out an envelope. Holding his stare, she threw it on his desk. "You might want to take a peek at these before you say anything else."

Nate broke eye contact and reached for the envelope. Dani waited patiently as he stared at the pictures.

"You have a picture of me leaving my house. Why?"

"Check the date stamp in the lower right corner."

The tension in the room grew as thick as year-old nail polish as Dani waited for his reaction. When he only stared, she nudged Nikki's shoulder.

"Come on, Nik. Nate should be alone. He has an important decision to make." She walked toward the door before turning back.

"Don't make the mistake of underestimating what I'm capable of doing to save my nephew."

Without another word, she led her sister from the office, careful not to slam the door as Nate leaned against the desk, his eyes on the photo.

Nate walked around the desk and sat in his chair, still clutching the picture. How had she gotten it? What did it mean?

He knew exactly what it meant. Dani would go to the police if he refused to help Casey.

The thought of his son made him smile. *His son.* All those years he and Janelle had tried to have a baby, and now he discovered he'd had a son all along.

He swiveled the chair and turned on his computer. He was amazed at the amount of information available when he Googled Fanconi Anemia. He opened the first reference and read about the disease he knew so little about.

After thirty minutes spent researching the information, he leaned back in his chair. How could he be Casey's father? Fanconi's was passed on by both parents. No one in his family had ever been diagnosed with it.

Of course, he'd never really known his dad's family. And his mother only had one sister.

He froze. He remembered how upset his mother's sister had been when her oldest son had died of cancer at age nine. When the boy's younger brother had died the following year of the same thing, she'd been inconsolable.

According to the information on the internet, cancer was a late development if Fanconi's didn't kill its victims first. Was it possible his mother had passed on the recessive gene?

He choked up, suddenly remembering the young boy sitting across from him at the dinner table that day. His first thought was that Casey was small for his age, a definite side effect of the disease. Then he'd noticed his pale skin and the fact that he stopped to take a breath every time he talked. More symptoms of Fanconi's.

Oh, God! The child with the laughing eyes and great sense of humor really was his. Casey carried the Randall genes, the Randall imperfect DNA. A gush of pride engulfed his heart.

I have a son.

Then a wave of depression hit him so hard, it nearly brought him to his knees.

His son would die before he ever got to know him. No ballgames or Boy Scouts. No hugs, no laughter. Only pain. Pain even worse than he was feeling right now.

CHAPTER TWENTY-THREE

He watched Dani pull into the garage. He'd caught a glimpse of her face when she'd rounded the corner at the end of the block and realized she was talking on her phone.

She wouldn't talk for long.

He waited a few minutes to allow her to get out of the car and into the house. Then he reached across the passenger side and opened the glove compartment, searching blindly until he found the disposable cell phone he'd bought several weeks ago. From memory, he dialed her number.

She answered on the fifth ring, making him wonder what had kept her. Had he caught her undressing? A vision of her naked body flashed in front of him, and he smiled. She had a great ass.

"Hello." She sounded breathless, like she'd run to answer the phone.

He inhaled deeply, and he could almost smell the spicy fragrance of the perfume she usually wore. Her favorite, *Spellbound*. He'd even gone out and bought his wife a bottle, but it didn't smell the same on her.

A familiar feeling tightened his jeans. Dani was one hot broad. Pity she had become a complication.

He took another breath and exhaled directly into the receiver.

"Who's there?"

Fear slipped into her voice. Slight, but there nonetheless. His breathing became heavier.

"Listen, you little jerk!" she shouted. "You're starting to piss me off."

He threw back his head and laughed when she hung up. He would have given anything to be in her house when those brown eyes darkened with anger. The woman definitely needed a little fire in her boring life. Needed to get laid by a real man. Too bad he wouldn't be able to oblige her.

He leaned back into the leather seat and closed his eyes. What a shame things had worked out the way they had. Just when his life was starting to look up, she had to up and ruin everything.

Well, maybe not ruin, but if he didn't stop her, that's exactly what would happen. Now that he was in a position to collect a lot of money, he couldn't let that happen. Couldn't let any bimbo mess things up, tight ass or not. He'd worked too damn hard to get where he was.

He sat upright and hit redial. With each ring, his anger increased. The bitch wasn't answering.

When it switched over to voicemail, he listened to her message. She sounded so sweet, but he knew better. Knew how fucking cold she could be. He breathed into the phone two times.

Then, just before he hung up, he whispered, "Bang, bang. You're dead."

Dani stared in disbelief after she opened the door to her office. "Oh, dear God!" she said aloud, despite the fact she was alone in the room.

Or was she?

She jammed her hand into her purse, groping for her weapon before crossing the threshold. File folders were strewn everywhere, totally blanketing the carpet. Everything on the desk had been shoved across the room, including the picture of her with Abby and Johnny at the state fair three years ago. It was shattered into a thousand pieces. The sight made her nauseous, and she tightened her grip on the trigger.

Slowly, she backed out of her office and made her way toward Harry's, her weapon cocked and ready. "I've got a gun, and I'm not afraid to use it," she warned.

Instinct told her she was alone. That whoever had done this was long gone. But she'd seen too many cops make mistakes when they relied solely on their gut. Cautiously, she opened the door to Harry's office.

After a thorough search turned up nothing out of place there, she walked down the hall. Grabbing the receiver from the floor, she dialed the Cimarron Police Department. The way things were going lately, it might be a good idea to put them on speed dial.

Dani knew she should have called them last night when that creep had first tried to scare her, but that would have been a waste of time. They wouldn't have found anything, because there was nothing to be found. No sense making someone come out and ask a lot of questions. The shooter had probably been some high school kid high on paint fumes or something. Still, she'd slept with her thirty-eight under her pillow.

After reporting the break-in, she tried Harry's cell phone, knowing he had a dentist appointment today. He'd picked a helluva day for a root canal. She left a short message on his voicemail, then flopped on the couch in the far corner of her office. Nothing to do but sit back and wait for the cops.

She took a deep breath and glanced around the room. It looked like a Texas tornado had blown in during the night. Swift and deadly and gone in a matter of minutes.

"Oh no!" She sprang from the sofa and ran to her desk, bending to look under it. She slammed her hand against the wood.

Her laptop was missing. She had a lot of important information on that computer, stuff that would be hard to replicate. Fortunately, all the client files were backed up on memory sticks. But that still left the websites she used for research, plus a lot of other sites she frequented. She'd have to spend a nice chunk of time reprogramming a new computer. Time she didn't have right now.

Her gaze moved lower as she noticed the bottom drawer of the desk slightly ajar. She reached down and pulled it open all the way.

"Son of a–" Her digital camera was missing, too.

She shoved her hand to the back of the drawer until her fingers touched an envelope. She pulled it out and tore it open. The fifty dollars she kept hidden for emergencies was still there. The thief had missed it.

Or had he? Why would someone tear her office apart and only take her laptop and her camera? Besides the fifty bucks, other valuable things were tucked way inside her desk. Just last week when her fingers had swelled, she'd taken off the opal ring Johnny had given her on their fifth anniversary, intending to take it home and lock it up. That had never happened.

She pulled out the middle drawer, fully expecting to see it gone, too. But it was there, next to her iPod and about five dollars in change.

Now she was really confused. Neither her laptop nor the digital camera would probably bring more than a hundred bucks at a pawn shop. Why would someone pass up a sure thing like cash?

Because the burglar hadn't been looking for cash. He'd been interested only in her computer and her camera. Her body stiffened as the answer came to her.

Randall.

She'd shown him the incriminating pictures yesterday. Today, her camera and laptop were missing. Coincidence? She thought not.

She whirled and ran to the file cabinet. Empty. Every single file had been tossed across the room like a Frisbee. Loose papers lay everywhere. She bent and grabbed one just as two police officers walked into her office.

"Are you Mrs. Perez?" the taller one asked.

Dani didn't recognize either of them, but that wasn't unusual. Only rookies caught the petty crimes that mostly went unsolved.

"Yes."

"Anything missing?" the other cop asked.

"Looks like my laptop and my camera, so far. I was just starting to go through my files when you arrived."

"Any reason someone might want a look into those files?"

Dani thought fast. She wasn't ready to give them Randall yet. She shook her head.

"I'm thinking a junkie out for a quick fix," she lied, knowing that theory was probably invalidated by the discovery of the money and the ring.

Both cops nodded. The taller of the two flipped open a note-book. "Let's get this report finished so you can start cleaning up. What time did you say you arrived this morning?"

Thirty minutes later, after the guy from the evidence team who arrived shortly after the cops found no detectable fingerprints on the drawer that had been jimmied, they left, promising to get back with her if any of the stolen items showed up around town.

The bastard probably used surgical gloves, Dani thought. *Must think he's pretty clever.*

Dani sat on the floor and sorted through the files. Thank God she was anal about writing the client's name on every page. As bad as this mess was, it would have been a disaster if she had no way of knowing where to put each sheet.

She jumped when her cell phone rang. "Perez."

"What the hell is so important that you called me at the dentist's office?" Harry growled. "I'm already numb."

"My office was ransacked."

There was a long silence. "Are you okay?" His voice no longer sounded angry.

"Yeah. It must have happened in the middle of the night. The police have been here and gone."

"Only your office?"

"Yes." She told him the details.

"I'll call the insurance company as soon as I'm through here. Hold on a minute."

He spit while she waited.

"Feel like I've had a stroke, dribbling all over my damn chin." He spit again. "Do the cops think it was a junkie?"

She hesitated. "That's their working theory."

"Dani, I can read you like a damn book. Are you thinking that maybe it wasn't a kid looking for today's fix?"

"What else could it be?" Dani hoped she sounded convincing. She hadn't told anyone about the phone call last night, and that's the way she wanted to keep it. God forbid if her dad found out. He'd never let her out of the house alone again.

"I'd better go, Harry. I've got one gigantic mess to clean up. Good luck with that root canal."

"Yeah, thanks. Let me know if you hear anything from the police. I'll see you tomorrow."

"Okay."

She flipped the receiver closed and leaned against the cabinet. She hated keeping her suspicions from Harry, but his knowing would only complicate things. He had no idea about her five-month investigation of Nate Randall before he became a client. No idea about the relationship between Nate and Casey. And Dani was pretty sure he would freak out if he suspected she was concealing evidence.

No, she'd keep that little secret to herself for now. At least until Randall agreed to be a bone marrow donor for his son. She leaned forward and started the tedious job of matching reports to folders.

About ninety minutes into the cleanup, she spotted the file labeled D.N. Romeo. Stretching her body across the stack in front of her, she retrieved it.

"Hmm," she mused, surprised to find it intact, the photographs still in the envelope.

That didn't make any sense unless Randall hadn't put two and two together with the play on his name. Nate wasn't an idiot. So why would he leave it behind?

She rubbed her stomach, trying to quiet the growls. She'd only eaten a bite or two of toast this morning before she picked Abby up at her grandfather's. Until this whole mess was settled, she had decided Abby needed to stay away from the house. It was an arrangement both Abby and her dad loved. Now she was convinced she'd be an idiot to stay at her house by herself. She'd stop by and pick up enough clothes for her and Abby for a few more days. Hopefully, the cops would come up with a suspect by then.

She glanced at her watch. No wonder she felt queasy. It was already after three. She pulled herself up, using the edge of her desk, experiencing pins and needles in her legs.

Plopping into her chair, she searched for her stash of crackers when her phone blared. Dani grabbed her phone and glanced at Caller ID. Why was Tino calling? She shoved it into her purse, in no mood to talk to him. No mood for the lecture she knew she'd get after what had happened at her office today. News traveled fast in the Cimarron Police Department, especially when it involved one of their own, or someone who had once been on the job.

Truth be told, the break-in had unnerved her more than she wanted to admit. Talking about it now would only make it worse. She needed no further reminder that her attempt to force Randall into giving up a little bone marrow had backfired.

She remembered the confused look on Nate's face when she'd shown him the pictures. Killers always think they're so much smarter than the cops. They're truly amazed when they're caught. Was that what the look was all about?

Instead of doing the right thing by his son, had Randall decided to take things into his own hands? Could she blame him for being angry when she and Nik told him he had a son?

Not really. You don't just spring that on someone and expect no reaction. They had crossed the line of common decency with the deceit, but they'd had no choice.

Maybe that wasn't entirely true. They could have gone to him the day they found out Casey carried his DNA and told him. In the short time she'd known Dr. Nathan Randall, she thought she'd gotten to understand him a little. Thought there was no way a guy like him would be able to say no to saving any child, let alone his own flesh and blood.

But she'd been wrong. Had she been wrong about everything else? She was beginning to think she was losing her ability to read people. Nate had fooled everyone, including her boss. Like a true sociopath capable of murdering without remorse, had he lulled her into letting down her guard?

No matter. She needed to have a talk with her dad. He'd know what to do, who to tell. As much as she hated to admit defeat, she had failed. Casey's fate rested in God's hands now.

Right or wrong, that conclusion made her feel better as she made a right turn and headed down the street to her house. Although Dani had made a promise to her sister to keep her nephew safe no matter what she had to do, she had run out of options.

Regardless of Nate's decision about the transplant, she would go to the cops with her evidence. Especially now that he knew about the photos and apparently hadn't been overly impressed with her lame attempt at blackmail.

She drove into the garage and lowered the door, ready to follow up on her decision. She'd call Nik as soon as she got inside the house and make sure she was on the same page.

He'd waited long enough. Dani wasn't going to go away quietly despite his numerous attempts to scare her off. She'd gone from a complication to a liability in the past week, and that demanded serious action.

Today was the day he'd tie up all the loose ends. Everyone would assume it was the same person who'd killed the druggie and shot up her house. They'd be right, of course, but there was no way to tie him to any of it.

He'd use the same gun then permanently retire it. Three hits were more than enough for one weapon. And that wasn't even counting the meth dealer in Mesquite who'd tried to scam him last year. He'd forced the guy to give up the cash hidden in the floor of the kitchen. The scum had crapped in his pants when he'd shoved the gun into his mouth. Then he'd put two slugs into the asshole's brain and rigged the house to blow.

Eighteen thousand dollars, tax free. He couldn't have gotten it at a better time. His bookie had been getting aggressive, even threatening consequences. Fucking Cowboys. How the hell could they have let Arizona whip their asses when they were favored by ten points?

The body had been so badly burned in the explosion, nothing was left to autopsy. Dumb-ass dope head. Shouldn't have screwed with him.

His attention was diverted as a car passed him and slowly made its way to her house at the end of the road.

Killing Dani just got a little easier.

CHAPTER TWENTY-FOUR

Something felt wrong. Dani sensed it the minute she switched on the light in the kitchen, just as she had the night someone shot through her living room window.

She scanned the room. Nothing looked out of place. Her half-eaten toast from this morning was still on the plate in the middle of the table right where she'd left it.

Still, something was different. Cop instinct or woman's intuition—whatever it was—made the hairs on her neck bristle.

She set her purse on the kitchen counter and opened the refrigerator, half expecting to see something weird.

Okay, Perez, quit acting like a paranoid wuss.

She inhaled slowly and reached for a bottle of green tea, then decided the less time she spent in the house right now, the better. The doorbell rang just as she shut the refrigerator door and threw the stale muffin into the garbage disposal.

She wasn't expecting anyone. Abby and her grandfather were at Chuck E Cheese, pigging out on pizza. She'd been invited but had declined. After the day she'd had, all she wanted to do was pack her clothes and get out of her house.

She turned on the light, crossed the living room, and peered through the peep hole.

What the heck?

She opened the door and stared at the two men on her doorstep shooting looks made to kill at one another.

"What's going on?" she asked.

Nate glanced at Spig. "I came by to talk to you about Casey. I tried calling Nikki, but she's not home." He pointed to Spig. "I have no idea who this guy is, or why he's here."

Dani shifted her gaze. "Spig?"

Her ex-partner glared at Nate. "I know you threatened to kill Tino and me, but we've been watching your house for the past few nights. You might want to ask your boyfriend why he was rooting around on your back porch about an hour ago."

"Boyfriend?" She turned to Nate. "Were you here earlier?"

"That's a damn lie. I didn't leave Dallas until seven. I wanted to catch you before you went to bed. I just got here. He drove up behind me."

"Ha!" Spig narrowed his eyes. "Explain why I found Dani's camera in your car." He pulled the digital camera from his jacket pocket and handed it to her.

"Oh, my God," she mumbled. "It really was you." She glared at Nate. "You broke into my office and tore the place apart looking for the pictures?" When he didn't answer, she snarled, "Too bad you didn't find them."

"What are you talking about?" Nate looked confused. "I was nowhere near your office."

"You know exactly what she's talking about." Spig turned to Dani. "What pictures?"

She hesitated then decided it didn't matter anymore. She'd already made the decision to go to the police. "Pictures of him leaving his wife's house at the time of her murder." She paused and met Nate's stare. "Pictures that prove he lied to the police."

Spig laughed out loud. "So you killed your wife. I gotta say, I'm surprised. I would never have believed a wimp like you had the balls to do something like that."

Nate ignored him and reached for Dani's hand. She jerked it away. "First off, I didn't kill Janelle. Second, no way I took your camera or wrecked your office. And finally, that's not me in the pictures. That's what I came to tell you."

"Yeah, right. And I suppose that's why it was so damn important for you to get rid of them." Spig's voice dripped with sarcasm.

"Look, asshole, I'm here to talk to Dani. I don't have to prove anything to you."

Spig lunged at Nate, grabbing a fistful of his shirt and slamming him against the door.

"Stop!" Dani yelled as another police car pulled into her driveway.

Nate's left fist connected with Spig's jaw, sending him backward just as Tino rushed to the porch and shoved Nate hard against the door frame.

Dani jumped between them, her eyes hard. "Cut it out. Stop acting like adolescents with a testosterone surge."

"What's going on here?" Tino asked.

Dani ignored the question and turned to Nate. "How could it not be you in the pictures? I followed you from your office to your house and waited until you came back out." The man was still lying despite getting caught red-handed.

"I don't have a clue how you got that picture, but I swear I wasn't in that car."

"Prove it." Spig's eyes squinted in anger, and he rubbed the right side of his face. His jaw had already started to swell. "He's the one who's been shooting up Dani's living room," he said to Tino.

"Dani?"

"I don't know, Tino. Spig found my camera in his car."

Tino pushed closer to Nate. "You bastard."

"Tino, stop, dammit."

"Like I said, I don't have to prove anything to either of you." Nate turned back to Dani. "Can we sit down and talk about this?" He flipped his head toward the two cops. "In private?"

Dani searched his face for any signal that he was lying. A twitch. A bead of perspiration on his upper lip.

Nothing.

Yet, as much as she wanted to believe Nate had nothing to do with Janelle's death, the photos said otherwise.

"How did you get my camera?"

Nate shook his head, his lips pursed. "He's lying, Dani. You have to believe me."

Tino grabbed her arm. "If you believe him, you're a fool. I thought you were a better cop than that. Can't you see he's a cold-blooded killer?"

Nate launched himself at Tino. "You son of a bitch." The weight of his body sent both of them into the house, over the back of the couch, and onto the floor, smashing into the coffee table and sending the lamp flying across the room. Spig tried to pull Nate off and ended up on the carpet with the two of them.

"Stop it!" Dani screamed.

But none of them were listening. Each was too busy kicking the other's ass. Dani grabbed a vase filled with silk flowers and threw it at the fireplace. As it connected with the bricks, it shattered into a million pieces, sending shards of colored glass sailing in the air as far as the window. All three men stopped and stared.

"Get out. All of you."

When no one moved, she ran to the door and opened it. "I said, 'get out'. Now!"

Without another word, the men walked past her. She slammed the door and leaned against it. Didn't even bother turning on the porch light. Let them break their stupid necks for all she cared. What in God's name were they thinking?

She stayed there until the cars pulled out of her driveway. Then she stood and slumped in the easy chair, her entire body shaking. Unable to control the emotions pulsing through her body, she did what she always did when she was mad enough to kill.

She cried.

Giant, wet tears escalated to full-blown sobs that racked her body, and she wrapped her arms around her knees and rocked. She hated feeling so vulnerable, so girlie.

She forced herself to take a few deep breaths as she reached for the box of tissues on the end table. Leaving the office today, she'd never dreamed this day could get any worse. And it had, big-time.

She glanced around the room, assessing the damage. Spying the broken picture frame in the middle of the floor brought another rush of tears to her eyes. It contained the picture of her and Nik with their mother, taken the Christmas before she was killed. The last picture of her before the accident.

Dani blew her nose, cursing the trickle of tears on her cheeks.

"Fuck," she said aloud, then smiled. She hadn't used that word since the day Johnny died. "Fuck, fuck, fuck, and double fuck!"

Somehow repeating the obscenity made her feel a little better despite her now owing the potty-mouth jar a hundred bucks. Or would that double fuck cost an extra twenty? No matter, it was worth every penny.

She got up and started toward the kitchen to brew a cup of coffee before heading back to her dad's. She had about an hour before he and Abby would get home. It was already way too late for caffeine, but she needed a boost. She might even throw in a healthy dose of Baileys.

Halfway to the kitchen, the lights went out. She froze, willing her eyes to dilate in the dark. She felt for the couch as she made her way to the hutch where she stored a flashlight for electrical emergencies. Since no storms were in the forecast, she figured she must have blown a fuse.

Then she heard it. A soft thud that was barely audible, like a movement in the dark, but her police instincts picked up on it instantly. The fine hairs on her arms stood on end.

She was not alone in the room.

"Who's there?"

Idiot! She had just given away her exact location to whoever was there.

She moved to her left just as a shot rang out, barely missing her. She slumped to the floor, as panic like she'd never known before welled in her throat. Someone was definitely in the room, and he wasn't playing games.

Her gun! She needed to get to it fast.

Crap! Her thirty-eight was still under her pillow from when she'd slept with it last night after the heavy breather called, and her purse was under the counter in the kitchen. Since the shot had come from somewhere on the side of the room closest to the kitchen, her only chance was to get up the stairs without getting killed.

She tried to breathe as quietly as she could, listening for anything that might help her pinpoint the intruder's position. Other than the chirping of the crickets outside, magnified by the contrast of the silence inside the house, she detected nothing except the thumping of her heartbeat.

Dani swiped her hand across her forehead, wiping away beads of perspiration. Her ragged breaths threatened to give away her position. She was more than a little scared.

She wasn't ready to die, not yet, not tonight. What would Abby do without her? She'd have nobody left.

A slight movement near the kitchen caught her eye. She held her breath and crawled in the opposite direction. If she could just make it to the stairs, she could rush up the steps and hope the bullets missed. It was her best chance.

She covered her mouth as a surge of queasiness threatened to bring up what little she had in her stomach.

Oh, God, not now.

She took several shallow breaths, trying to block out the smells in the room. The sweet fragrance coming from the bowl on the TV was enough to gag anyone. Why had she filled it with orange potpourri?

Easing her body from the floor she positioned her self on her knees. If she was going to make a run for the stairs, she had to move soon. She had no weapon. Whoever was in the room would figure that out soon enough when she didn't return fire.

Suddenly, the back door creaked, and all Dani could think about was how she'd meant to put WD-40 on its hinges months ago.

When her assailant fired a couple of shots into the kitchen, she stood and bolted for the stairs, taking them two at a time. A single bullet zinged past her and grazed her upper arm. She grabbed her burning flesh and raced toward her bedroom, not slowing until she was safely behind the closed door.

She ran to the bed and reached under her pillow.

Nothing.

She picked up the pillow, then the other one before flinging them to the floor.

Where in the hell is my gun?

215

Hurling herself across the top of the bed, she shoved her hand between the headboard and the mattress, in case it had fallen during the night.

Footsteps echoed in the hall, and she twisted her entire body toward the door. Sucking in a gulp of air, she held it as the doorknob turned slightly. The streetlight cast an eerie glow on the knob as it turned slowly. Her entire body shook, the pounding in her chest so loud she was sure whoever was on the other side of the door could hear. She snatched the phone from the nightstand.

Dead.

Jerking her hand to her mouth to cover the scream, she scrambled to the door and flattened her body against the wall behind it. Perspiration trickled into her eyes, setting them on fire as she waited. Frantically, she searched for some sort of weapon. Her eyes zeroed in on the trophy Johnny had won in the police bowling tournament the year before he died. Could she make it all the way over there?

She had to. She was out of options.

She lunged from behind the door just as it opened. Before she could reach the trophy, an arm circled her neck, and a hand covered her mouth.

Her scream stuck in her throat.

CHAPTER TWENTY-FIVE

"Shh," Nate whispered. "I managed to knock the gun out of his hand, but it won't take him long to find it. How do we get out of here?"

He slid his hand from Dani's mouth. Should she scream or make a run for Johnny's trophy? Or both?

"Dani, hurry. He's coming." Nate released his hold on her.

She sprinted to the dresser, grabbed the trophy, and thrust it out in front of her. "Don't come any closer, Nate. This thing is heavy enough to kill you."

His eyes questioned, and confusion creased his forehead. When he took a step toward her, she lifted the statue over her head.

"I'm not kidding, Nate."

"Spig's on his way up here to kill us both. You've got to trust me. We have to get out now."

She held his stare, wanting to believe him. But if she did, that meant Spig was a bad guy. Spig, who'd ridden with her on the job all those months. Spig, who'd comforted her at Johnny's funeral and helped her with the investigation.

She jerked her head toward the door when footsteps sounded in the hallway. They were coming this way and getting closer.

Nate grabbed the dresser and shoved it across the carpet in front of the door just as it creaked open. For a split second, Dani glimpsed Spig's face. He had a crazed look in his eyes.

Holy mother of God! Her ex-partner really was trying to kill them. But why?

She had no time to think this through as Spig slammed his body against the door. She grabbed Nate's arm and pulled him toward the window. "It opens over the patio roof. We can jump into the backyard."

"It's better than nothing. Come on."

Nate unlocked the window and pushed on it, but it wouldn't budge. The Texas summer had been brutal, and the window hadn't been opened in a while.

"Stand back." Dani raised the trophy over her head and threw it at the window. She turned away but not fast enough. A searing pain tore through her face as a shard of glass speared her cheek.

Nate reached over and pulled it out in one quick motion, then broke the remaining glass from the edges with his elbow. He shoved her in front of the opening. "Go."

Just as Dani crawled through, her bedroom door splintered. With a glance over her shoulder, she read the rage on Spig's face as he struggled to push the dresser out of the way.

"Hurry!" she screamed.

Nate pushed her out the window onto the patio roof, then slid through just as Spig fired the gun.

Dani was near the edge of the sloping when the shot rang out. She turned and stared at Nate in horror. He had stopped halfway through the window, and from the look on his face, he'd been hit. Quickly, she ran back and pulled him through, knowing every movement was killing him.

"Run, Dani. You can't help me. We'll both die." His eyes pleaded with her to go.

But she couldn't.

Somehow she lifted him to his feet. In the faint glow of the full moon, she noticed a dark red circle spreading on the back of his slacks from the hit to his lower leg. She glanced into her bedroom as Spig shoved the dresser away from the door and squeezed through the opening.

She hurried to the edge of the roof with Nate limping beside her. "Jump," she commanded.

When he hesitated, she pushed him, then held her breath as he tumbled to the ground and rolled on his side. There was no mistaking his scream. He was in agony.

Then she jumped, landing a few inches away from him.

"I can't go any farther," Nate said, pain evident on his face. "Go get help."

Her eyes widened. "He'll kill you."

"I'll hide in the bushes. He'll think we're both running." He tried to smile. "Hurry and bring back the whole damn cavalry."

She stared into his eyes for a second. He was right. Together, they'd both be killed. If she could make it to her neighbor's house, they stood a chance. She prayed nosy Mrs. Manahan would be awake, though she never stayed up past nine.

Dani helped Nate to a hiding place behind the tall scrubs, then turned and sprinted through the back gate. Halfway through her front yard, a stinging spread through her upper arm. When she reached for it, she lost her balance, tripping on a tuft of grass and landing hard on her tailbone.

Before she could pull herself up, Spig pushed his foot into her chest and shoved her back down. His face was evil incarnate. She shivered.

"You can't run from me, Dani. Don't even try." He turned his body completely around, scanning the darkness before pointing the gun at her head. "Where's your boyfriend?"

"Why, Spig?" Dani asked, confused. "We're friends."

He laughed. "You just couldn't leave well enough alone, could you? IAB was ready to close the book on Johnny's case. You could have taken the money and run. But no, you had to go and screw everything up."

"Screw what up, Spig?"

"Everything." He sneered. "Thought you were too good for me. Still think that?" He wiped his forehead with his sleeve. "I tried to warn you, Dani, but you were too goddamn stubborn. Just like Johnny."

Spig did another 360 with his body. "Randall, I'll kill her if you don't come out with your hands in the air," he shouted in the dark.

Dani propped her upper body on her elbows. "You killed Johnny, didn't you?" She prayed he'd answer, 'no,' the alternative too horrible to consider. She and Spig had been friends since high school and partners for over two years.

"What difference does it make? He found out someone was shaking down the pushers for heroin and made it his personal mission to find out who. I couldn't let that happen. He got too close for comfort."

Dani lowered her head. "So you did kill him."

"Didn't have to. Apollo was more anxious to keep our little arrangement a secret than I was. The plan was to make it look like Johnny and Tino had walked in on a drug deal. Apollo said he would kill them both and be long gone before the cops showed up. But Tino, the perpetual screw-up, went and put a bullet between Apollo's eyes before he could finish the job."

Dani's mind refused to register the significance of his words.

Spig smiled. "The beauty of the whole thing was that Johnny hadn't shared his suspicions with his partner, so nobody was the wiser." The smile turned into a big grin that covered his face. "Kind of brilliant, don't you think? I get rid of the cop who could take me down, the newspapers label him a bad guy, plus the middle man gets knocked out as an added perk."

Dani lowered her head so Spig couldn't see the pain that tore at her heart, didn't want to give him the pleasure. Out of the corner of her eye, she spied Nate in the shadows, hobbling slowly toward them. She had to keep Spig talking. "But why, Spig? You hate drug dealers."

"I know, but I got in a jam a few years back with some bad guys." His face tightened. "When I couldn't pay up, they threatened to kill me. I didn't have much choice. So what if a few scumbag dopers ended up dead?"

"Johnny wasn't a doper," she said, rage spreading through her entire body.

Spig smiled. "Saint Johnny? Shit, no. He was just like you, a self-proclaimed do-gooder who couldn't leave well enough alone. He ended up dead, just like you're gonna be."

"Spig, we can work this out. No one has to know."

"Shut up, Dani. Don't make this any harder."

He was caught off guard when Nate threw his body into him, sending the gun skipping across the lawn.

"You son of a bitch! I'll kill you if you hurt her."

As the two men wrestled in the grass, slick with dew, Dani crawled to the weapon, her hands shaking. She raised the gun and fired a single shot into the air, piercing the quiet night.

Both men stopped and stared. She lowered the weapon, aiming it directly at Spig. "On your knees, you bastard, and pray I don't blow your head off."

That was not a stretch, considering how much she hated this man right now. A mental image of Johnny walking into Apollo's house thinking he was about to make a routine bust flashed in her head. She prayed he never knew his good friend had betrayed him.

A porch light came on, further illuminating the three of them in the front yard. When Mrs. Manahan poked her head out the door, Dani shouted, "Call 911. Tell them to send the police and an ambulance. There's been a shooting."

Spig took a step toward her. "Dani, we can talk this over like you said." He inched closer.

She fired into his thigh.

"Fuck!" he screamed, as he crumbled to the ground. "You bitch! You shot me."

"The bigger surprise is that I didn't kill you, Spig. That was for Johnny." She stared at the man she'd considered a brother. A man who had just confessed to killing her husband, and for the first time, she wished the bullet in his leg had been higher. Like between his eyes.

She forced herself to look away and walked toward Nate, who had collapsed on the ground. The right leg of his trousers was soaked with blood. "Do I need to put a tourniquet on that or something?"

He tried to smile but couldn't quite pull it off. "I'm okay. The ambulance will be here soon." He crinkled his eyes in another attempt to smile. "What about you?"

She glanced at her left shoulder, aware of the throbbing pain. "I'll live." She sighed. "Too bad the same is true for him." She glared at her ex-partner, now crying softly and holding his leg.

Big baby!

The next fifteen minutes went by quickly after the police arrived. When they handcuffed Spig and led him past Dani to the waiting ambulance, he wouldn't meet her eyes.

Freakin' coward.

The cops insisted she ride in the ambulance to the emergency room despite her protests. Why couldn't they load her into the cruiser and follow behind? Reluctantly, she climbed into the back of the emergency vehicle. At least they hadn't put her on a gurney the way they had Nate.

On the way to the hospital, neither she nor Nate spoke, both absorbed in their own thoughts. Both trying to make sense of the past hour. Dani wondered how she could have misjudged Spig so badly.

She was jolted from her thoughts when Nate's hand covered hers. She didn't pull away. No matter what their history was, she was warmed he was there for her. Had been willing to die for her.

She squeezed his hand. The man had saved her life. No words were necessary.

Dani turned her head as the ER doctor stitched her upper arm. Luckily, she only had a flesh wound. Other than it hurting like heck when the doctor used forceps to make sure a piece of the bullet hadn't lodged in the wound, it wasn't a big deal.

The cops had already been here and taken her statement. She was alone in the room with the young doctor stitching her arm.

"You're a cop?" the doctor asked as he finished with her arm and leaned closer to inspect the wound on her cheek.

As he prepared to work on her face, Dani noticed for the first time how good looking he was. She smiled. "Used to be. Never got hurt as a cop, though."

He laughed. "Maybe you should consider a career change."

The door opened, and a lab technician walked in. "Want me to come back?" she asked.

The physician shook his head. "You can work on that side."

Fifteen minutes later, when Dani was finally alone in the room, her thoughts returned to Nate. What was happening to him now? They'd whisked him down the hall to another room as soon as the ambulance had pulled up to the emergency room dock.

The rush of feelings surprised her. Even when the hot young doctor had been close enough to her face that she could feel his breath on her cheek, she'd hadn't been able to get her mind off Nate.

What was that all about? Surely, she wasn't falling for him. She couldn't. Not when she had the evidence to prove he was with his wife the day she was murdered. The day he'd sworn he was nowhere near her.

She should have turned the pictures over to the Dallas police a long time ago.

What had stopped her? And why was he still insisting he hadn't been in the car that day after seeing the pictures that proved he was.

She wanted more than anything to believe him. She prided herself on her ability to tell the good guys from the bad ones. Nate didn't fit the profile of a killer, but she'd been wrong about Spig—and that had almost gotten both of them killed.

She relaxed into the pillow, wincing when her shoulder hit the mattress too hard. She remembered Nate's scream when he'd rolled on the ground after she'd pushed him off the roof. She hoped they'd given him something strong for the pain.

Her thoughts went back to that night in his hotel room, smiling as she remembered how nervous he'd been. He'd treated her more like a first date he was trying to impress than a working girl.

Having dated Johnny since junior high, she hadn't been on many first dates, but she knew enough to know they didn't go the way that night had. A visual of his wet body, hard with desire, in the shower caused an unexpected flush on her cheeks.

"Good grief, Dani! You're going to be the death of me yet."

She looked up at her father, hoping he couldn't read her mind. "I'm okay, Dad."

Hector Ramirez hugged her, then held her away from him to get a better look at her injuries. "All that money I spent on braces and cosmetics when you were a teenager. Wasted," he said, trying to make light of her injuries.

"I could have been killed, and all you worry about are my looks?" she teased. Then she turned serious. "The doctor said I'll only have minimal scarring." She pointed to her left shoulder. "This, on the other hand, will be tougher. I'll have to wear a sling for at least a few weeks."

Hector exhaled noisily. "I'm never letting you out of my sight again."

'Yeah, right." Dani grinned. "If I remember correctly, you were the one always pushing me to get out more. To meet Spig and the gang for a few drinks. Or have you forgotten?"

His face twisted with anger. "I'll kill that little scum with my bare hands if I ever get the chance. He's more than a disgrace to the shield. Anybody who would shoot an unarmed female can't even call himself a man. He's nothing but a coward." He sat on the edge of the bed and grabbed her hand, and the hard look in his eyes softened. "What about Randall? How bad is he?"

Dani's eyes clouded. "I don't know. I've been trying to get them to tell me something, anything, but they won't. All they'll say is that his injuries aren't life-threatening. He lost so much blood, I'm worried."

"Tino called," Hector said, changing the subject. "Said Nate saved your life."

"He did. That's how he got shot."

The door opened, and the doctor walked in, his eyes moving to Hector.

"My father," Dani explained.

He shook Hector's hand. "We're ready to discharge your daughter. She'll have to take it easy for a few weeks, but she should recover nicely."

"What about Dr. Randall?" Dani asked.

"All I know is they took him to surgery. Let me make a call to find out more." He turned back to Hector. "I need to go over Mrs. Perez's discharge instructions with her. Now is a good time to pull your car around to the ER door. We'll bring her out in a wheelchair."

Dani opened her mouth to protest.

"Hospital policy," the doctor said, anticipating an argument. "No exceptions."

Dani pursed her lips. "Okay, but I'm not leaving until I find out about Dr Randall."

Hector bent and kissed Dani on the cheek. "You always did hate it when you didn't get your way." He grinned. "Back in a flash." He followed the doctor out.

When the doctor returned, he placed his hand on Dani's back and helped her sit up so he could adjust the sling around her neck.

"Like I said, two weeks of taking it easy should do the trick. I'm sending you home with a prescription for antibiotics as well as some pain medication. Take the antibiotics until they're all gone in ten days. You'll need to make an appointment with your family physician to get the sutures out, or we can remove them. Either way, that needs to happen in about a week."

He adjusted the splint. "Keep this on for a few days after the sutures come out. If it still hurts, wear it longer."

"Can I see Dr. Randall before I leave?"

He shook his head. "I called. He's still in surgery. They had to sedate him to get the bullet out and tie off the bleeders."

"He's going to be okay, isn't he?" Dani held her breath for his answer.

"He's lost a lot of blood, so they're keeping him overnight, but he'll be fine. You two must have had someone up above watching over you."

Dani sighed. No truer words had ever been spoken. She looked up. *Thanks, Mom.*

The doctor walked around the bed and placed another piece of tape on her cheek. "Try not to get this dressing wet until you get the stitches out."

He walked to the door before turning back. "And Mrs. Perez, you might want to make an appointment with your obstetrician."

Dani sucked in her breath.

"When you gave the nurse your medical history, you mentioned you've been having some queasiness lately. I ordered a pregnancy test." He smiled. "It was positive."

CHAPTER TWENTY-SIX

Nate grinned when he opened the door. Dani looked so adorable with a bandage on her cheek and her left arm in a sling.

"I went to the hospital, but they said you'd already gone home." Her face creased when she spied his knee brace and crutches. "You're here by yourself?"

"Came home right after breakfast. And yes, I'm alone."

"Are you managing okay?"

He opened the door wider. "This is a hotel, remember? With enough money, I can get them to do anything for me." Noticing her hesitation, he stepped back. The room probably brought back a rush of unpleasant memories. "You want to come in?"

"I thought money was tight right now." She looked embarrassed, dropping her eyes to the floor. "I could scrounge up a little to help out until you're on your feet again."

He laughed. "I'm fine. Really. The manager worked out a deal with me." He hobbled over to the bed and sat on the edge of the mattress. "Sorry, but I have to get this leg elevated before it swells and hurts like hell again."

She was at his side in an instant, lifting his leg onto the bed with her good arm. "When did you take your last pain pill?"

"About ten minutes before you got here. It should start working soon."

She shoved the pillow under his leg. Then she picked up the warm ice bag. "Where can I get this refilled?"

He looked into her eyes for a moment, remembering the last time she had been this close to his bed. Even with the pain medicine on board, his body responded to her nearness. He pulled the sheet over his waist.

"Ice bucket is in the bathroom. The machine is down the hall to your left. Thanks."

He exhaled as she retrieved the bucket and opened the door, pulling off her shoes and wedging one of them against the door jamb so he wouldn't have to get out of bed to let her back in. He hated having someone take care of him, but he was in no shape to argue. He'd already tried stumbling down the hall for more ice and ended up in a cold sweat after only a few feet.

Once he got past the weak male issue, he had to admit he was glad she'd come by to check on him. When he had awakened in the recovery room yesterday, he'd been disappointed she wasn't there waiting for him.

Not that she had any reason to. Still, he'd hoped. When he'd asked about her, the nurse had said her dad had taken her home hours earlier. He'd assumed he wouldn't see her until he was more mobile and could drive again. According to his orthopedic surgeon at Cimarron County General, that would be in about four weeks.

In the few short months he'd known Dani, he'd developed a growing connection with her. The fact that they'd nearly lost their lives together only strengthened his feelings. He'd read somewhere that when people go through life-threatening experiences together, they form a special bond. Something special had definitely happened between them.

Yeah, right.

Who was he kidding? He didn't feel a special bond to Dani because they'd nearly died together. He was in love with her. Hopelessly, completely in love with a woman who believed he was a killer. Freud would have a field day with that.

When had it happened?

He fought to control his swirling emotions. Somewhere in the back of his mind, he'd known she was special that first night when she'd told him her name was Sophie.

Sophie? He'd thought it was a weird name for a hooker. And now, after meeting the real Aunt Sophie, it took on a whole new dimension.

He glanced up when the door opened, thinking it was probably a good idea to keep his feelings under wraps for now, maybe forever. But how could he do that with Dani so close?

He stole a glance at her as she filled the bag with ice before filling two glasses on the bar.

"Got any soda?"

He pointed toward the mini-bar.

"Won't they charge you an arm and a leg?" She grinned. "You only have one good one left, you know."

"Part of my deal with the hotel. I only have to give up my Mercedes." He smiled. "And my firstborn." When her smile faded, he realized what he'd said. "I'm sorry, Dani. That was only meant as a joke. I wasn't thinking about Casey."

"I know."

She opened the refrigerator and pulled out a soft drink. For having only one good arm, she managed pretty well.

She walked over and set the drink on the nightstand beside him, leaned in, and for a second, their eyes connected. "Lift up, Nate, so I can fluff your pillow."

With her so close, he had to use all his willpower to keep from taking her in his arms and pulling her into bed. "You smell like flowers," he said instead, eliciting another smile.

After she fluffed the pillow, she met his gaze again, this time with her face only inches away. Then she did something he wouldn't have expected in a million years.

She kissed him. Not a lust-filled, I-want-to-jump-your-bones kind of kiss, but it might as well have been. It had the same effect on Nate.

He took both her cheeks in his hands and drew her to his lips, this time for a more demanding kiss.

"Nate, I–"

"Shh, Dani. Don't say anything." He patted the mattress next to him. "Lie down with me. I have some things I need to tell you. Things I wanted to say the other night before Spig arrived."

She glanced at the chair by the desk, obviously trying to decide what to do. Then she pulled back the covers and slid in beside him.

"I promise not to touch you," he said. "Unless you want me to."

228

Having her so close and not putting his hands on her body would be a major challenge to his self control. One he had to win so he didn't scare her off.

Who was he kidding? He was the one scared to death by his feelings. Look what had happened the last time he'd fallen in love. And his history with the woman beside him wasn't terrific, either. She'd already admitted to deceiving him. What made him think he could have a relationship with that as a first date memory?

Like she'd even want to have a relationship with me. He was nearly penniless, on trial for murder, and at the moment, so high on hydrocodone, he slurred his words. What made him think a woman like Dani would even give him the time of day, much less her heart?

He almost wished he didn't know about her lie. Wished she still needed his specimen. That right now she'd turn to him and work her way up his body with her sweet mouth.

His eyelids fluttered as he struggled to keep them open. He leaned closer until his head rested on her shoulder. To his surprise, she didn't pull away. Instead, she put her good arm around his shoulder to allow him to nestle closer.

With his head on her chest, the beating of her heart echoed in his ear. Like a soft lullaby, it lulled him to sleep.

When Dani opened her eyes, she was surprised to find Nate still asleep in the crook of her arm, snoring softly. She lifted her head to see the clock on the nightstand. Almost five o'clock. They'd been asleep nearly three hours. Her dad would be frantic.

She eased her arm from around Nate's neck, trying not to wake him. She almost made it before his eyes slowly opened and he smiled at her, melting her heart. Something about a man when he first wakes up reminded her of a little boy, vulnerable and trusting.

"What time is it?" he asked, his voice thick with sleep.

"Ten till five." She freed her arm and sat up in bed. "We've been asleep a long time."

He looked surprised. "You slept, too?"

229

She nodded. "And now I have to call my dad before he sends out the entire Cimarron Police Force to look for me."

She slid over the side of the bed and walked to the dresser to use the phone. When her dad answered, she felt like a teenager again, explaining why she'd missed curfew.

She'd been right. He was like a crazy man, but she managed to calm him down by promising to head home after rush hour traffic. She couldn't blame him for being overprotective. She'd certainly given him more than enough reason to worry over the past few weeks.

After she hung up, she turned to Nate. "Can you stand me for another hour or so?"

"Only if you'll call and order some dinner. I'm starving."

The thought of food made Dani's stomach growl. "Sounds like a plan. What can you eat?"

He smiled. "I have a bum leg, not a stomach ulcer. I'll eat whatever you're eating, only a lot more. Did I mention I was starving?"

If he flashes that great smile at me one more time, I won't be responsible for my actions.

"Okay, okay, I got the message." She reached for the phone on the desk.

After placing an order for two chicken sandwiches and fries and a large order of onion rings, she made another trip to the ice machine. Nate had gotten out of bed and was in the bathroom when she returned. She leaned over to grab two sodas from the minibar, just as her phone rang.

"Hey, Tino," she answered, out of breath from popping up so quickly.

"I've got news, Dani."

"I'm almost afraid to ask what."

"It's about Spig. They got a warrant and searched his house and his car last night. They found enough evidence to link him to at least four murders over the past three years."

"How could we have misjudged him so badly?"

Tino sighed, and Dani realized this was just as hard for him. He had also considered Spig a friend.

"Yeah, and we call ourselves cops."

"Did they find anything else?"

"Your laptop in his trunk. Forensics has already dusted it, so I'll bring it to the house tomorrow."

"Why did he come after me?"

"He thought you were collecting evidence. Said you were getting closer. Apparently, his paranoia skyrocketed." His voice cracked with contempt. "That and the crank he was shoving up his nose."

"Crystal meth? Oh, God. Has anyone talked to Joanne yet?"

"That's another thing. Spig was screwing around on her. She always thought you and he had something going on."

"Me?"

"Yeah. Funny, huh? I've been trying to talk you into going out with me for over a year, and now I find out Spig had the hots for you, too."

"I never knew."

"Maybe you never knew about him, but I made myself perfectly clear."

"Tino..." Dani started.

"I know. You love me like a brother. I finally get it," Tino interrupted. "I took a hard look at my life after I lied to you about flirting with that girl at the bank. You'll be glad to hear Alana and I are talking again. Maybe we can give it another shot."

"I hope so, Tino."

"Oh, and Dani?"

"Yeah?"

"We found Johnny's bank book in Spig's locker."

"Huh?" She was really confused now. "What does that mean? Did Spig open the account to make everyone think Johnny was dirty?"

"Johnny opened the account."

Dani groaned. Not what she wanted to hear. "When?"

"About a year before he was killed, Spig caught Johnny writing a deposit in the book one day, and Johnny fessed up. Said he was going to surprise you and Abby with your dream vacation. I think he said Hawaii."

Dani couldn't stop the cry that escaped her lips.

"He said Johnny socked away about a hundred dollars every week just by cutting out Starbucks and bringing a sandwich for lunch. Gave the bank book to Spig so you wouldn't find it. Apparently, he thought I couldn't keep a secret."

A flash of guilt pulsed through Dani's body. All this time she'd wondered about that account. On a bad day, she'd even doubted Johnny because of it. Hearing how much he'd sacrificed for her and Abby tore her apart.

"And one more thing..."

She choked back her emotions. "Yeah?"

"They found your thirty-eight in Spig's glove compartment. As soon as ballistics releases it, I'll swing by with that, too."

When Nate came out of the bathroom, Dani turned quickly to hide her face from his view. "Gotta go, Tino. I'll see you tomorrow. Thanks for calling."

She flipped the receiver closed, making sure she kept her back to Nate. She took a deep breath to get her emotions under control.

"Dani?"

When she didn't answer, couldn't answer, he was beside her, his hand on her shoulder, gently turning her to face him. Concern clouded his eyes. Gently, he pulled her against his chest and held her close.

Finally, he asked, "Why are you upset?"

She didn't want to tell him. Didn't want him to think she was weak. She tried to smile, searching for something flippant to say about girls and hormones. She couldn't pull it off.

"I just talked to Tino. He called to tell me Johnny–" She paused. "My husband–will probably be cleared of all charges of being a dirty cop." Her voice cracked, but she forced herself to continue. "I tried not to doubt him, but God help me, I found so much evidence against him. It was hard."

Nate slid his hands up and down her back, causing shivers to skitter up her spine. He grazed her temple with his lips, then moved to her ear, and her muscles relaxed.

"Sometimes things aren't always the way they seem, Dani. You're human. Humans make mistakes. The important thing is to not let them eat you alive. Forget the past and concentrate on the future. In your heart, you always knew Johnny was a good man. That's what counts."

She lifted her face to his and finally smiled. Then she pulled free and walked to the dresser to retrieve her purse.

She handed him the envelope containing the pictures. "I've decided not to go to the police with these. They're yours to do with as you want."

Nate stared at the envelope.

"The only other copies are on the hard drive of my laptop. They found that in Spig's car. Tino said the cops dusted it for prints already, and he's bringing it by tomorrow. He would have mentioned if they had discovered the pictures."

"Will you do me a favor, Dani?"

She nodded.

"Will you go with me to the police station tomorrow?"

"Nate—"

"I've told you all along that I wasn't in the car that day. Hopefully, the cops can find out who was."

"In all probability, they'll use these as evidence to convict you," she warned. "You might want to talk to your lawyer first."

He brushed back a stray lock of hair from her face. "That's a chance I'll have to take. Will you go with me?"

"If you're sure."

A soft knock at the door ended their conversation. Dani walked over and stood to the side as a bellman wheeled a cart of food into the room. After signing for it, she ordered Nate back to bed and placed a makeshift tray across his lap. Then she climbed in on the other side and curled her legs under her, facing him.

They ate in silence, polishing off the food in record time. Dani caught herself stealing glances at him, trying to decide if she should tell him about the pregnancy. Since she'd heard the news, that's all she could think about. No wonder she was so emotional about everything.

Nate had been kept in the dark all those years about his first child. He deserved to know about this one.

And she would tell him. Eventually. But not now. Not when they had so much else to deal with.

233

She wondered how Nate would react to the news he was going to be a father again. Maybe it would take the pressure off Nikki and Bobby if he had another child. Maybe he wouldn't demand as much from them.

He glanced as she scrutinized him, and he shrugged. "What?"

She smiled and shook her head. "I was just thinking about how much you ate and wondering why you don't weigh a ton," she lied.

"Look who's talking," he teased back.

She stood and stacked their empty plates on the tray. When she was through, she walked back over to the bed.

"I'll refill this, and then I need to head home." She reached across him for the ice bag.

He grabbed her hand. "Can I ask one more favor?"

"Do you need another pain pill?"

"Yes, but that's beside the point. I need to do something really important before I dope myself up again. I need to talk to someone."

Her eyes questioned him.

"Will you drive me to Nikki's house?"

CHAPTER TWENTY-SEVEN

Nikki rushed out when Dani and Nate pulled into the driveway. Bobby was right behind her. She pushed the door open to allow Nate to navigate inside on crutches.

"Come into the kitchen. I've put out some snacks." Nikki pointed up the stairs. "Casey's playing video games."

Dani hugged her sister, who was unable to hide the fear clouding her face. Nikki's eyes, red and swollen, were hard to miss, and they matched Bobby's. Nate wondered how they would deal with what he'd come to tell them.

"How's your leg, Nate?" Nikki asked when they were settled around the table with cups of hot chocolate.

"I need to talk to you and Bobby about Casey." His voice grew soft, almost sorrowful, as he dispensed with the small talk.

Dani drew in a sharp breath and bit her lower lip.

Watching Nikki's hopes die was going to be difficult for her. Knowing he was the one responsible would be worse. But he had to tell her now. Making her wait would be cruel.

"Before I left the hospital yesterday, I called the Mayo Clinic. After about an hour, I finally spoke with Casey's doctor, David Juliana." He looked at Nikki. "Fortunately, I'm on the record as Casey's father, so he was able to discuss his prognosis with me."

The silence that hung over the room was thick enough to cut with a carving knife. Nate paused to sip his hot cocoa, and Bobby reached across the table for Nikki's hand. He hated that the news was so bad.

"Anyway, after talking to Juliana, I had the lab draw some blood for the specific tests he recommended." He swallowed the lump in his throat before looking directly at Nikki. "I'm not a match."

"No." Dani cried. She was out of her chair and at her sister's side in a flash.

"I'm so sorry," Nate whispered.

"We already knew." Nikki's voice cracked with despair. "Dr. Juliana called about an hour ago with the results." She lowered her head, unable to go on.

"He thinks we need to aggressively pursue the transplant bank for the most suitable donor," Bobby said, picking up where his wife left off. "Since Casey is doing so well after the blood transfusions, we have a few months to play with before it becomes critical. We've already called the transplant nurse in Dallas. She put him on the list."

A heaviness settled in Nate's chest. "I can't even begin to tell you how much I wanted to match. How much I wanted my bone marrow to save your son."

A suffocating sensation tightened his throat. "But I can't help him. I came here to tell you that in person, but there's something else I wanted you to know. I've given this a lot of thought."

Out of the corner of his eye, Nate noticed Dani leaning closer to her sister. "I'll never interfere in Casey's life. My lawyer is drawing up the paperwork to terminate all parental rights. I'll sign it as soon as he completes it." He turned to Bobby. "Then you can adopt Casey and legally be the father you've always been."

Bobby's eyes glazed over with pain, and he turned to his wife, the spark of hope gone from both their faces. Then he stood and walked to the foot of the stairs.

"Casey, will you come down here, please?"

Nate's pulse raced. He'd vowed not to complicate Casey's life any more than it already was. If that meant giving him up completely, he would make that sacrifice. But seeing him one last time might be too much.

As the child walked into the room, Nate's heart nearly exploded. Even his most honorable intention to give up Casey came under fire. He had to stay strong. Seeing his son now made it almost impossible. Casey was perfect, even with his small stature and pale skin. Nate prayed for the strength to do what he knew was right.

Then Casey smiled at him, and Nate cupped his head in his hands, unable to speak, afraid to speak. He would gladly give his life for this child. But he couldn't. No one could.

A hand touched his shoulder, comforting him, almost caressing him. He took several deep breaths until he was strong enough to raise his head, surprised to see Casey standing beside him, smiling.

"My mom said you're my father," Casey said, giggling now. "It's cool having two dads."

Nate's heart squeezed in anguish as his eyes connected with Nikki's.

She drew in a deep breath before she smiled, swiping at her own tears. "We told him last night."

"We decided Casey has a right to know his biological father," Bobby said, softly. "His life can only get richer with you in it."

Nate finally found his voice. "I don't know what to say." He glanced toward Dani for the first time since they had arrived. Judging by the expression on her face, she wasn't doing so well with this, either.

"We would never pressure you, but we'd love for you to get to know your son. Maybe take him for a week or two in the summer. Obviously, this is still so new, we haven't worked out the details."

Nate felt drained. All he could do was nod. He'd just been handed the greatest gift in the world, access to his son.

He noticed Casey staring at him.

"I have your eyes," Casey said, matter-of-factly. "And maybe even your nose. What do you think, Mom?"

Everyone at the table laughed. It was just what they needed to lighten the heavy moment.

"I think you might be right, kiddo," Nikki said. "Now, say good-night to your new dad and your Aunt Dani, and get your cute butt up to bed. Dad and I will be up in a minute to tuck you in." She winked at Bobby.

Casey ran to the stairs before turning back. "I'm glad you're my other dad, Mr. Randall."

"Call me Nate, Casey." His heart ached with an acute sense of loss.

Jesus. He hadn't been this emotional since—well, never. All his life, he'd swallowed his feelings. It was a miracle he'd made it this long without an ulcer. A nine-year old had forced him to finally unlock his emotions. He'd had no idea a child could bring this much joy or cause so much pain, all at the same time. He had a new respect for anyone who had ever raised a family.

He swallowed the last of his drink. When Nikki stood to refill it, he waved her off. "I have to get back to the hotel and elevate this leg. I'll call a cab."

"I'll drive you," Bobby offered.

Nate shook his head. "Thanks, but that's not necessary."

With all the excitement tonight, he'd shoved the increasing pain in his leg to the back of his mind. Now he was paying the price for letting it hang down. Not even a Vicodin would control the throbbing now.

He reached for his cell phone and dialed information. Before he could punch in the number for the taxi service, Dani was beside him. She grabbed the phone from his hand and laid it on the table.

"I think you're going to need something stronger than hot chocolate. Unfortunately, it wouldn't mix very well with your pain meds."

She picked up his empty cup and walked to the counter, offering no explanation. After she'd refilled it, she twisted her head to glance over her shoulder. "Marshmallows?"

"No, thanks," he replied, suddenly nervous. She was acting really strange. He braced himself for more bad news.

All eyes focused on Dani as she slowly refilled the other cups. Finally, she sat and faced Nate.

"I'm pregnant."

Unable to speak, Nate blew out a long breath. No one else said a word, either.

Finally, he found his voice. "You're sure?"

Dani nodded.

He choked back his emotions. For so long, he'd wanted a child so badly it hurt. Now he had two. No words could express how he felt at this moment.

"I've been queasy a lot lately. Since my periods have always been irregular, I didn't make the connection. They ran a pregnancy test at the hospital yesterday."

Nikki sprang from her chair to kiss Dani. "I am so freakin' happy for you. Abby will be ecstatic." She tugged at Bobby's sleeve. "Let's go up and kiss our son goodnight, so Nate and Dani can talk in private."

Finally alone with Dani, Nate was unable to take his eyes off her face. If he'd thought she was beautiful before, knowing she was carrying his child elevated her to goddess-like status.

A sudden thought sobered him. Dani had never said she was carrying his child. He'd only assumed.

"Are you wondering if you're the father?" she asked, reading his mind.

He nodded. "I don't really know anything about your personal life."

"Unless my name is Mary and yours is Joseph, I'm one-hundred percent sure your swimmers are the guilty culprits."

He threw back his head and laughed. "I didn't need you to get that specific." He furrowed his brow as another troubling thought crossed his mind. "Will you have the baby?"

"I'm Catholic, remember?" she said without hesitation. "After the shock wore off, I let myself get excited about him or her." She fidgeted with the napkin. "But don't worry. I would never expect you to contribute to the care of this child, not financially or emotionally."

"What if I want to?" His words brought a half-smile to her face. "What if I told you I'm so damn excited about this, I could kiss you?"

She lowered her head and sighed.

"And then, what if I told you I think I'm falling in love with you?"

Her smile faded, and she turned away.

Christ! He'd done the one thing he didn't want to do. He'd scared her off. Despite the pain in his leg, he stood and walked around the table to stand in front of her. He would have preferred to go down on one knee, but that was physically impossible right now.

"I can't offer you anything, Dani. There's a good chance I'll spend the rest of my life in jail, I know, but I couldn't leave tonight without telling you how I feel. And it has nothing to do with the baby. I've felt this way for a while now, but I didn't want to scare you off. I've hidden my feelings all my life, and look where it's gotten me."

She held his gaze.

Why didn't she say something? He plunged ahead. "I want you to know that whatever happens between us, I'll always be there for you and the baby."

She bit her lower lip. He cursed the fact he didn't know her well enough to interpret the gesture. But even though he didn't know much about her past, he'd come to know her character. He'd seen firsthand her fierce loyalty to her family, her love for her daughter. He was still amazed at the way she'd taken care of him, even though she suspected he might be a killer. Without a doubt, this woman was the strongest person he'd ever met.

And he was sure of one other thing. He loved her, probably had from that very first night.

Finally, the beginning of a smile returned to the corners of her mouth. "I have feelings for you, too, Nate. I just don't know what they mean. What I do know is that a child needs two parents to guide him through life." She inhaled before continuing. "Whatever happens, this baby is just as much a part of you as it is me. I would never keep you away, but I need time. This is happening too fast."

He lowered his head. "I know. I can't even promise I'll be around to see the baby born. What kind of life can I offer you?"

She touched his cheek and lifted his head to meet her eyes. "I'm only saying let's take this slow. We've been through hell the last six weeks. Any decision we make will affect more people than just you and me."

He bent and kissed her lightly. "I'm a patient man, but you need to know I usually get what I want."

For the first time tonight, she gave him the grin he loved.

"I'm counting on that."

Just then, Bobby and Nikki reappeared, questions covering their faces as they sat back down at the table.

"Well?"

"Nate and I are going to take some time to get to know each other. Whatever happens, happens." Dani smiled at Nikki. "How's Casey?"

"He's so excited about meeting Nate, he can hardly get to sleep. For once in my life, there's no second guessing. We made the right decision."

Nate studied their faces. "Six weeks ago, work was the only thing relevant in my life. I can see now I was merely existing, not really living." He stopped. "I'm grateful you've allowed me into your family, if only a little, to share a small part of the unbelievable love you have for each other. I just wish I could repay you by erasing the pain from your heart."

"No one can," Bobby said. "It's in the hands of a Higher Power."

"I know. But at least now Casey will have a half brother or sister to—" He stopped mid sentence. "Holy shit!"

"What, Nate?"

He looked first at Dani, then turned to Nikki. "Identical twins like you two have identical DNA. That means this baby will be like a true sibling to Casey."

Nikki cried out, and a spark of hope ignited in her eyes.

Nate turned to Bobby and Dani, who were trying to figure out the significance.

"This child might be a match."

CHAPTER TWENTY-EIGHT

Plans were made to fly to Minnesota in two weeks—Nate included—to run DNA tests on Dani's unborn child. She'd been so jazzed, she hadn't even minded the occasional vomiting that accompanied her daily nausea bouts while they waited.

But even with the hope and the excitement that her unborn fetus could quite possibly save her nephew's life, she'd awakened a week before they were to leave with a feeling of doom and gloom. Today was the day she was meeting Nate at the Dallas Police Station so he could turn himself in, along with the picture she'd snapped the day of Janelle's murder.

For some odd reason she'd believed him when he said he wasn't driving his car that day, although she'd still tried to talk him out of giving the DA evidence that might put him in jail for the rest of his life—or worse. But he'd been insistent.

After eating a piece of dry toast and keeping it down, she got into her truck and headed downtown. At nine in the morning the drive into Dallas wasn't too bad since most of the commuters were already at work and traffic had thinned. After parking in the lot next to the police station, she walked slowly to the entrance, unable to shake the feeling that this would not end well. The minute she stepped inside the station, she spotted Nate sitting in a corner by the window, his crutches leaning against the chair next to him. When their eyes met, he smiled and motioned for her to come over.

"Was traffic bad?" he asked when she was beside him.

"No," she replied before exhaling noisily. "What are we waiting on?" She knew she sounded impatient and scolded herself. Just because she was a nervous wreck didn't mean she had to make him feel that way, too.

"The officer at the desk said it shouldn't be long." He reached over and grabbed her hand. "No matter how this turns out, Dani, it's the right thing to do."

"I know, but—"

She was interrupted when the desk sergeant walked up. "Mr. Randall, Detective Markle is ready to see you now."

When Dani stood up, the officer shook his head. "Just him, ma'am."

"She goes with me," Nate said, grabbing her arm again.

For a minute Dani thought the officer was going to protest, but then he shrugged. "Follow me." He led them to one of the interrogation rooms in the back where two men were already seated around the table.

Nate greeted the police officer and held out his hand. When it was obvious the man had no intentions of shaking it, he pulled it back.

"Sit," the detective commanded, finally noticing Dani. "Who's this?"

"Dani Perez. You might know my dad, Hector Ramirez. He has a lot of friends in this house," she said, feeling absolutely no shame for name dropping.

Markle smiled. "And why are you here with Randall?"

"She's a friend," Nate answered for her. "And she's the one who took the photos I'm about to show you."

"Photos?"

"Yes. May we sit down?"

Markle nodded. "Hope you don't mind that I asked DA Romero to sit in on our little chat."

Nate shook his head and leaned forward to offer his hand over the table. When the DA accepted it, the scowl on Markle's face deepened.

"Okay, let's get to it," Markle said when Dani and Nate were seated. "Where's the pictures?"

Dani reached into her purse for the photo of Nate's car leaving his house with a date stamped at the bottom.

Markle stared at it for several seconds before handing it over to Romero. "This is your car, right, Randall?"

"Yes, but I wasn't driving it."

"Oh yeah. I forgot that you were conveniently asleep in your office—a fact we can't verify with any of your colleagues or the woman who runs the deli downstairs."

"I know how it looks, but I wasn't in that car. I brought you the photo because I thought it might help you find the person who killed my wife."

Markle threw back his head and laughed. "And we appreciate that, although for my money, it looks like the guy sitting across from me right now fits that bill."

"Thanks for making my case, Randall," the DA said sarcastically before turning to Markle. "I can't stay much longer. I assume we can wrap this up soon?"

Markle never took his eyes off Nate. "For the life of me I can't understand why you'd hand over evidence that very clearly puts you at your house when your wife was murdered. We already have motive, and now you've given up opportunity as well."

"Can't you even entertain the possibility that someone else was driving the car?" Dani asked, unable to hide the disgust in her voice. "He's a doctor, for godsakes. You think he'd be dumb enough to walk in here and show you the pictures if he was the one in the car?"

"Who else could it have been? No one else had a reason to kill the woman or access to his vehicle."

"How can you be so sure of that?" Dani's voice escalated a notch. "Have you checked out everyone in Dr. Randall's building?"

"In respect to your father, I'll let that one slide. I don't take well to people telling me how to do my job, Ms. Perez. Of course we checked everyone out."

Dani fumbled in her purse and pulled out a stack of papers held together with a rubber band. After glancing momentarily at them, she slid them across the table. The DA scooted his chair closer to get a look for himself.

"These are the bank statements from Nate's practice for the past six months. You'll notice a monthly payment to Brown's Janitorial

Service." When Markle's head shot up, she continued, "His monthly rent comes with free janitorial service, and the building owners use a different company." She had no idea if that meant anything, but she was desperate.

Just when she thought it had been a useless ploy, she noticed the look that passed between Markle and DA Romero.

"What?" When neither man responded, she stood. "I guess I'll have to chase down this lead myself."

Again, the two men stared at each other before Markle motioned for her to sit back down. "Brown's Janitorial Service is well-known to us," he said. "They're currently the focus of an ongoing investigation."

"Investigation into what?" Dani asked, narrowing her eyes.

"I'm not at liberty to divulge that information, Ms. Perez."

"Well, that's too bad because I'm at liberty to check this out myself," she fired back. "I sure hope I remember not to mention that you're watching them."

"I'll file obstruction charges so fast, your head will spin," the DA said angrily.

"You do that, Mr. Romero. I'm sure a jury of my peers would only see it as a slip of my tongue."

The two men again faced each other before Markle spoke up. "We think the company is a front for an organized crime operation heavy into gambling and money laundering. We've had the owner under surveillance for several months now but haven't been able to catch him doing anything illegal."

"Surveillance? You have tapes?"

Markle nodded.

"Can we see them?"

"Why would we let you do that, Ms. Perez," the DA asked, his face now flushed with anger.

"Because apparently, someone in Dr. Randall's office is making payments to them. If we're lucky—and your guys tailing Mr. Brown are as good as you think they are—we might notice a familiar face on those tapes."

Markle hesitated for only a few seconds before he picked up his phone and dialed. "Get me all the tapes the organized crime guys have on Brown's Janitorial Service and set them up on my laptop in the conference room," he barked to someone before hanging up and turning to Dani. "I think this is a long shot, but I'm willing to pacify you so you don't screw up about six months worth of undercover work."

He stood and motioned for them to follow him. Once in the conference room, they waited nearly ten minutes before a female officer delivered the tapes.

"How far back do you want to go?" Markle asked.

"How about if we start a month or so before Dr. Randall's wife was killed?" Dani suggested.

"You got it." Markle touched his laptop and the surveillance pictures appeared on the screen in front of them.

"As much as I'd like to stay and watch this useless attempt to pin a murder on someone else, I have to be in court in fifteen minutes," DA Romero said. "Be sure and read him his rights," he said over his shoulder to Markle as he made his way to the door.

Markle pointed to the picture on the screen. "The guy you're looking at is Randy Brown, the owner." He stood. "Sit back and relax. You're gonna be here a while. I'll be in my office."

Once they were alone, Nate smiled at her. "Remind me never to get on your bad side." Then the smile turned into a full-out grin. "Oh wait, I've already been there and got to see firsthand how forceful you can be."

When she smiled back, his face turned serious. "No matter how this turns out, Dani, I can't thank you enough for coming down here with me even though you tried your damndest to talk me out of it."

She lowered her head. "What we did to you—what I did to you—was unconscionable, Nate. And for that, I apologize. In our defense, though, we were desperate to save a little boy's life. You've met Casey, so I hope you understand."

He nodded before settling back in his chair and turning his attention to the overhead screen. "Wish we had popcorn."

Two hours later, Dani had seen about as much of Randy Brown as she could stomach. She was about to suggest they go out for a bite to eat before a few more hours worth of watching the boring tapes when Nate jumped up.

"Oh my God!"

"What?"

"He pointed to the screen where Brown was standing near the ticket counter of the racetrack on the outskirts of town, talking to another man.

"What are you seeing, Nate?" Dani asked, not sure why he'd reacted the way he did.

"Take a closer look," he said as the photos clearly showed the men arguing now.

She studied the screen before it hit her. Staring out at her from the screen was a familiar face she recognized from Nate's office.

She leaned in closer. Without a doubt, they were looking at Nate's partner, Roger McMillan, in the middle of a heated conversation with Randy Brown.

EPILOGUE

Seven Months Later

"Nik, it's time. The doctor—" Dani doubled over when another contraction ripped across her lower abdomen.

Okay, little boy, I know you want out of there, but give me a freakin' break.

She took a deep breath and exhaled slowly. Where was Nate?

"Dani?"

When the contraction ended, Dani wiped the perspiration from her forehead with her sleeve. "Nate's on the way. We'll meet you and Dad at the hospital."

Nate's car roared up the driveway and screeched to a halt as she hung up the phone. She peeked out the window just as he tripped and tumbled to the ground in his haste to get out of the car.

She giggled. The man was more nervous than she was.

He burst through the door, the concern on his face quickly changing to a sheepish grin when he realized she was laughing.

"You saw?"

"Oh, yeah. I thought doctors were supposed to be calm and collected."

He snorted. "Only when it's somebody else's baby."

"Kinda like the old saying, 'it's only minor surgery when it's happening to someone else.'"

He bent down and brushed her lips with his. "Exactly." His grin faded as he touched her abdomen. "How far apart are they?"

"About fifteen minutes. We need to hustle. I was only in labor six hours with Abby."

Nate glanced up the stairs. "Where is Abby?"

"With my dad. Nik's stopping by on her way to the hospital to pick them up." She touched his arm. "We really need to go."

Nate lifted the overnight bag that had been parked by Dani's front door for the past two weeks. After two earlier trips to the hospital, she'd learned the hard way that first babies aren't the only ones who produce false labor pains.

But these contractions were the real deal. She'd noticed a slight backache when she'd gone to bed, and she'd taken a couple of Tylenols. When the pain grew worse, she suspected the baby was on the way, but after those two embarrassing trips to Cimarron General, she'd wanted to be sure. Two hours later, she was convinced.

"Hurry, Nate, I don't want to have this baby in the car." When she read absolute horror on his face, she was immediately sorry. "I don't think I will, but we really should go."

Nate popped the trunk and threw in the luggage just as he'd done the other two times, then helped her into the front seat. Within minutes, they were speeding down I-20.

Nervous about her day ahead, Dani gazed out the window on the drive. Except for nausea and occasional vomiting the first six weeks, her pregnancy had been uneventful. She hoped labor and delivery followed suit.

She leaned back in the seat and blew out a long breath

"Another one?"

She nodded. If they didn't get to the hospital soon, Nate was going to unravel right in front of her.

She thought about the last seven months. So much had happened since the day she'd told him she was having his baby. She remembered the way her sister's face had lit up with renewed hope when Nate had suggested the baby might be a match for Casey. Nikki had immediately called Dr. Juliana, who was almost as excited as they were, further fueling their spark of hope.

The following week, all of them had flown to Minnesota so Dani—or rather the baby—could be tested. Dani still got choked up remembering that day.

Dr. Juliana had walked into the room, his own eyes wet with tears as he told them the results. If everything went as expected, this baby would save Casey's life.

Even strangers in the room had cried with them when they'd gone to the hospital chapel to thank God for the miracle. Dani had gone to church every Sunday since.

She scrunched her face as another contraction hit, moaning softly and squirming in the seat.

"Breathe, Dani, just like they taught you." Nate started the who-who-who breathing exercise they'd learned in Lamaze class.

If she didn't hurt so much, she would have cracked up.

When the contraction finally ended, she glanced at her watch. "Seven minutes since the last one, and they're longer now. You'd better floor it."

Five minutes later, she was in a wheelchair on her way up to the obstetrics floor. Nikki and Abby were in the waiting room when the elevator doors opened. Even Aunt Carmella and Aunt Sophie were there, anxiety covering their faces. Dani smiled to reassure them.

Nate stepped back when the nurse punched the button to open the automatic double doors. "I'll wait out here until you call me."

"Stop," Dani ordered the nurse. She twisted to meet Nate's eyes. "I need you with me."

His smile broadened as he followed the wheelchair through the doors.

"Get Nikki," Dani commanded.

Her eyes met Nate's briefly. Over the past seven months, she'd spent a lot of time with this man. True to his word, he hadn't pressured her about their relationship. Other than a few kisses, some hotter than others, he'd kept his distance, even when she wished he hadn't.

Somewhere around the fifth month, her hormones had gone into overdrive. At times, she'd wanted to jump his bones so badly, she ached. Wanted his hands all over her swollen body, making her feel the way she had that first night. But she'd held back, knowing sex between them could no longer be casual. She had to be sure. Loving a man like Johnny had raised the bar.

Truth be told, Nate was up to the challenge. Over the past months, she'd discovered his kind, compassionate side, as he'd transformed into a great father to Casey. And Abby adored him. That said a lot, since Dani believed her daughter's judgment was usually better than her own.

After Nate closed his practice in Dallas and moved to Cimarron to be near Casey, he was at Dani's house almost daily, usually bringing Casey over to play with him and Abby in the back yard. Sometimes, he showed up after a hard day at the hospital and talked her and Abby into eating out that night. She hadn't missed the glow on Abby's face when he was around.

Closing up shop in Dallas hadn't been as difficult for Nate as Dani expected. After the police dropped the charges against him, he never looked back. Said he felt like he'd been given a new lease on life, and he wanted to start fresh.

The cops had been surprised when Nate recognized his partner on the surveillance tapes from an investigation into Brown's Janitorial Service. Once confronted, Roger McMillan had confessed to everything. Apparently, he'd been up to his eyeballs in debt and had skimmed off the top for several months. When he'd learned that Janelle had ordered a special audit, he'd panicked. Then she'd threatened to reveal the gory details about their year-long affair to his wife if Roger didn't basically become her puppet.

With Brown's goons prepared to seriously hurt him if he didn't come up with more money, he'd felt trapped. When he'd found Nate asleep in his office, taking his car seemed like the perfect solution. That way, no one would get suspicious seeing the familiar car at that time of day.

In the end, Roger agreed to testify against Brown in return for a lighter sentence. He was currently at a federal prison under special guard, awaiting trial. Brown was in Huntsville Prison, no doubt trying to figure out how to permanently silence Roger before he testified.

Dani's first impression of the man had been that he was a slimeball, but she'd never dreamed he might be a killer. The fact that he'd been willing to let Nate take the fall for the murder only made him more despicable in Dani's eyes. What kind of man did that?

"Dani, are you ready to have this baby?" the obstetrician asked, interrupting her thoughts.

"The boy's ready. I'm not sure I am, but I guess I don't get a vote."

"Unfortunately, no. We're taking you straight to the delivery room where we have Lab standing by."

Dani's smile quickly turned to a grimace as she squirmed with a new contraction.

"How long since the last one?"

"Three minutes."

The doctor glanced at the nurse. "Get her on the table and hook her up to the monitors. I don't think we're going to have to wait long for this one."

Two hours later, with Nikki on her left side and Nate holding her hand on the right, Dani delivered a beautiful seven- pound baby boy who cried the minute he took his first breath.

After the doctor cut the cord, she placed the baby in Dani's arms.

"He's gorgeous," Dani said, holding him up to show Abby who had been escorted into the room.

"He looks just like Casey."

Nikki drew in a sharp breath and turned to meet her sister's eyes.

I love you, Nikki mouthed the words.

"Me too."

When the placenta was delivered, everyone in the room held their breaths while the lab technician milked the umbilical cord for every last drop of blood. Quantity was critical. Anything over two ounces was good.

Finally, the tech looked up, a huge smile spreading across his face. "Three."

Even the nurses choked up as the tech rushed to the lab with the cord blood to prepare it for the transplant. Nikki had booked a morning flight to Minnesota to hand deliver it to the clinic. Bobby and Casey were already there waiting.

As soon as Nikki heard there was enough, she called Bobby so they could start the preliminary treatment on Casey. Although the actual transfusion wouldn't take place for about three weeks, he had to undergo seven days of powerful chemotherapy to wipe out his damaged immune system so his body could regenerate a healthy one from his half-brother's blood.

"When will we know if Casey's all right, Aunt Nik?"

"About three weeks after the transfusion." Nikki's voice relayed her optimism. "We have to keep praying until then, Abs."

"Can I see him?"

"No, sweetheart, he'll be in a room all by himself to protect him from germs. Only Uncle Bobby and I can go in. But he'll have my laptop. He can e-mail you every day."

"A girl in my class had leukemia and lost all her hair." Abby scrunched her face. "Will Casey?"

"Probably." Nikki smiled at her niece. "Uncle Bobby is going to shave his head, too."

Abby's face lit up. "Cool." She turned to Nate. "Are you?"

Nate frowned. "I never thought about it, but now that you mention it, that's a terrific idea."

Just then, the newborn's eyes flickered open.

"He smiled, Mom. Did you see that?"

"He recognizes his big sister already." Dani squeezed Abby's hand, knowing the baby only had gas, but never in a million years would she say that to her daughter. She winked at Nikki when Abby wasn't looking.

When the nurse walked over, Dani handed her the baby. "We need to clean him up so he can have his first feeding," she explained when she saw the worried look on Abby's face.

Dani yawned, suddenly feeling exhausted. Giving birth was not for sissies.

Nikki guided Abby toward the door. "Come on, munchkin. Let's go tell Gramps and your aunts about the baby. Then we can call Casey, and you can tell him, too."

When Nate and Dani were finally alone, he leaned in and kissed her. "You were amazing."

Dani could hardly hold her eyes open. "I was, wasn't I?"

"Have you picked out a name?"

"Several, but now that I've seen him, none fit. Do you have one in mind?"

He reached for her hand. "John Nathan Randall."

"Perfect," Dani whispered, sucking air into her lungs to help her hold back a sob.

He kissed her again. "I'm in love with you, Dani, but I've made so many mistakes in my life. I don't want to make another one."

She stared into his eyes. If ever she was sure of herself, of him, now was the time. After all the deaths, the deceit, and the lies, the unthinkable had happened. She had fallen in love, too, but like Nate, she wanted to be sure. "I feel the same way."

He threw back his head and laughed, but when his eyes met hers, they were wet with tears. "I want to know everything about you, about Abby. What would you say to a real date after you get home?"

Dani pulled his face down and brushed her lips against his. "You're on, Randall. But first, I have to know how you'll deal with a dirty diaper."

"Like every other man on this planet." His grin widened. "I'll pass him to you."

The End

ABOUT THE AUTHOR

Liz Lipperman started writing many years ago, even before she retired from the medical profession. Wasting many years thinking she was a romance writer but always having to deal with the pesky villains who kept popping up in all her stories, she finally gave up and decided since she read mysteries and obviously wrote them, why fight it? She now calls what she writes Romantic Mystery (RM) since there is always a little romance involved. Two years ago, she signed her first contract with Berkley to write a cozy series called "The Clueless Cook Mysteries."

Having lived in Taiwan and Saudi Arabia, she and her HS sweetheart hubby now reside north of Dallas. When she's not writing, she spends her time doting on her four wonderful grandchildren. She writes the Clueless Cook Mystery Series for Berkley Prime Crime, the Dead Sister Talking Mysteries for Midnight Ink and her romantic suspense/mysteries are available on Amazon.

BOOKS BY
LIZ LIPPERMAN

~~~~

Clueless Cook Mysteries
Liver Let Die
Beef Stolen-Off
Murder For the Halibut

Jordan McAllister Mysteries
Chicken Caccia-Killer (coming December 2013)

BOOKS BY
LIZBETH LIPPERMAN

~~~~

Dead Sister Talking Mysteries
Heard It Through the Grapevine (coming May 2013)
Jail House Glock (coming May 2014)

SWEEPERS, Inc. (Romantic Suspense)
SWEEPERS: A Kiss To Die For (coming December 2013)
SWEEPERS: Die Once More (coming July 2014)

Other Books (Romantic Thrillers)
Mortal Deception
Shattered

MAR 0 2 2016

Made in the USA
San Bernardino, CA
05 May 2014